For Senenti, forever

Contents

'The blues is an art of ambiguity, an assertion of the irrepressibly human over all circumstances, whether created by others or by one's own human failing.'

Ralph Ellison

Beach Boy

And so it happened almost as soon as he landed, dropped his bags into the guesthouse and was walking along white sand. Twisting ends of locks between his fingers, eyes hidden behind Ray Bans, focused on the curving sheen of her body. She was wearing a pink bikini, sitting with her chin against one knee and smiling as he approached. He matched her enthusiasm, using the slow tick of passing moments to survey his surroundings. The twinkle of ocean, yards away. Dark heads above waves. Donkeys trotting slow like old men. *Dhows* that rolled at the shoreline, captained by youths he guessed were no older than twenty-one, twenty-five at the most.

He failed to see the group to the right of him until he was almost parallel with them, his shadow stretching across faces. There were six or so. They who he'd been warned about in his guide book, by the friends he'd made in Nairobi and the porter that carried his bags. Some were chewing *miraa*, what he knew back home as cat. Others lay with their eyes closed while a few passed a joint. Most had shoulder-length locks like him, although the ends were tinged blond and their skin glowed from trapped sunlight in a way his never had. Their eyes were white and watchful, all on him. He released the lock he'd been twisting and raised his hand in the universal gesture of peace.

'*Habari*,' he said, feeling the clumsiness of the Swahili against his lips, smiling around the thought, down onto the boys. They looked away in mute discontent, staring around, behind him. He could feel quick breath in his lungs, his heart pattering against his chest, and then he was striding without seeing, the moment reverberating inside him.

'*Habari*!'

He frowned without knowing, determined not to answer. Realised it was her. Deep caramel, a dark star placed against the undulating white of the sand. Long, untamed black hair, cascading to her waist. Thin arms and legs that matched her face, bangles and rings everywhere, eyes hidden by huge black shades. Beneath the glasses Palermo could see the white of a smile, enclosed by the curving roundness of her cheeks. He stopped before her makeshift island of beach blanket, novel, suntan lotion.

'*Musuri sana* . . .' he murmured, and now the words came easily. 'You speak Swahili?'

'Oh *no* . . .' She was blushing, loose fingers combing her hair, leaning back on her free hand. '*Kidogo* . . .'

'Just a little, huh?'

'Yeah . . .' She giggled, looking past him out to sea. 'Just a little . . .'

He followed her gaze towards the thin wooden boat carving through calm waters. The young captain stood with one foot on the prow, waving in the direction of the beach as though he was the tourist, not they. When Palermo looked at the girl she was waving back, although she wasn't looking that way anymore. Her eyes were fixed on him.

'Would you like to sit with me?'

He snatched the opportunity like a stray Lamu cat, letting his actions be her guide, sitting beside her on the makeshift island without reply and lifting his shades so she could see him properly. The girl did likewise. All his previous girlfriends had told him that he had nice eyes, shaped in part by his Chinese–Jamaican cousin on his father's side, or so he believed. They were doing their work even then, roaming the girl's body a second time, taking in all the details; the mole on her left cheek, the darkened cups beneath her eyes, her eyebrows, plucked to perfection, the baby hairs that ran along her temple. She was Indian, so gorgeous his heart kept its stuttered pace, forcing him to take deep breaths. It had happened so suddenly he'd hardly had time to think.

'Palermo,' he said, sticking out a hand in hope she would do most of the talking, at least for now. She took it gently, as though he'd offered a delicate gift, and shook it once, seemingly unsure.

'Uh . . . Yes . . .' She smiled again, less confidant. He was completely bowled over.

'That's my name. Palermo . . .'

'*Oh!*' Laughter like birdsong, bright and pretty, over in seconds. 'I thought you were speaking Swahili again . . .'

'I wish. I can say *Jambo, Musuri, Asante Sana, M'gappe* and *Samo Hani*, but that's about it.'

'Oh,' she said, quieter. She was looking him over like a counterfeit note she'd found on the beach. 'You're not from Lamu?'

'No, I'm not.' Palermo wasn't sure if he saw disappointment or curiosity. He felt the hollowness in his gut, that dislocation, the feeling of not belonging. 'I'm from London. And your name is?'

She covered her mouth again, giggled. Palermo was reminded of the countless Hindi films he'd seen one teenage summer, dating a Gujerati girl behind her parents' back. He laughed along with her.

'I'm sorry, that's so rude . . .'

'Don't worry about it.'

'My name's Shalini. Nice to meet you.'

They shook hands again, Shalini pumping his. She was a PhD student from Vancouver studying pharmacology and writing her thesis. Her parents were Kenyan but had left for Canada as children and met years later, during their own PhD studies. She had family in the country and had been there before, but on this occasion she'd returned for a wedding in Nairobi, after which she'd decided to travel by herself and see the places she usually missed. She was staying another four weeks, during which she planned to go back north to Malindi and up the Rift Valley, on towards Mount Kenya. There she would take a plane to Nairobi in time to catch a connecting flight back to Canada. She was leaving for Malindi in three days.

'You should take the train from Mombassa to Nairobi before you go home,' she told Palermo when he said he'd gone south by bus to save money. Her eyes had widened with respect, although she thought he was missing out on a great experience. 'One night I was sleeping in my cabin and it was so hot I thought I'd leave my window open to catch a breeze. In the middle of the night, it must have been like one or two in the morning, I heard a noise that woke me. When I looked at the window there was a man crawling across the side of the train like a spider or something, trying to get in! I screamed so hard the train staff came running, but by then I'd already slammed the window shut. The guy went rolling off the side of the train. I don't know what happened, I mean he must have been badly hurt to take a fall like that. I felt bad, but I would've felt worse with a knife against my throat and all my money gone and he might've even raped me. You never know.'

'Sounds like an experience I could do without,' he told her. Shalini laughed some more and said he was probably right. She stretched herself out on her blanket and put her head on a beach towel. Her legs were smooth and shiny from suntan lotion and her breasts were barely withheld by the pink bikini.

Behind her, the beach boys were staring in their direction, looking at her, at him, at them together. He held their gaze for a moment before he reminded himself what he had promised when he'd left London. No arguments, bad looks or vibes. He was leaving that behind in the city of smoke where it belonged. He ducked his head and returned his eyes to the beautiful young woman.

'And what about you?' she said.

So he told her about himself, that he was a poet from London writing the final pieces for his second collection, one that concerned the worldwide African diaspora rather than those that had settled in London; that he was travelling on an Arts Council grant that could possibly keep him for the next few years if he budgeted correctly; that he had read about Lamu on a plane while heading to a reading in Italy and immediately fell in love with the Island, its heritage and backpacker atmosphere even though he'd never heard of the place; that he was single because he was married to the words he wrote and the art that was created by people of various ages, races and creeds. He told her of his travels across Africa, from Morocco, to Egypt, Sudan, Ethiopia, and finally Kenya, where he planned to rest. Of his proposed travels to Uganda, Rwanda, Burundi and Tanzania, working his way southwards until he reached Johannesburg and the land of new beginnings that was South Africa. He told of poetry, literature, art and artists, of slang, murder, clubs, London and its comparisons with the iron-red land of the continent.

They talked until the sun had moved across the sky, from above them to behind, lengthening shadows. The beach, deserted apart from donkey caravans led by skinny kids with sticks and the occasional European tourists, was beginning to cool. The winds were picking up. Gusts of sand flew into their faces, which bothered Palermo, although Shalini seemed not to mind. She was looking into his face, and even though her glasses were lowered, Palermo could feel the weight of her eyes. Their warmth pleased him; with reluctance he told her he was going back to the guesthouse to put his feet up and read, maybe even write.

'Where are you staying?' she asked, still shy.

'*Pwani*,' he told her. 'It means *sea* in Swahili.'

'I know,' she said. 'That's where I'm staying. I mean, I would have stayed in Peponi, its lovely and everything, but with my budget . . .'

And so it was settled. They decided to meet for dinner that evening at Peponi, the Swiss-owned hotel with the Italian name where neither could afford to stay. Palermo knew he should leave; it was unwise to overdo a first encounter, no matter how sweet. He got up, kissed her cheeks three times as was the custom, and walked away hoping she caught the swing in his step, accentuated by his jean shorts and fitted vest. He was so caught up he completely neglected the gathering of beach boys that remained in the spot he had passed hours ago. He looked down into the sea of firm faces and was jolted from his fantasy, back to the beach.

'Ay, asshole.'

Their faces were so free of emotion and filled with sullen dislike it was difficult to see who had spoken. He scanned the gathering and focused on one, the guy with bleached blond locks and red Oakley sunglasses, a T-shirt with a head-and-shoulders portrait of Bob Marley, spliff in hand. He was staring with double the intensity of the others, lip curled, *miraa* stem jutting from his mouth like a toothpick. Palermo didn't know what to say. After a moment of shock and a dose of fear, he was about to turn away and walk on, when the blond dredd took the *miraa* stem from between his teeth, brandishing it at him. It had been chewed free of leaves, a sure sign, Palermo knew, that he was high as the fast-moving clouds. A bag of un-chewed stems sat by the young man's feet.

'Ay, asshole. That one is mine, you know. You stay away, *mzungu.*'

He knew that was Swahili for white man, but to hear it referred to him meant they knew where he came from but didn't give a damn about heritage and culture and roots, or any of the things he'd been writing about for ten years, possibly more. He wanted to shout it at them, that they were wrong and had misjudged him, that he wasn't *mzungu* but one of them, a prodigal brother returned with arms opened wide. He opened his mouth to say as much and then it came from behind him, a shouted word that sounded more like a call to attention than a greeting, loud, powerful, confident.

'*Jambo!*'

He looked up just in time to see the real *mzungu* wearing a short-sleeved shirt and khaki shorts, thick red legs kicking up sand as he walked. The gathered beach boys raised their hands palms upwards, muttering '*Habari*' and '*Jambo*', wearing smiles. His head shot around, taking measure of what had happened, unbelieving, heartbroken. The man walked on, down the sand towards Shalini and her beach-blanket island. He could almost see her watching them. Palermo turned away, returning the mute anger on their faces, which were as blank as they had previously been. This was not how he'd imagined Africa.

'I'm no *mzungu*. I'm African,' Palermo spat, spearing the group with his eyes. He walked across the sand, desperately trying to ignore the burst of laughter that gnawed at his spine.

* * *

In his small room, he wrote at the shaky desk. He'd thought his twin encounters would inspire poetry, but found himself writing his journal. He penned his first impressions of Lamu, the shock he'd felt when he stepped from the boat and was rushed by the crowd of people begging to take bags, the fly-infested room, the donkeys and the smell of their leavings. He wrote of the beautiful buildings, the silent reverence of mosques, the familiar chatter of lounging men. The women covered in black from head to toe, stepping through narrow streets like a shadow of royalty. It hadn't been quite what Palermo had expected from his seatback magazine, filled with tourists and hustlers, open hostility. He'd stayed one night in Lamu, scanning his guidebook. The next morning he'd packed his bags and taken the ten-minute boat ride to Shella.

They met outside the guesthouse door where she was sitting on the purpose-made porch shared by all the buildings. The heavy wooden door was carved with Islamic designs. Palermo ran his hand along bumps and knots, waiting for her to finish a conversation with one of the cooks, Hassan, the young one with a swollen belly, trying to ignore the way he looked at her. She had changed into a simple green dress, low on the shoulders, the hem caressing her ankles. Her hair was tied back and wrapped in a similarly coloured headscarf, only the baby strands of her temples exposed. She wore gold earrings, bangles and anklets. The dark and light shone together, even in the night.

They crossed a small patch of grass into the Peponi grounds, situated next door to Pwani, and there, standing by the bar in a tight knot of around six people, were the young men he'd seen on the beach. They stiffened. Palermo stiffened. Shalini seemed not to notice. She waved and called *Habari* to one and all, even the guy behind the bar. The young men seemed caught between the urge to smile or frown. They raised sweating pints of Tusker, silent, watching Shalini and Palermo walk into the restaurant. As the couple stood in anticipation of the waiter, Palermo could hear shouted Swahili, felt his forehead tense even as Shalini talked of all the great places to eat on the island, how good the food was in Vancouver, especially the Sushi, which Palermo didn't eat because he hadn't the stomach for it.

They were guided to a table, surveyed the prices, and complained about the cost. He'd already made up his mind that he was paying, but it pleased him to see her talk as though he wasn't. Peponi was packed that night, filled with the wealthy and image conscious, everyone from Notting Hill women who owned glossy magazines and Shella summer-houses, to young Africans on holiday with their European girlfriends. The table they were led to looked out onto the expanse of channel separating Lamu Island from Mandu. *Dhows* and the public waterbus crossed the water. The constant lap of the tide. When the waiter returned they ordered curries and rounds of *roti*, a half bottle of white.

Shalini told him of the *dhow* ride she'd taken two days before, out onto the open sea searching for dolphins. They'd only made it halfway, the calm of the channel giving way to rocking waves that covered her in seawater and caused the boat to dive and dip until she threw up over the side. She'd been disappointed in herself, forced to ask the captain to turn back. They'd given her weed in commiseration and she'd hung out with them for the night, at a party in one of the bars between Lamu and Shella. That was how she got to know the beach boys, although she admitted they'd been making varied attempts to talk with her since she'd arrived.

He wanted to ask whether she'd slept with any of the young men. After all, they were supple and attractive. Many female tourists did, maybe even some men.' Pulling on ropes and lifting heavy goods instead of the metal weights of some sterile gym had toned their bodies. Usually they could speak at least three European languages as well as Swahili. They were quick-witted and charming, nubile movers on the dance floor and probably in the bedroom too. He forced himself to bite the question back, where it blocked further conversation, silenced his voice.

Their food came. Shalini was looking at him with double her previous focus. He noticed gold eye shadow cast across her eyelids. Glitter sparkled under the Peponi lights.

'They're really not as bad as they seem, you know,' she said, lowering her eyes towards her plate. 'They can be a bit territorial, but then it's a small place. You should ignore them, they'll soon get used to you.'

'I'm trying. They don't make it easy.'

She smiled in sympathy

'It's hard for them, eh? They want what you've got. The accent, the European passport; even more than that, the money.'

21

'I understand that. Meanwhile, the irony is, I – I mean we – want what they have. The language, the culture, the good weather . . . They're comfortable in a way we never are.'

'Yeah, but imagine living here permanently, with very little prospects and no way out. Gentrification buying up land you can't afford. Money coming from tourists, alcohol and food from tourists, even sex from tourists.'

He took a chance, raising his glass of wine. 'Not all of them.'

Shalini blushed and looked at her food, though he could tell she was pleased. He took the opportunity to change subject, telling her of his desire to leave London and live abroad. She was adamant that he came to Vancouver. She borrowed a pen from a waiter and gave him her full details, even as he said there was no hurry, until she reminded him she was leaving in three days.

They talked about their families, her sister and mother, his four brothers and parents. They talked about his work, Palermo remembering the slim book in his bag, giving her a signed copy of his first collection. She squealed with delight, reading his inscription. She told him of her secret passion, photography, producing her Canon Rebel and showing him the pictures she'd taken. He was surprised to see she had real talent, 'competition winners' as he called them, an eye for the unusual and beautiful. By the time she'd showed him everything, he was looking at her differently. She would have been a photographer of some kind, she told him, had her mother allowed it. Her father had been a doctor before he'd died. The family wouldn't hear of her doing anything else.

When they looked around themselves, blinking their way back to reality, the other diners were gone. They were alone, left to their own devices by waiters sitting at the bar, smiling as one stood and brought over the bill. He insisted on laying down his dirty notes, fully expecting her protests, gentle belligerence winning her over.

'I'm paying next time,' Shalini said, eyes sparkling. He was warmed by her assertion.

They walked the small grass patch towards Pwani, his stomach clenching in anticipation of seeing the beach boys. No one was there. Palermo was tempted to suggest a walk along the cool sand, and though he tried to convince himself he wasn't scared of them, or even rejection, he kept his silence. They let themselves in with Shalini's key, climbing the steps to their rooms. On the first floor, she stopped. They kissed, a slight pressing of her lips against his, which surprised him. Shalini touched his hand and turned away, rattling her keys in the door as he walked the stairs to the rooftop, his own room.

At breakfast he met the other guesthouse residents. Two women, obviously lovers, one tall, skinny and quiet, the other short, stocky and talkative. A young, sporty-looking German couple. A friendly, middle-aged Canadian clutching a Nikon and Shalini. They gathered on the rooftop just beyond his room, sitting at the long table where they ate together. Below them lay

Peponi, the channel, the *dhow* captains' meeting and greeting that morning's dolphin-chasers. The sun had risen over the building, warming the rooftop, the sky an unbroken blue. The perfect day was enhanced by her arrival, wearing another dress, red with a matching head wrap. He was pleased to see she respected Islamic tradition enough to dress accordingly.

He was also pleased to note the attention she gleaned from the other residents. They made a fuss, moving chairs and the table to make room for her, calling the staff so she could order breakfast. She took the space next to him, whispered good morning. The German young man, Michael, gave Palermo a wink. The group talked in a manner they might not have had there been the segregated breakfast area found in most hotels. They swapped stories of their travels, their work at home and their island experiences.

After breakfast everyone went separate ways. Shalini said she needed some money. The only ATM on the island was in Lamu, so they decided to make the half-an-hour walk into town together. The Canadian, Gaetan, said he would join them, an offer which they accepted. While he showered and dressed more appropriately for the heat, Palermo sat on the rooftop, pen and notebook in hand, jotting down a poem that had come to mind. Shalini sat on the opposite side of the rooftop reading a book, her legs raised and the novel placed on her thighs. He couldn't take his eyes from her. She looked like some wild creature, all tousled hair and gleaming skin. When he sighed and stared into the distance she came over, sitting close enough for her thigh to rest against his, peering over his shoulder. She read the poem aloud, her rhythm and intonation surprisingly good. Palermo thought he'd disguised the fact he was writing about her. When she asked he couldn't lie and tore the page from the book, gave it to her. He was sad to lose the poem, as he'd written well, yet the way she regarded him afterwards told him he'd done the right thing.

In town, she retrieved her money and paid for lunch at a nearby restaurant not far from the pier. The streets were busy with tourists and locals. Kids making their way to school. Music blasting from an unseen CD shop. Gaetan, who had been coming to Lamu for years, got into conversation with a man who was apparently running for town mayor. While they talked in French, Shalini and Palermo faced each other over milkshakes.

'So, d'you like it?'

'It's great,' he told her. 'I might stay for a while longer than I planned. I think they're having some kind of literature festival in the next few weeks. It would be cool to hang out and meet African writers.'

'Sounds good. I wish I could stay.'

'You could,' he said, keeping his gaze level.

'I could not. I have to get back to my studies. My mother's already tearing her hair out.'

'Surely if you're doing a PhD you can take as long you want.'

'Yeah, but I *want* to get it finished. Besides, I could always come back.'

'Or I could come and see you.'

'You promised you would. We have literature festivals in Vancouver you know, and African writers.'

'I know. I just never had a good enough reason to visit.'

'And now you do.'

He liked her boldness, the way she said whatever was on her mind.

'Yes. Now I do.'

They sipped their milkshakes. More laughter from Gaetan's table.

'You don't have a boyfriend do you?'

She shook her head.

'We broke up. He was meant to come out here with me, but . . .'

'Oh. I'm sorry.'

'He's a prick.'

'Well I'm not.'

They laughed. Shalini blew bubbles into her shake, caught herself and smiled, embarrassed.

'I'm like a kid sometimes, I swear.'

'It's OK.'

She rotated the straw, working up a thick froth.

'I'm not sure he was capable of dealing with my ethnicity, if you know what I mean.'

'I do,' he said.

'He called Diwali a pagan ritual.'

'Oh.' Palermo looked down at his own shake. 'So. If we went out for dinner tonight . . .Would that be a date?'

Shalini grinned.

'Only if you took me dancing.'

'They have clubs here?'

'Practically every night.'

'Then I'd love to.'

They had a moment. A genuine, no-holds-barred stare into each other's eyes. He relished what was happening, even as he wondered how real it could be, even as he heard the shouts from outside and saw him, the beach boy with the bleach blond locks and Oakley sunglasses, standing with his back toward them. There was a tourist, large enough to be American, though Palermo was only guessing. He was shouting too, but he looked wary. His skinny wife and two kids stood behind him, frightened. The guy in the Oakley glasses threw up his hands and walked along the cobbled street. Palermo felt himself tense, hoping he wasn't coming their way, but the beach boy headed further down the street, away from the outraged American and his family, who were left down-mouthed, unsure.

Another burst of laughter from Gaetan and his friends, discussing what everyone had seen. Shalini reached over the table and held his forearm. She rubbed thin hairs the wrong way in consolation.

They walked almost halfway back to Lamu in total darkness, along the beachfront road. Even though they each had a torch, Shalini was still frightened. He was almost glad. Fear caused her to clutch his arm tight and press her body against his so that he could feel her curves, although it also made him nervous. The moon was bright in the sky, the heavens cloudy. Sometimes they would see distant shards of approaching torch beams, waving erratically. Usually a dark-skinned figure would emerge from the gloom empty-handed, walking past without a word. Shalini had some weed the beach boys had given her, which they smoked to calm their nerves. They stumbled on pebbles and driftwood.

Music pumped from the small bar two hundred metres before they got there. Shalini floated up the stairs into the packed venue, waving and smiling. He was coming to understand that was her way. It was as though she knew every face. Palermo ducked his head, smiling when he caught a stray eye, pretending not to notice them staring. The place was full to the brim with beach boys and the women he presumed were their foreign conquests, moving together in the coloured lights projected from the DJ booth. Once they'd looked him over they went back to their dance steps, fists clenched, eyes cast at their feet. He looked around for the guy with the Oakley glasses, hoping against hope, found he wasn't there. He tried to let his shoulders drop and lounge his way into the venue, look comfortable like the dancers. Shalini approached the bar, ordering large Tuskers. He ignored the barman leering at her breasts, the way the burly man glared at him before he turned to get their drinks.

And so they had a perfect night to end their day, dancing close to the selection of R&B, hip pop and reggae. The DJ played with a passion that caused Palermo to raise his Tusker bottle high in salute, shaking his head so his locks flew from side to side. He was hamming it up for Shalini and he didn't care. She led him into the thick of the crowd where they stayed, vacating their spot only to make trips to the toilet or bar, sometimes even receiving the smouldering end of a passing joint. They built a few of their own and sent them back around the shuffling people. She threw her arms around his neck when the DJ selected Siźla, pushing her firm body against his and letting her hips writhe to the bump of the beat, looking into his eyes in a manner that was slightly frightening, even though he couldn't break that gaze, couldn't resist staring at her.

The German couple from Pwani turned up hours later, with some people who had arrived that afternoon. The DJ switched to Crunk. They bounced on the balls of their feet and yelled along to the chorus with the crowd until Shalini rested her head against his chest. He looked at his watch; it was three in the morning. The night was young, their dancing comrades told them. Nevertheless, they waved and shook hands with their newfound friends, stepping down onto the sand. Hand in hand, they turned in the direction of their guesthouse.

An older man with thick locks that hung to his shoulder blades was sitting on his *dhow*, drinking a beer with friends. When he saw the couple he warned the tide had risen, and the path to Shella was deep under seawater. He offered them a lift in his boat. When they asked how much, he said they should give him what they could. Palermo was unsure. The guy looked trustworthy enough, but how could you tell?

Shalini beamed, said thank you. They stepped onto the rocking boat and settled in the aft, arms wrapped around each other as the man wrenched the engine into life. The journey was like a romance movie – the chill of the pitch-dark night, the lights from the houses that lined the shore, the pinprick stars and the sway of their captain guiding the *dhow*. Palermo caressed Shalini's hair, amazed by its softness, desperate to retain every aspect of their journey so it could be regurgitated onto blank paper. Their captain pulled towards shore what felt like too soon, holding their hands as they stepped from the boat so they could alight with ease.

Then they were entering the guesthouse, creeping upstairs to the first floor, Shalini holding him by the hand as she unlocked her door, tugged him inside. They were kissing before it was closed, Palermo kicking the door with a foot and listening to the lock *snick* shut, guiding her towards the bed where they descended, still kissing, searching for heat beneath garments, gasping, squeezing, biting flesh and tender spots, tugging clothes from limbs until they were exposed before each other, naked and unafraid.

They spent most of the next day in bed, had breakfast in her room. Lovemaking became a hunger they fed at regular intervals, discovering more with each encounter. They were shrouded by a mosquito net, mingled shadows entwined, ruffled by the breeze of the overhead fan. Palermo didn't think about the other residents, but when they eventually emerged from her room around five and bumped into Gaetan, the Canadian wore an unmistakable smile. Shalini was unfazed, as was Palermo, though they began to feel uncomfortable when faced with the wide grins of Hassan and the other cooks. They left Pwani for the approaching night, taking the seafront road a quarter of the way to Lamu until they found a small, barely populated restaurant that sold lobster, fried chicken and fish.

The floor was smooth concrete, the windows free of glass. Empty wooden tables and chairs were loosely grouped throughout the restaurant. When the meal came, it was tasty; nevertheless, Shalini was reticent as she peeled meat from his chicken bone, popped it into her mouth. Lamu cats gathered around the legs of their chairs and ankles, rubbing soft fur against warm skin, expressing plaintive mewls. She dropped her fish head onto the floor. The cats nudged it with their foreheads and turned away, going back to the circular vigil at their feet.

'I shouldn't eat meat,' she told him. 'Hindus are mostly vegetarian.'

'Does your mum know?'

'Yeah . . .' She gave him a *what-the-hell?* look. 'She eats it too.'

'I bet there's a lot of things you're not supposed to do. Culturally.'

She gave him her gorgeous smile, the one that first charmed him. The thought that he would miss her materialised and he quashed it with a memory of how she had felt between thin bed sheets. He would keep those recollections close like a keepsake.

'Loads,' she told him. Palermo grinned with her. He hadn't noticed how much her eyes resembled those of the cats.

There was a clatter from a table behind them. He turned to see a group of beach boys that had arrived while they ate. They were leaving, talking close with their waiter, clutching open bottles of beer and sneering.

'Ignore them.'

'I am,' he said, turning back to face her. 'I am.'

'I'm leaving tomorrow.'

'I know. What time?'

'Early. Around six. I have to catch a flight at one. That road to Watamu is terrible.'

'Yeah.' He looked down at the scattered collection of bones on his plate. He picked a dry chip and placed it between his teeth, crunched. 'Have you packed?'

'No. You could help.'

The lump in his throat was a liability, restricting anything cool he may have said. She probably wasn't bothered. After all, she'd thought he was one of them when she'd first seen him. A beach boy with a London twang.

'Will you miss me?'

'Would you care if I did?'

She was aghast; he should have known better.

'I've only had three boyfriends.'

Palermo stared at her, blinking.

'I get quite attached. Just so you know.'

'Have you been to London?'

'Once.' She looked over the channel. A bat flew low, squeaking over their heads. 'I bet it would be different now I know someone.'

He nodded. She took his hands in hers.

'Come to Vancouver.'

He smiled at their empty plates.

'I mean it.'

'Then I'll come.'

They stared into each other's eyes.

* * *

When he woke it was to growing daylight, her empty room. He yawned, rolled over in bed. The smell of Shalini hung in the air like a hazy spirit. The dilapidated wardrobe was bare. The space on the floor where her backpack had been was vacant. He rubbed his eyes, telling himself it would make no difference.

On the rooftop they were all there, trying not to look. Shalini was their new taboo, the avoidable subject that replaced how the female couple felt about Hijabs, how the German couple felt about beach boys, how Gaetan viewed the corruption. Now they talked of dolphins, new places to visit in Africa, the world. He sat and ate his breakfast somewhat quieter than he had been, unsure why his mood was so sour. She'd left her details, including a Kenyan mobile number. They could speak any time. There was no reason for melancholy and yet he felt it. The others noticed and kept a close eye on him, Palermo resenting the new drama he provided until he realised they were concerned because they were kind.

And so he found himself wandering the narrow Lamu streets by himself, oblivious to the stares, occasionally taking pictures of running, playing kids. He sat in a coffee shop attempting to write until his loneliness chased away words. Eventually he found himself on the main street, by the docks. He knew it would be cheaper to wait for the public boat to Shella, but he couldn't see one, so he decided to grab the first captain he found and pay the extra. Palermo was adamant that he preferred Shella to Lamu by then. The clean streets, the quiet stretch of beach, the camels that walked in single file, their driver far behind. The plethora of

Notting Hill types was a bit of a pain, but they could easily be avoided by steering clear of Peponi. Shella was a quiet haven; the yin to Lamu's yang, the place Palermo had imagined when he'd originally read his seatback magazine. He was grateful he'd found the town, and in turn, found Shalini. The relaxed comfort he felt there made sense.

He spoke to a young boy, no older than thirteen, who motioned him towards the edge of the jetty, disappeared. He looked around at the gathered young men and dirty water as though he was the subject of some joke, only to feel relief when the boy called from a small, thin *dhow* that rocked beneath him. There was another young man in the boat, taller and older with short locks and a beard. Palermo made his way down concrete steps dampened by the rising tide. He stepped onto the unsteady boat, helped by the younger boy.

'My brother,' the boy said, indicating the older youth. Palermo waved in mute greeting and sat at the stern, back turned. He heard them mutter amongst themselves and felt bad, but he really didn't have the energy for talk, especially not in broken English. The engine expelled black smoke, an odour of petrol that spread over the jetty. He held the sides of the boat, steadying himself.

A few minutes along the channel, the young men began to chatter in their tongue. Palermo ignored them, realised they were arguing. He noticed the throaty growl of the engine change to a lower key. Turning to see what had caused this new song, he saw a huge unfurled sail daubed with the Lion of Judah, red, gold and green colours, a smell of weed only now reaching him on the wind. The beach boy with the Oakley glasses was standing at the stern as his *dhow* bore down on their little boat, one foot raised in imitation of Vasco de Gama. Oakley had his mirrored red glasses lowered, though Palermo could tell he was staring right at him.

'Ay, you!' Oakley called over the noise of the engine, a finger thrust at him. 'I want talk with you!'

Palermo stood, stumbling as the waves from their boat reached them, finding his feet. He felt worry on his face.

'Ay, asshole, it's you. I want talk with you.'

The young men in his *dhow* were either looking towards the bottom of the boat or over the channel at the land. The opposite bank looked far way, the expanse of water threatening. The waves flowed diagonally in an appearance of calm.

'Ay, asshole! Didn't I tell you to stay away? Asshole, I'm talking to you!'

Oakley's Rastafarian *dhow* had drawn closer. There was a matter of yards between them. Palermo shot another glance at the young crew and guessed there would be no help. He looked into Oakley's face. It was rock, twisted with anger, a tendon protruding from his neck as he shouted over the engine noise. He wondered if Oakley had a machete. It seemed the African weapon of choice. He leaned over the edge of the boat, cupping his hands around his mouth.

'I haven't done anything to you,' he shouted, loud as his voice would allow. The thud of his heart made his voice tremble. The *dhow* showed no signs of slowing and Oakley showed no sign he'd heard. The boat drew closer.

'Tell him I've done nothing,' Palermo said to his young captains. They each looked at their feet. He faced Oakley. The young man was shouting in Swahili, arms flailing. His boat was even closer.

Palermo dropped his bag into the sodden bottom of the boat. Bracing himself, he stepped towards the prow and leapt into the sea.

It was colder than he had thought, but that wasn't a surprise considering he hadn't swum since his arrival. There was something about the water that was different from Mombassa, where the sea was pea green and bathwater warm, filled with families, couples, children. Here it was a pale blue that looked as icy as it felt, the current tugging in one sure direction. Palermo tried to swim against it; he was reasonably good in the water, and had won his bronze award when he was eleven; yet he wasn't sure what was wrong, whether the weight of his clothes was a hindrance or the current too strong. He heard shouts of panic from the thin boat beside him, saw hands reaching for his. He let the current take him and only saw it was pushing him into deeper water when the shouts became shrill, turned into screams. He heard Oakley's coarse voice, *'Ay, asshole!'* and suddenly realised it was getting louder, along with the sound of an engine. He tried to swim and listen, but waves lapped seawater over his head and into his ears.

He made an attempt to move his arms and legs, to propel himself into some forward motion, but could not. He was moving away from the bank, into the depths of the channel. After that, he wasn't sure what happened. One minute he was swimming and then he was hit by a blast of stronger, colder water, thrown off course. He fought his way to the surface. It felt as though it took some time. He was splashing and spluttering as he broke waves, only to find himself pushed along by cold current, faster than he could anticipate. There was the very definite sound of a splash. He tried to swim away but Oakley was beside him, negotiating the water like a fish, reaching for him. A huge wave emanating from the boat ducked his head, silencing the assorted boys' screams. He went under.

A sizzle of popping air bubbles. The louder noise of the engines. A clanging metallic sound somewhere far beneath him. The hard push of cold water. Dark so thick he couldn't see.

Arms wrapped themselves around him, lifting him away. He broke the waves, still fighting, Oakley shouting at him to calm down. His *dhow* was metres away, the engine silent, and his duo of crewmembers looking into the water, solemn. Oakley swam one-handed, dragging Palermo like an empty sack. When they reached the boat, the crew lifted his weak body aboard.

He collapsed into the dank boat and rolled onto his back, dribbling water while they argued. He was shivering, partly from the cold, more from embarrassment. His teeth chattered. His eyes closed. As the young men fired up the engine, still arguing, Palermo forced himself to wrench them open, to see. The bone-white sun might have blinded him if it hadn't been eclipsed by the Lion of Judah sail, dancing with the wind.

Fresh for '88

I never found out why P. Nutt and Sy Rocc hung me from Reason's front steps. Mind you, it wasn't exactly something I could ask. I loved those Harrow Road flats, they reminded me of *Cosby Show* brownstones and made it easy to imagine I lived in Brooklyn, like the raregroove tune we'd heard a million times that summer. I'd gone outside for half a loose because Reason's mum Barbara didn't like us smoking cigarettes indoors, although anything with a bud was cool with her. I was sitting on the steps thinking about my lyrics, murmuring beneath my breath and trying to correct mistakes I'd made while Reason performed flawless spinbacks on his 1210's, Big Daddy Kane's *Raw* instrumental thundering through my brain. Maybe that's why I never saw them. Next thing I knew, the whole world was upside down. There was a tight grip on my ankles. I could hear my loose change hit the ground as though a money storm had broken somewhere above.

I screamed. Begged for them to let go, which they didn't. P. Nutt and Sy Rocc were at least half a foot bigger than me, which meant they would bully me until I grew big enough to fend them off, or at least until I left school. I put my hands out to stop my head smashing into the concrete. They dangled me that way until Barbara came out to complain about the noise. Not the fact that a duo of teenage brutes were swinging a kid half their size like a trapeze artist beneath their fists. Just the noise.

P. Nutt and Sy apologised and pulled me back up, sweating as much as me. Once my feet touched solid ground I collapsed in fear, knees weak. They were laughing so hard their faces were red and their eyes were leaking as they slapped their thighs. I lay with my spine against the hot front door, getting my wind back, feeling dry flakes of paint tickle my neck. Downstairs I could hear Reason had changed the record to *Rebel Without a Pause*, the wall of sound and noise that was already a classic. He was spinning back on Chuck D's line, 'Radio; suckers never play me.' Making him repeat the words like a taunt.

That was the year young London went hip-hop crazy. When kids wore jeans two sizes larger than necessary, and rocked Pumas or Adidas with fat laces, sometimes no laces at all. When the original Nike Air Max hit the stores and *Recognition*, the classic Demon Boyz album, made a firm mark for UK hip-hop. It was the year of Gazelle sunglasses, leather Goose jackets and fur-lined hoods, the Godfather of Soul's *Static* with hip-hop artists who'd sampled his music. The year of the Juice Crew All Stars, the rise of the bedroom producer, of house parties and all-dayers and rap battles on misty London streets. 1988 was the year my mother began wondering where I was for the first time, and I fell head first into an all-encompassing culture that spoke in a deafening scream. Long before the close of the decade was christened hip-hop's golden age, I wallowed in a period I'd come to think of as the best days of my life.

I went back inside the flat, leaving P. Nutt and Sy to their laughter. The corridor was a solid wall of shadows. I poked my head into the living room and found Barbara building up with her lodger, Richard. They both looked at me quick, ducked their heads. Heat washed my face. They knew they should have said something.

'Y'all right, Stone?'

Richard swivelled in his seat. He was a whole head bigger than P. Nutt and Sy, forearms bulging with veins. Richard was a black belt in tae kwon do. He could have helped.

'Yeah, man. Could I borrow a chip please?'

'Borrow?' Barbara said. 'You gonna give it back?'

'I might. If I go shop.'

'Alright then.'

She handed a third of cigarette to Richard, who passed it over. I stood in the doorway a second longer, stalling.

'You shouldn't let dem man bully you, Stoney . . .' Richard began, packing the spliff down with the wheel of his Clipper.

'What's he s'possed to do? Fight dem?' Barbara piped up.

'Nah, I'm not sayin he should fight dem . . .'

'I'm gonna go down,' I said.

'Alright, later yeah?'

'In a bit,' I told them.

It was difficult negotiating the steps down into Reason's bedroom. They were always dark and the light switch never seemed to work. I stepped slow and careful, one hand on the banister, alert for my friend's dog Brute, who was known for vicious attacks and was locked in a back bedroom where he barked and snuffled doggie threats. Once I got to the landing I was on safer ground. The heavy thud of music had stopped, but I knew where I was going. I put my hand out straight in front of me, walking forwards until I felt my palm against the cool door. Pushed inside.

Reason was sitting on his bed, Sega gamepad in hand. He'd just bought the new Mega Drive and spent most of his free time playing *Golden Axe*. His room was a crazed mix of order and calamity. Decks were set up on the right, opposite his bed; crates of records were piled all over the floor, mixed with games cartridges and VHS cassettes. His walls were filled with posters, car stickers promoting various bands, and newspaper cuttings featuring him on the decks performing some unearthly trick or another. His clothes spilled out of an open wardrobe. Ashtrays were everywhere.

There were three others in the room. My DJ, Reka, wearing large headphones and performing silent cuts on the decks, practising for the big day. MCP, a tall, dark-skinned rapper sitting on a wooden chair smoking and staring into space. And Calalloo, a stocky mixed-race MC who partnered Reason on *Golden Axe*. No one was talking. I waved a nervous hand, feeling as though I'd walked in on some secret meeting.

'Rizla?'

Spitting the word like a code that ensured safe entry, looking from face to face.

'Why you always beggin, man? You got weed? Or d'you want us to roll it too?' MCP sneered.

'Fuck you, man. . .'

I stretched out my hand. Reason paused his game and dug in his jeans until he found a pack of blues.

'Don't try it, y'know, Stone; man'll cuss yuh raas . . .'

'Cuss me den! Go on, cuss me!'

'Bwoy . . .' MCP lay back on the bed. 'I don't feel like it now . . .'

'That's cos you was up all night. Park bench hard innit, P?'

Howls of laughter from Reason and Cal. Reka noticed the look on my face and lifted one headphone, a smile on his face. MCP's expression stiffened.

'Don't try it, Stone . . .'

'Tell the truth, blud; you ain even got a house have you? No gyal's yard where you can lay yuh head . . . You grind against grass every night, innit?'

Everyone laughed. Even MCP was smiling, though he was trying to hold his face rigid. Reka reached over the decks to touch me. Cal and Reason slapped palms with me, quite hard too. MCP jumped up to stop them, but he was only messing.

'Don't test me, man. True say I'm buzzin,' I crowed, taking a seat next to my defeated friend. I built up quick and passed it to MCP first to show there were no bad feelings. He was a good rapper, one I respected. P took three big pulls and passed it back. After that I'd caught a vibe again. I got up and joined Reka by the Technics.

'Wanna run through?'

'Yeah, man. Come we go,' I said, taking the mic.

We went through our routine a few times. On some occasions it went better than others, but most of the time either I messed up a particular line, or Reka brought the beat in too early. If he fumbled a cut or made the record skip I'd take two draws and wait for him to cue up again. It was difficult not to notice my friend was distracted by the tiniest occurrence. If MCP said something, Reka would lift his headphones. If Reason and Cal screamed laughter during their game, he did the same. It was kind of annoying because all I wanted to do was practice enough so I could feel good about my performance, maybe have a chance of actually winning, but Reka didn't seem that bothered. I kept at it though. Soon enough, maybe the fifth or sixth time, we connected and it all fell into place. Reka was mixing Grandmaster Melle Mel's 'Pump It Up' with Run DMC's 'Peter Piper' instrumental. He'd bring in the intro to the first and cut in the second, mix the two, and then fade the former gently. I'd start to rhyme, the crowd would be rocking, fit gullies would be screaming my name and we'd hopefully win ourselves some cash.

There's something about rhyming I've always found difficult to explain or recapture in the years since my youth. That sheen of anticipation coating my palms, the hard feel of the mic. The hot blood that pumped through my chest, soothed by the cool intake of breath I'd sucked inside before I began my verse. Once I'd watched the Winter Olympics and caught the start of a downhill toboggan race. Rhyming was a bit like that. Once you'd taken the initial leap and launched yourself into the air there was nothing to stop that headlong rush, faster than you'd imagined or experienced, the roar of the wind loud in your ears. And if you found the right line – if you did that, you enhanced your forward momentum, doubling your speed. That made the run more exciting, but also dangerous. You could slip up, crash and burn. For me, nothing supersedes that split-second moment of finding my flow and placing the words exactly on the beat, so they fit like bricks in a wall. Sometimes I would forget what I said, how I'd said it. That would piss me off, especially when me, Cal, MCP, P. Nutt and Sy Rocc would freestyle and I said a few dope lines. I tried to urge Reason to tape our sessions but he never would, saying it was a waste of TDK's.

P. was leaning forward on the bed, pumping his fist in the air aggressively. I finished my rhyme, bigging up my DJ while Reka cut up Original Concept's *Can You Feel It*. When I put down the mic, Reka hit the stop button. A second later P. was up in my face.

'Oh my days, that was live, blud, yuh gonna mash it up nex week, I'm showin you . . .'

'You reckon?' I panted, knowing. Reason and Cal had paused their game and turned, offering fists. I tried not to smile, even though I gave Reka a look of congratulations. We'd done it. We were in with a chance.

I gave it another few goes, and we were good, just not as energetic as we had been. I was about to try again when the bedroom door opened. P. Nutt and Sy breezed in. Everyone gave us a look. Me and Reka knew what that meant. Reka tried to defend it a little, refused to move. Sy took one glance at his resolute face and made a beeline for him.

'Wha you screwin me for, blud? Man'll tuck you in yuh nuh . . .'

'Move from the decks, rudebwoy . . .' P. Nutt added.

There was nothing we could do. I gathered my rhyme book and paperback then unplugged my mic, sliding both furtively into my rucksack. Reka busied himself putting away records and avoiding slaps to his head. Reason gave me a sorrowful look, but didn't say anything. No one said anything when those guys were around.

Westwood had been playing Wormwood Scrubs Park for the last two summers. No one knew how long it would last. Everyone from every manor in London came, which made it a mad, bad and dangerous place to be. Last year a few of the local shops had been raided – kids were mugged for their trainers with CS gas and there were lots of irate residents. There had also been fit gullies, dance battles and live performances from the top UK MCs of the day. I'd managed to get off with a green-eyed, light-skinned girl who looked like Mr Tibbs' wife from the TV show *In The Heat of The Night*. I even went out with her for a few months, although she lived in Harrow, which was too far for me and I called it a day. Reka met a girl who claimed she was a cousin of the Wee Papa Girl Rappers and granted him a series of sexy liaisons on the South Acton Estate. He cut her off too, mostly due to the potential danger of visiting an area where he didn't live. This year

Westwood promised an MC battle that would net the winner a whole £50. Not enough for crate loads of Bacardi and Coke, or even my favourite Peach Canei, but we told ourselves prestige was worth more than money. We'd been practising our routine every day since Westwood broadcast the prize on KISS. Secretly, although I didn't find out until years later, me and Reka both hoped we'd get a spratt if we won.

The coins lay on hot concrete, glinting in the sun. I was surprised to find them still there. After we'd collected my scattered change Reka and I walked to the bus stop. Sometimes we caught the 31 and got off after four stops, where either a 7 or a 70 would take us home. But on long summer evenings when the sky was still bright and there was a chance of seeing girls, we sauntered down the Great Western Road taking in sights. Sometimes we even bought a cold beer. Shopkeepers would never serve me, so I usually talked a passing adult into going while I waited outside. Reka, who had a full beard and was pushing six feet, had no trouble buying alcohol.

I remember the world as bright, colourful, full of music blasting from car speakers and noise and summer heat. It was the school holidays, perfect for entire days spent hanging out. Carnival was less than a month away. Part of me didn't want to think about that. The festival, billed as Europe's largest street party, signalled the unofficial end of summer. A week after that we'd be back in school.

We cut through the flats and hit the bus stop, which

was packed with people. A sweet smell of baking bread wafted from the Domino's Pizza a few yards from where we stood. I tried to ignore it; neither of us had any money, even though we both had the munchies. There was a number 7 Routemaster at the bus stop, but it must have been waiting for the driver to change, as he wasn't letting anyone on board. I was cussing because I'd scuffed my Cross Trainers on the curb when we'd run across the road. Reka ignored me as usual, beat-boxing into his cupped hands. I began to rhyme. People were looking at us, some of the adults smiling at the ground as though they liked what we were doing but didn't want to let on. Everyone else ignored us, barring a toddler who stared up, confused, toothless mouth gaping.

A group of kids our age came out from the corner store opposite the stop. I turned my head and watched from my peripheral vision. Reka hadn't seen them. I was willing the bus to get started when they began to cross, holding up their jeans as they jogged around cars and gathered in front of us. Reka stopped beat boxing. I trailed off into half-formed mutters.

'Ay my yout, where you goin wi dem jeans y'ave on?'

I looked down at my Pepe's, up at the kid who'd spoken. He had dry lips and dry skin. Even the hair beneath his Laker's baseball cap resembled dusty desert weeds. You could see the dandruff trapped between his tightened curls from three steps away. I measured my thoughts, trying not to laugh, knowing I stood a good chance of feeling cold steel between my ribs if my lips even twitched.

'Uh . . . What d'you mean, my Pepe's?'

'What the fuck d'you think I mean, you chief?'

Dry Head was up in my face, all cheesy-Quavers breath. I looked beyond him at his crew. Every one wore the same pair of Pepe's as mine, baggy loose-fitting denim blues with lime-green stitching. I looked over at Reka, who was biting his lip and looking around the street, nervous. Willing him to get involved. He must have felt what I was thinking because all of a sudden our eyes met, and I saw the shift in his stare, his pity.

'Ah come on, man, 'llow the brer . . .' he finally said, trying to insert himself between the sweaty body of the kid and mine. Even Dry Head's BO smelt old, like a sandy patch of parched musk beneath his arms. The other youths began jostling Reka, trying to get a reaction.

'Take em off . . . *Now*! I ain' jokin wid you, rude-bwoy . . .' Dry Head muttered, eyes cast down at my jeans.

Another kid came out of the corner store, saw what was happening and ran to join his friends even as I protested. He looked eager to get involved until he reached us. His face went pale. He stared at his livid friend, who was shouting loud enough for everyone to hear, and then back at us, unsure. The adults moved away. I had a hand on my silver name buckle, ready to comply if knives were produced. Reka was keeping the others away from me, long arms outstretched like Mr Tickle. New Kid made up his mind.

'Blud, you know P. Nutt an Sy, innit?' he said, pushing Dry Head back with a sweeping hand.

'Yeah. So?' Reka's face was screwed up as though he'd been forced to chew grit. He actually looked like he would have fought, had it come to that. I was surprised.

'See what I mean about you, man?' New Kid said to his friends. 'Leave dem, man, let dem go bout their business, yeah? I don't want trouble wiv none ah dem bwoy deh . . .'

It was as though he'd said the secret code. His crew stepped back, as one, leaving Reka with ample space to approach. They grunted apologies as they backed off. I watched them re-cross the road, feeling as though I was dreaming. When Reka put a hand on my shoulder I almost jumped. The bus driver, who'd been sitting in his cab the whole fucking time, told the conductor he could start letting people on. We climbed aboard the Routemaster and took the stairs to the top deck.

We talked about it on the way home; the deck was empty so we took a whole seat each, talking loud and cussing the youths. The conductor didn't even bother to come up, knowing we had child photocards. Reka was laughing, saying I actually looked like I was going to drop my jeans. I laughed with him, denying, even though it was true.

At Ladbroke Grove station there was a thump of heavy feet on the narrow stairs. Two girls, both dark-skinned, wearing short skirts, leggings and trainers, both with baseball caps perched on relaxed hair. They were giggling and laughing, even more so when they saw us. We stopped talking, waiting to see what they'd do next.

One walked all the way to the front seats. The other

sat at the back. They continued the conversation they'd been having on the stairs about some girl from their estate they didn't like because she thought she was too nice to sleep with the first girl's cousin, but had slept with a world of men from Kilburn Estate. I looked at Reka. He rolled his eyes. The girl at the front told the girl at the back she couldn't hear, she would have to come closer. Reka began to smile. The first girl walked all the way to the back of the bus, gave me a pointed look, smiled and sat next to me. Her friend laughed as though that was the funniest thing she'd ever seen. We ignored them both, playing it cool and looking out of the window at the big houses on St Mark's Road. When we got to the roundabout on St Helen's, the bus threw us against the windows as it turned. The first girl made an obviously exaggerated attempt to fall on my shoulder.

'Oops, sorry,' she said with a grin.

I laughed and asked her name.

'Desiree.' She turned to the girl behind her. 'That's Myanna.'

I introduced myself and Reka, asking where they went to school.

'Sion Vaughan.' That was an all-girls school, five minutes from St Helen's. 'Don't you guys rap with P. Nutt and Sy? We heard you on Isis.'

I was slightly pissed that the names had come up yet again, the emotion much diluted by the fact these lovely ladies had heard what would probably be my only live broadcast; on that particular pirate at least. I'd thought it had gone well enough, and so did Reka actually, but when we came out of the studio all the

Isis guys were locked in a backroom. Reka and me weren't allowed in, but P. Nutt and Sy were. They were there fifteen minutes while the DJ played Jazzy Jeff and Fresh Prince's *Live at Union Square '88*, and Reka studied the cover of *Criminal Minded* as though searching for a hidden message in Scott La Rock's face. He wouldn't look at me, even once. When they came out everyone was cool, but when we walked home P. Nutt said the studio manager told him there were too many MCs on Isis already, and they were cutting down, so I wouldn't be able to come back. Reka kept his head down and didn't say a word. On the way home we talked a bit about jealousy and that was it. Done.

I told the girls we would be performing at Scrubb's, if they cared to come along. Myanna leaned forwards. She had an expansive dark cleavage and a tangled jumble of gold chains that glittered all the way down.

'Maybe you lot should make a date an' ting innit?' she chewed around her gum. 'Desiree thinks you're nice. D'you think she's fit?'

I told her yes, though I'm sure that my eyes expressed my lust more sincerely. Desiree licked her lips, leaned back and assessed me. I felt like she was testing her power.

'Meet me by the stage at five?'

I said cool. Reka nudged my elbow. We had to get off. Waving goodbye, I took the stairs down without looking back in case I tripped, bust my head and fell out of the open door onto the street. We waved the girls off as the bus trundled away in a blast of diesel smoke. Covered our noses and walked home.

Reka could have gone one stop further, so I was grateful he'd stepped off with me. We crowed, beginning to plan what we would do with Desiree and Myanna if they gave us their numbers. Reka lived on Greenside Close, a collection of relatively new blocks across the road from the underground station. My home was an exact clone of all the others on a quiet street beneath the shadow of the A40 Westway. He walked me as far as the warren of subways that snaked beneath the overpass, where we touched fists, wished each other luck, went on our separate ways. I'd taken a few steps before I remembered to tell him to keep practising. I trotted back and yelled into the subway but all I heard was an echo of my own voice, fading into silence.

I lived with my mother and younger brother in the three-bedroom council house I was born in. It was small and cramped but according to my mother the house was heaven compared with the mash-up flats on Greenside. I liked it well enough, although given the choice I would have lived on the estate where most of my school friends were. Mum, who had a good few friends on the estate too, was always going on about how lucky it was that we'd never had to move when Dad died. I'd long been tired of hearing her try to turn something so morbid into a supposed luxury I didn't even care about.

My brother was still in primary school, and even though I loved him loads our objectives were poles apart. He wanted to watch cartoons and talk forever about his collection of Matchbox cars. I wanted to talk hip-hop and girls. I supposed it would get better in a few years, when he joined my school and caught up with the rest of the adult world, but for now my brother was nothing more than a pleasant distraction from the most important things in my life. Mum, much as I hated to say at the time, was a schoolteacher, of all things. She worked on the other side of London, which was great when school was in, but murder during the holidays. My friends would have their places to themselves, but oh no, not me; every day I had to come back to Mum's scowling face, asking where I'd been, whether I'd been smoking. A long ting. The worse thing was the books. Stacked everywhere, falling off shelves, packed in boxes that suggested they'd never even been read; fuckin books everywhere. OK, even I had to admit she would sometimes catch me sitting with my back against cardboard, an open novel resting against my knees. It helped with rhyming to learn new words, didn't it? On the rare occasions Mum came home from work to find me like that, she'd tousle my hair and smile, even though she looked tired. I hated the snide twist of her lips, the look of triumph on her face as she walked into the kitchen and asked what I wanted for dinner.

That Sunday was the hottest day of the year so far, which meant Scrubbs Park was rammed. The maximum-security prison sat on the horizon, an ominous threat. You could see the haze of heat rise across the shorn expanse of corn-yellow grass, making hundreds of bodies shimmer like trees in a wildlife programme. Me and Reka were disappointed to see the huge main stage Westwood usually had was gone; instead, there was a rickety sound system set up between towering black speakers. When we got close it was difficult not to trip on thick cables, making the Cat security members, who were not known for their kindness, stare us down until we eyeballed our identical pairs of trainers and the tiny mounds of mud left by worms. We signed our names on a sheet of A4 offered by a pretty girl in a pink rah-rah skirt and fishnet tights, topped off with a skin-tight red T-shirt. I would have chirped her if I wasn't so nervous. Nothing was happening, but my insides were alight with fear. Westwood was playing *Rock Creek Park*, the bass echoing over the grass. Families laid rugs down and ate from picnic baskets. Teenagers wandered from spot to spot.

'How we gonna meet dem gullies if the main stage's gone?' Reka said when we'd signed up.

'They'll see us when we go on, don't watch dat . . .'

My casual air was a blatant act. I'd been thinking much the same thing. Reka wasn't buying it. He seemed worried.

'Yeah but look how much people's about, if we go on early they might not see us . . .'

'Wha you worrying about anyway, man, they weren't chirpin you . . .'

That caused Reka to thump me. I thumped him back and pretty soon we were kicking at each other until we got too hot. We stopped, panting, went looking for our friends until we saw MCP, Calalloo and Reason not far from the speakers. They were blazing. Reka and me joined them. They looked lean up already, even though Westwood only started an hour before.

'Yes, my youts . . .'

'What's every man sayin?'

Fists knocked against fists.

'You sign up den?' MCP asked.

'Yeah, mate, blatant . . . You?' I said, taking the zook when offered.

'Nah man, fuck dat shit . . .'

'Why not, man? You should show man what man's dealin wid . . .'

Reka gave me a look and we tried not to smile. We were secretly glad P. and Cal weren't rhyming. They were stiff competition. The MCs leaned back and looked at the sky as if they knew this was the case and couldn't be bothered to argue. Then again, maybe that was just the green.

P. Nutt and Sy Rocc bowled past, their tall, lean figures looking even more monstrous from our reclined positions. My breathing got faster as they looked at me; I swore they were gonna try it, fuck up my vibe for the competition, but for once they kept going, bouncing on Nike Airs, open shirts fanned behind them like superhero's capes, exposing bird chests. Our group had fallen silent when the older kids bopped past. When their shadows moved on and the sun fell on our patch of grass, we continued as though a spectre had passed overhead.

The call for rap crews came not long after we crushed our last spliff. We stumbled to our feet, made our way to the sound system. Westwood was still calling MCs and their DJs when we got to the criss gully in the rah-rah skirt; he didn't even look our way as we queued with other hopefuls; only five or so, mostly solo rappers. We ignored each other, watching Westwood, who was dressed in a purple fur Kangol and dark shades with his trademark black bomber jacket and black 501s; a kind of punk-meets-hip-hop look. The crowd gathered around the sound system. All I could see were dark faces. Reka pushed my shoulder, waking me. We touched fists hard, ignoring the pain. Reka was sweating. He wiped his palms on his jeans repeatedly. The first act was called.

I honestly can't remember whether the people who went before us were actually good or not, just that I sneered my way through their performances and when it was our turn we elbowed past the rappers, up to the decks. There was a weighty silence as Reka fumbled records from sleeves. A spotty girl at the front with Salt-n-Pepa blonde highlights said, 'Look, his hands are shakin,' which couldn't have helped. I could feel the stickiness of sweat between my fingers and the mic. The hot sun made my temples pound.

I heard Reka cutting 'Pump Me Up' just the way we'd practised. I watched the crowd react with enthusiasm as they realised they knew the tune. When he dropped 'Peter Piper' and the beat kicked in everyone went wild. One girl was doing the Wop so hard it looked as though her head would fall from her neck, throwing her arms back and forth, fist-fighting air. The front row threatened to bury the sound system as the crowd surged forwards. Westwood had a tiny, rarely seen smile on his face. I let the beat roll for another two bars and launched into my rhyme.

It was better than anything I had dreamed. My nerves and the crowd response had hyped me up, and the words came out stronger, faster and with more clarity than they ever did in Reason's basement. I was flowing like liquid gold, melting everything in my path. I caught sight of my friends bouncing in the thick of the crowd, watching me with wide eyes, urging me on. It felt good. It felt *great*. I was *slaying* the MCs before me . . .

A white brer dancing in the front row had the Kangol snatched from his head. First he tried to grab it, then he tried to protest and before anyone could react, the snatcher swung a wooden baseball bat into his face, hitting at least two people on the backswing. The white brer fell to the ground, clutching his face.

There was pandemonium.

Girls ran screaming. Some bait guys did too, although they'd never admit it. The snatcher kept hitting the guy even though he was down. Fights broke out everywhere. When I turned to look at Reka, he was hastily putting the needle on another wax. I wasn't sure what he was doing until he cued it up, flipped the fader and began to cut the opening line from 'Can You Feel It', which was actually 'Can You Feel It . . .' I wanted to say maybe that wasn't a good idea, but before I could Westwood snatched the needle from the wax, yelled, *'You're disqualified!'* then ripped the record from the decks. I stood there holding the mic, my heart pumping, the crowd still yelling, feet rooted to the spot. Reka looked dismayed. I could tell he knew he'd fucked up. I switched the microphone off.

* * *

We saw who won when Cat Security calmed everything, mostly by cracking some heads. MC Byron, some brer from East who wasn't even all that. He was smug and loud and I hated him on sight. Westwood said a lot of shit about the battle being close, waved the edge note in the air, and announced the winner with over-hyped flourish. It was obvious Byron totally knew the Bobby Moore when he looked into the crowd and everyone fell silent. There was withheld violence in the air, the thick feel of an approaching storm. I'd never felt an atmosphere like it. Byron took the edge note from Westwood, cried, 'This is for you, London!' and threw it into the crowd. Arms and legs were still flailing like a hundred drowning swimmers when we turned our backs and left.

Reka and me walked to the edge of the park, where the grass thinned into black dust and the one block housing estate began. There were others who'd left when the fighting erupted again, walking in threes and fours, scuffing black clouds with their trainers. Reka and me were silent. There was nothing to say. He knew we'd stood a good chance of winning the fifty pounds; we knew we'd have never left the park with the money.

We saw them when we got to the edge of the path, by the noisy main road. P. Nutt and Sy Rocc with their arms curled around two fit gullies, whispering in their ears, making them squirm. Reka looked at me. It was Desiree and Myanna. Our girls. They didn't even have the grace to look shamed. Myanna took no notice. Desiree smiled and snapped her gum before turning her head and burying it in Sy Rocc's chest. Neither of the older youths saw us; they were totally caught up by the girls. I wanted to say something to Reka, but I held my tongue and walked on.

The walk continued in silence until we got to the underpass. We stopped and looked at the Westway, the speeding cars and Central Line train beneath us, clattering westwards in a thunder of metal wheels. I wanted to tell Reka what I'd been thinking since I'd seen the older youths holding what was rightfully ours; that maybe the rap thing wasn't for me; maybe what had happened on Scrubs was a sign; maybe I was fooling myself about the whole thing, being part of a global hip-hop culture and all, maybe the London scene would never match the States. I wanted to tell him everything, but when I opened my mouth I heard myself say something that surprised me.

'Look, Reka blud, I know we're boys an all dat, but you gotta tell me the truth, yeah? You think all dis shit happens to me – to *us* – because I'm white?'

And I have to say one thing about my friend – the friend that I have to this day – he never once blinked, hesitated or looked away. Instead, Reka put a firm hand on my shoulder.

'Nah, blud. Wha you talkin bout? No way. I'll see you tomorrow yeah?'

He walked down the concrete steps into the underpass. I watched, thinking he probably would.

Spider Man

It had already begun when we saw the spider. There we were, lying on my bed, sweat drying on our bodies, breathing fast and noisy when I noticed. Hanging upside down. Perched like a predatory bird. It could have been looking at us from its upturned position on the ceiling, but then, how could we tell? I watched it for a long time that night, though to be honest I wasn't entirely surprised. Three nights ago I had gone to bed alone and laid eyes on the spider. I'd been tempted to get out my newly purchased Goblin vacuum cleaner, suck the creature into dusty oblivion. I would've done it too, but it was late, around three in the morning. Besides, I'd thought, it would probably be gone by the time I got up for work. Now here I was, looking up at the same spider on the same spot of ceiling, wondering why it was still there. Surely it needed to eat. How long could an animal stay in one spot, rigid as a corpse, without some kind of food, however alien it might be?

'Shit, Darren, you know there's a massive spider on your ceiling?' You saw it and instantly freaked out, like usual.

'Yeah, I know. It's been there a few days. I'm gonna Hoover it up if it don't move.'

You looked at me, frown lines on your forehead running left to right. I loved it when you frowned. By then, I'd pretty much realised that I loved everything you did. Every word and sigh, every groan as you bent to take off your boots when you came in at night. Every step, every smile, every gesture.

'You can't! It's not right. The poor thing's frightened. It's probably sitting there thinking we're gonna kill it or something, scared out of its wits.'

'I doubt it.' We were both looking up at the dark-brown creature, immobile on the stark white of my ceiling. 'I think its dead.'

'It can't be. Wouldn't it fall?'

'Dunno. Don't think so. It's been there four nights and it hasn't moved.' I sat up a little, getting closer but not close enough. Visions of John Hurt from the *Alien* movie lurked in my mind. Ridiculous as the possibility seemed, I was spooked. 'D'you think a spider loses its ability to climb when it dies?' You shrugged in reply and thought about it afterwards, as was your fashion. 'I thought it was scared at first, but it must've just kicked the bucket standing up, or in this case standing upside down. One of those freaks of nature you hear about all the time, never see.'

I looked back down at the bed, feeling clever, wondering what you would make of that. Lying back on the pillow, hair fanned out around you, arms framing your head as if in horror, you were already lost in thought.

'I suppose . . .' Now you were looking up, dark eyes wide, mouth open. At that point I had one of my moments, an emotional rush of feeling. Right then I loved you more than ever and I leant over your face, blocking your view of the still, eight-legged body, kissing you full on the lips. Before long we were making love again, rocking back and forth to a rhythm that was all our own, the spider forgotten as fresh sweat began to course the contours of our bodies.

Temporarily banished from our thoughts, the image of the spider returned during our last few weeks together, still and silent, appearing like a portent of some terrible thing, though I barely knew.

And why should I? It had been love at first sight, as sure and undeniable as anything found in novels and rom-coms. Me walking into All Bar One for a drink with Richard, Johnny, Mika and a few other friends from work, you already there, invited because you were cousins with Richard and you'd both grown up as close as index and second finger, and everybody who'd met you liked you, probably even fancied you, but were scared to say anything because you were like a sister to Richard and he was built like a professional wrestler. I walked in, I remember like it happened five minutes ago, shouting and being generally rowdy as was my fashion, hugging Richard as hard as a footballer, clapping him hard on his back. Then I looked over his shoulder, saw you. As much as I tried to hide it – because I knew who you were through Mika and Johnny always going on about you – I couldn't help staring into your eyes. All the shouting suddenly got caught in my throat. I remember you looking back at me, unabashed, a tiny smile at the corner of your lips and your wine glass half-raised so it caught the overhead lights, glinting like a distant star. The overall effect was like being pounded over the head with a plank of wood. You raised the glass higher, sipped and mouthed 'Hello', but by that time Richard, who was wondering what was going on, was shaking me and saying, 'Good you could make it, it's been ages, man,' and Mika and Johnny were laughing because they'd seen the whole thing and you were just standing there smiling into your Chardonnay because you knew. You bloody well knew.

When it seemed appropriate and I had calmed myself enough to speak coherently, I made my way over to you armed with a pint of Belgian courage – Stella Artois. Our conversation began with a brief introduction and then moved on to mutual acquaintances, before eventually progressing to our appreciation of art in its many forms: literature, contemporary visual art, music, modern dance and, of course, film. I had just watched *The Sea Inside*. You, the Korean art-house flick *Oldboy*. We discussed differences in taste and themes until the bar closed. Mika and Johnny had long gone home, much to your dismay – you told me that you were disappointed you hadn't got to talk. I felt a pang of something, I wasn't sure what, but held it down; after all, I hardly knew you. We swapped numbers. I felt better after that, forgot my earlier annoyance. Richard and I both walked you to the tube station. When you left, Richard told me that you made it a point never to give out your mobile, let alone your landline number. You liked me, he urged. I was probably the first guy you'd truly liked in a long time.

I was happy, of course; this gave me the confidence to ring a few days later to discuss the terms of our first date. When we met, it was at that Thai restaurant above the pub in Farringdon, a compromise between your

North and my West London home. You were wearing a burgundy dress and were even chattier than before, full of smiles and compliments, which I easily matched. You seemed relaxed and free of hang ups, unlike most girls I'd dated. Our topics were wide ranging, covering everything from the latest bashment artist to the recent Turner Prize winner. We even talked about sex (or the lack of it, in a conversation centred on Viagra). You were (and still are, I might add) prettier than most of the women I'd dated, the type of girl I'd long eyed from afar but never quite managed to talk to. Richard was right and I was grateful, I concluded, ordering for you and myself.

The food was excellent, company better. Conversation flowed so well it was difficult to eat without talking with my mouth full. I found myself relaxing in my seat, able to say anything and not worry about offending you, or at the very least being misunderstood. I tried not to get too comfortable, but both of us bloody well knew by that time, and we were both fine with the thought.

I invited you back to my house. Explained that I had no plans to try to get you into bed, that I'd order and pay for a cab whenever you wanted to leave. To my surprise, you said yes. We caught the train to Belsize Road, the food working on me like a narcotic, so I was in no position for any unclothed gymnastics once the door was shut behind us and we were sitting on the sofa watching late-night TV. We drank a little more and then I fell asleep on your shoulder, you rubbing my head like a baby. A couple of hours later you woke me, saying you were ready to leave. I called the cab.

I was already missing you by the time the sound of the rattling engine died. Still, I knew that I'd done the right thing and scored irreplaceable brownie points.

The rewards of my forward thinking became very much apparent over the next few months. We began meeting on a regular basis. You finally invited me to your house after an evening at your local cinema. Would you mind if I admitted now that I knew, from the moment the door slammed behind us, what you wanted? Probably had known from outside, when you first asked me in? We hadn't kissed, or even touched (I had fallen asleep in the darkness, mouth open although silent, and you didn't notice until the film was nearly over). Somehow, as quietly as the breath I had expelled, we had decided. What followed happened without words or questions. That was the thing I loved most about our relationship.

It all fell into place as the night was reaching middle age. I thought I'd do the gallant thing and ask for a taxi number. You said you didn't have one, smiling in that beguiling fashion you had, letting me know even though I'd already guessed, and that was when I leaned forward and kissed you, as lightly as I could. You turned your head upwards, tasting of peppermint tea and popcorn and at all once I knew that was how I must taste too. I remember thinking how much of your-self you placed in that one kiss; how you surrendered, let go, allowed me inside with no restrictions. We took our time, savoured each other and the moment, not touching, or even breathing heavily, just enjoying that taste and feel of each other, appreciating the warmth, every nerve and sensory path wide open. I hadn't been expecting the feeling of giving myself over, of being accepted totally. It took me to places I'd never been. When we eventually fell asleep that morning, the sun was creeping upwards and orange light was flooding the room. I held you close. This time it was different, there was no denying. I had finally found someone good.

As the months passed my feelings grew deeper. And with them came a new emotion I had never experienced. Jealousy sneaked up like a jewel thief during our first night together. It snatched my heart right out of my chest when I wasn't looking and was miles away before I'd even realised it was gone. The first I knew of this was the night of our first real get together since All Bar One, the drink up at your flat. You often threw drinks parties, you'd told me two weeks before. They usually involved the same circle of friends and workmates coming over with a dish, or some booze, preferably both. There would be music, a little dancing, but mostly good conversation, good food and lots of drinking. This particular night was homemade-cocktail night. Each guest had been instructed to bring a mixer. You had got your long disused blender out, and Richard had promised to stay in the kitchen mixing drinks until the alcohol was gone. When I look back, given my state of mind, it was a recipe for bad things to come.

At first, everything had been fine. We'd got the flat ready together, made love just before the first guests arrived, done our own thing as the doorbell began to ring with increasing regularity. Neo-soul was on the stereo. I'd drunk two glasses of champagne and had stimulating conversation with a Chinese student from the London College of Fashion, so I was feeling pretty damn good. Until I looked for you. The sight of you talking close with Mika, your lips next to his ear and a hand on his biceps began to make something smoulder inside my belly, something I'd never even known was there, something that had me clutching my white plastic cup until it scrunched in my hand, making the nearest people turn and look. I backed away and headed for the kitchen. Richard was there, chatting to the Chinese student, who seemed to be eating up his every word.

'All right, bruv,' he said, snatching a glance at me while making sure the student (Wai, wasn't that her name?) didn't think he was losing interest. I was nodding, reaching for the large glass bowl of a brownish-looking liquid I hadn't encountered yet.

'I'd watch that if I were you, mate; it's got some kick. There's about different four spirits in it.'

'Yeah?' I paused, the ladle dribbling alcohol back into the bowl. I could smell what he meant from the splashes dancing around me like fireflies. Wai raised her cup. She'd been drinking champagne when I'd been speaking to her, and her little white cup wasn't even a third full.

'Take your time,' she advised. 'Drink *slow*.'

Of course, macho as I was feeling, that left me no other option but to half fill my little white cup, ignore Wai's shaking head and Richard's questioning glance, leaving them to their own courting devices. When I got back into the living room you were dancing with Mika; not touching, or even close up – but even you have to admit that it *was* slow and sensual enough to make spectators clap, make Mika wipe his forehead when you wound down low in front of him, doing moves like the girls in those videos. The embers of my fire caught, began to emit dark smoke. I stepped back a little, shielded by your friends, watching you dance and Mika feign resistance, sipping homemade cocktail in an attempt to douse the growing flames. When the next tune ended, someone put on bashment. I waited to see what you'd do, feeling faint pleasure when you threw your hands in the air and shook your head, gave Mika a kiss on the cheek and left the room to come looking for me. With your back to him, you couldn't see the expression on his face. I did. As we both looked over your shoulder from opposite ends of the room, we caught each other's eyes. Mika instantly turned away, running a hand through his hair, face reddening, realising I knew what he was thinking. My fire became a blaze. By the time you got to me it was already way out of control, turning reason into black, smouldering skeletons, charred remains of rational thought. You were smiling until you saw me avert my gaze. I was looking at the floor. I still remember how my eyes, on their rapid journey downwards, couldn't help but pass my empty plastic cup.

'Whassup?'

'Nothing.'

You peered at me. Through my haze of drunken thought I still had time to notice how pretty you were, to find sympathy for Mika, who had been single so long even his mother was beginning to ask what the problem was.

'It doesn't look like nothing from here.'

'Well it is, seriously. I'm just not feeling too good, probably had too much to drink. Maybe I should go home.'

You grabbed at my arm. Just like you grabbed at Mika's, I thought to myself. The flames caught again, fanned by irrationality. I snatched away, relishing the flash of shock on your face. It came from nowhere, fast as sheet lightning but just as bright, and before I knew it you had become a solid rock before me, eyes hard and jaw held rigid. You glared at me a moment, straining for neutrality. I watched, waiting to see what you had to say.

'Why are you being like this?' Your whisper managed to scrape my ears and give me a moment of reproach. Unspoken accusation was alive in my body. I leant towards you for better effect.

'I *saw* you – with Mika . . .'

You were looking at me, blinking slowly, not getting what I meant. When your eyes lit up I knew that I was wrong, even though I held the hurt close to my chest, unwilling to take back my manufactured falsehood, even though it was shared.

'Are you serious? Are you really gonna come to me with that kind of stupidness? You might as well go home for real if that's what you think –'

'Fine. I'll talk to you tomorrow.'

I left the flat with my fire bright, no cause for the blaze. Mika stared, somewhat triumphantly, as I passed his shoulder and the urge to strike him caused the flames to rage and roar. I forced it down as I grabbed my coat, not looking behind me in case I saw your face and the glare in your eyes, urging me to come back inside and stop immersing myself in the heat of my own self-pity.

We made up quickly. Following twelve hours of body-numbing silence, you turned up at my flat that Sunday evening with a downcast face, eyes hazy from drink, your very physicality begging forgiveness. I let you inside, knowing you had done no wrong, accepting your apology. That night, for the first time, you told me you loved me. I felt triumph, though little belief. Hours later we saw the spider on my ceiling. Without knowing, we were approaching the end.

For what I had realised in the living room, staring at you dance with Mika, was that you were too good for me. That while I shuffled about in complacency, immersed only in the simple joy of being with you, others would be waiting for me to make some fatal mistake. Friendship would provide no protection. You told the best jokes, had the most interesting stories, danced harder, wore tight dresses, smiled and entranced the world. I, on the other hand, was nothing more than a sprig of moss growing at the foot of a mighty volcano. Brave, when looked at in isolation. Strong. Hearty even. Unnoticeable beneath the eternal shadow cast by my nearest neighbour.

I began to take closer note at the effect that you had on people. Seeing what I had first thought of as the visual epiphany that had been mine alone replayed in the faces of various men stung like a nettle. And there was nowhere I was safe. Walking along the high street in Stoke Newington, seeing the way shop-keepers, butchers and newsagents alike would stand to attention, smile your way and wheeze a hello, eyes focused on nothing but you. The way we would walk into a restaurant and seated men would obviously forget what they had been saying, trailing off into nothing, averting their eyes only when I stared just as hard in return. The overzealous courtesy of waiters. The eager determination of guys at parties who would box you into a corner like a championship fighter, forcing you around the ring, pummelling your defences, pushing you against the ropes until you would shoot me a resigned look, imploring me to come over and throw in your blood-stained towel. And even then, I suppose, that hurt me the most. The resignation in your eyes, the pity you showed as you walked home, bruised and tired, aware that your beauty was a cross to bear in life, a burden hefted by us both. I resented being forced to carry such an unwieldy object, one I'd had no knowledge of when we had met. I think my arms grew weary.

A few weeks after the homemade cocktail party we attended a film screening as part of Black History Month. It was a cold, rainy Sunday. Attendance numbered at somewhere around twenty, sat in a theatre built to house hundreds. The film was a documentary about the cultural, social and literary activist that had been the late John La Rose. It had been your choice and, as the programme began at twelve p.m., I had been reluctant to get out of bed. However, sitting in the dark of the Renoir in Russell Square, sipping on a lukewarm coffee, I began to relax and focus on the life and times of someone who had been a great, if not infamous, man. A silent, focused calm saturated the cinema. The feeling was pervasive, generated mostly, I believe, by the image of the man himself, talking in a soft yet urgently passionate voice, his toughest comments sweetened with a smile. I felt you relax against my shoulder, place a hand on my biceps and rub. When the lights came up you shook your head and began to curse the apathy of black people for their lack of attendance. A man seated behind you heard what you had to say and voiced well-natured disagreement. And that was it. The man, who had come to the Renoir on his own, spoke to you for forty-five minutes, first in the cinema, then afterwards in the café area when we had been ejected to make way for the next film. I took a limited part in the conversation but was mostly ignored, owing to my lack of knowledge on the subject and the fact that the man, whoever he was, just didn't see me. Whenever I looked at him it was clear his eyes were only filled up with an image of you, leaving me to wander the area making silly small talk with people I didn't know, or browse the selection of indie films with no idea which director I was looking at, or even the style of filmmaking. Again, I had proved my ineptitude. I knew nothing of John La Rose or New Beacon Books, the publishing company he had run, although I was familiar with some of the authors he'd had in print.

When I saw the man touch your shoulder and watched you back away, I immediately felt vindicated, although when he got out his mobile and made you recite your number an arc of pain leaped through my body. I saw your mouth move, form silent digits. Imagined you were my very own Judas, whispering subtle words of betrayal.

I turned my back, fingered the DVDs before me. You touched my arm moments later and we left. I know you sensed my anger, because I said very little on the journey underground. And still, varied men rocked back and forth in the cocoon of the tube carriage encouraged by my silence, eyes travelling up and down your body while you read a Sunday paper discarded by some other passenger and I scanned them from the corner of my eye. Every page you turned made my jaw clench tighter. Every moment you ignored them made me angrier.

Walking up the steps to my front door, I felt like I was going to explode. You rested your head against my cheek as I fumbled with the keys because my hands were shaking. I had to try three times. You never even noticed. Instead you smiled to yourself, hummed a jazz melody and didn't say a word.

Inside I threw down my keys and stalked into the kitchen. I was thinking maybe a drink of water would cool me down. I turned my cold tap roughly and blasted some in a glass, listened to see what you were doing. Silence. I walked out of the kitchen. My front door was at the bottom of a thin set of stairs, wide enough for just one person to climb to the top, where he or she would find the living room and bedroom, the kitchen to the right, the bathroom to the immediate left, and the door to the spare-room directly opposite the kitchen. You were bent over at the top of the stairs, one hand against the bathroom wall, attempting without success to take off your boots. They were calf-length leather, ending just beneath the knee, and along with your black stockings, short corduroy skirt, and fitted black jumper, they only served to amplify your image as a sexy, yet entirely classy breed of female. You always had trouble taking off those boots. Usually you would call and ask me to help, but on that day you had sensed my mood acutely enough to struggle on your own, mute, red-faced. You were so intent on your task you didn't even notice me. As the thought made me smart my ball of anger flared like a sunspot. Before I knew what I was doing I had crossed the few steps it took to reach you, raised my hand behind me as far as it would go, let it fly, bringing it crashing against your cheek.

The angle of the blow made you stumble. The awkwardness of your position meant you fell back against the bathroom wall, arm crooked so that for one moment it looked as though you would fall down the stairs and crash against the front door. I hardly believe it myself, but my fires were raging so bright that I almost wished you would tumble down the stairs and land there, curled beneath my feet in an undignified heap. I watched and waited; it did not happen. In a moment you righted yourself, clawed your way back to the top step, holding onto the wall with both hands. It was only then that you could look me in the eye, see me standing with what must have looked like the fury of God in my eyes. And you're such an intelligent, understanding, empathetic woman that you saw everything. Even though you had ignored it all until this point, your understanding was crystal clear. I felt the glass of water I'd gulped enter my stomach, slow and cold.

You bent over again, getting to work on the boot.

For a moment I thought that you were going to forget what I'd done, take off your shoes and banish yourself to some lonely corner of the flat. I would be ignored, denied once more. Before I could even contemplate the irrationality of that, I realised in fact that you were putting the boot on. When it was secured you stood to your full height, towering over me by at least two inches. You spat in my face. I can still feel the heat, the thickness, the shock of it landing on my nose, cheeks and eyelids. I wiped. The door had already shut. You were gone.

When my fires had been put out, partly by more water, mostly by a lack of flammable materials, I came to terms with what I had done. I phoned you, many times, but there was no answer. You had spare keys to my flat, and I wasn't surprised when I came home from work one day to see that everything belonging to you was gone. Your cuddly toys, CDs and DVDs, your postcards from the Tate Modern and your many, many books. The keys were placed on top of the long-dead fireplace, together with a note that said 'You Bastard'. That was our final communication. It shouldn't have been that way. I only kept the note because you were right.

Not long afterwards, I heard my buzzer go around ten p.m. I suppose I was a little complacent after being alone for a week or more. I was probably hoping it was you, though I can't remember that now. When I opened my door, Richard was swaying in the cold like a reed on a riverbank. I know that he was drunk now, but if I had then I probably would have been more cautious. His face contorted when he saw me.

His fist connected with my nose. When I came to an old woman was standing over me in hysterics. I was laying half in and half out of my doorway, a huge bruise on the back of my head and blood all over my house T-shirt. I shook off her concern, told her repeatedly I was all right and there was no need for her to come in. When I had brushed her off I retreated into the house holding my dripping nose. It was broken, I was sure. I had to call an ambulance.

I wandered in the kitchen and opened the freezer door, looking for a packet of ice. Grabbing a half-filled bag, I stumbled into the bedroom, still dizzy, collapsing onto my bed. Face up on the mattress, I lay there making an attempt to stem the blood.

There it was. The spider. Hanging upside down, staring with its double row of unseeing eyes. Trapped within the thin coffin of a body, doing nothing more than drying up and rotting on that very spot . . .

I realised my mistake. The spider was in a different place. When I had noticed it that first time it had been near my wardrobe. Now it had walked a miniscule two steps to the right. My spider had moved. Which meant that it wasn't dead. Which meant that it had been fooling me all this time.

I jumped up from the bed and wandered out into the passage. I grabbed my vacuum and came back brandishing the hosepipe and brush. One minute the spider was there and then it was gone. I stared at that blank, white spot. The patch of ceiling looked like the page of a book that had previously harboured some secret talisman, some etching of ancient symbolism wiped clean. I felt as though I had committed a terrible sin, an action of high treason or blasphemy. All of a sudden the noisy whooshing of the Hoover seemed too loud, too intrusive, and I turned it off, sat on the bed. My guilt came in an instant. My eyes and nose began to leak simultaneously and I couldn't move to wipe them. I sat there and let them run like an eager child.

All Woman

She complain about it las year an the year before dat, but I don't give a shit; as far as I'm concerned it's tradition, y'get me, we've always done it, so when I hear Sianna tell her bredrins she wanna go Neighbourhood an sweat her clothes off I thought right – me too. An I didn't say jack at the time, cos that's how yuh hafta drop it wit Sianna, play foolish to catch wise as me Gran Gran used to say, God rest her soul. So dat's what I did, just sit in the kitchen an listen to her an her mates chat fart an me nah say nuttin, y'unnerstan? I jus wait until the whole ah dem pick up an gone home an I sip my JD an coke. When Sianna come to see what I was doin, all meek an dat, talkin bout:

– Mum, yuh got any green?

I had to smile to myself an say Lawd God; me know me chile well.

So I break off a lickle ah the skunk, though to be truthful, I wish I had some Mersh dese days. I tink is the skunk weed mash up de youts in dis country, mek dem stab up security guard an shoot innocent people on road, dem way deh. You can't get decent weed in dis city fuh love or money, not like when I was Sianna's age. Anyway, I give her piece an say:

– So what, yuh goin Neighbourhood an you never did say?

Sianna do her usual ting innit.

– Mum man, why yuh lissenin my business again? You always stressin me!

Stress! Wha she know bout stress? She's a watless seventeen year old, stress don't lick her yet! Wait until she's eighteen if she thinks life hard – from den it's downhill all the way, truss. Sianna don't understand the lengths I've gone to keep the outside right where it should be, beyond the four walls of our yard. She don't know as hard as she tink life is in the bits, as dem yout's call the neighbourhood, it's twice as tough if you don't ave a stable parent. Two if you can afford it, but not everyone can, y'get me? An as much as she try to go on like I'm always in her face, I know say Sianna loves me bad. I could see it even then, because she was smilin an sniffin the weed, tryin not to make me notice, knowin she was lucky because none ah her friends got a mum like me.

– How am I stressin you? I'm only sayin you never tell me nuttin, as usual . . .

– Mum man, see what I'm sayin about you?

An dat's how it went, back an forth until she give up an say yes, I could come to her birthday drink up at Neighbourhood an have a good rave with my daughter on her eighteenth. After dat she was only thinkin about the spliff she was gonna blaze, so she disappear upstairs in her room. Marcia, who lives two doors down, is always sayin what a good relationship I ave with Sianna, how it's nice we can smoke, drink an rave together like we do. I like it. It means if I run outta ciggies she might have couple, an if I'm bored on a Saturday night she might know somewhere decent to go. I've had some of my best nights out since I was teenager wit her an her bredrins, times when I don't fall into bed until sunlight beam tru my window an I have to pull my curtains dem shut tight tight, otherwise I can't get no sleep.

I must admit, I felt good dat night as I sat at the kitchen table an bun. Glad me an my one pickney so close. After I went into the living room an end up fallin asleep in front ah the TV – again. Next day when I got up for work, I felt stiff bad, an slightly hung over. I promise myself I wouldn't mix the skunk an drink on a weekday night, but still find myself goin home dat evenin an doin the very same ting.

When Sianna's birthday come Saturday I get up early even though I wanna sleep another two hours. I get her present from where I have it hidden an go down the passage to her room. When I knock the door I hear her groan an shuffle; I feel a sharp pain in my stomach, like I'm queasy. I start to wonder whether Simon Bassey stay again. I step back from her door.

– Hello?

My daughter's voice crackle like an old forty-five.

– Hey, bub, it's me! Can I come in?

– Yeah, Mum, come!

I ease the door open, fearful, only to see Sianna an Tarryn, her best bredrin an Marcia's eldest, loungin in bed watchin CBeebies. The room dark and smoky. I walked further inside, more confident, resistin my urge to pull the curtains open like the mothers do on dem TV shows. Sianna beam at me, her pink flower duvet pull up to her chin. I beam at both girls, feeling teary-eyed, though I try not to let dem see. I always feel dat way when the girls are together. They been friends since Nursery school, always at each other house. They remind me of the friends I had before I'd moved out my manor an down to West London, away from the people I grow wit.

– Happy birthday, bub!

My daughter's face scrunch up like her hairband as I smother her with kisses. I can't help feelin bad about dat, although I try. Tarryn start smile as I hand over Sianna's present, a tiny box covered in pink wrappin paper wit a bright red bow. It's kinna obvious it's jewellery, but I can't help dat.

– Ah, thanks, Mum. I love you!

– Mornin, Kay! Tarryn says in her too-cute way.

– Hiya, babes. How are you?

I give her a kiss as well, just so she don't feel lef out an stand back while Sianna struggles with my wrappin paper. Lookin at them both, I'm proud, but I try hold it down. I know what people say about vanity, though you can't fault truth. My daughter an her sister friend are the best-lookin girls in the manor, I don't care what no one thinks. They're always get chirped by local boys. One time I even had to step in, heart racin, when I see some guys from the bookies on the corner try move to dem on their way home from school. I know a few of those lot, so I asked dem man to step in, have a word. Sometimes, when I look at the girls, it's difficult not to think I can't really blame dem fuh gettin hot an dat.

Their looks are so similar they could be related.

Bright brown eyes an flawless red-brick skin, Sianna's inherited from her father (he's a good-lookin bastard, I can't take dat away). Perfect white smiles, both way taller than me an Marcia, with long gleamin legs an curvin figures. Bottoms like an open drawer, natural dress sense dat makes dem look like actresses, even though Sianna wants to be an accountant and Tarryn a poet . . . When us three step tru Portobello market on a Saturday, boys are hypnotised by the junk in our trunk an men drool. Sometimes they think we're all sisters. I tell em I'm still young yuh nuh, not even in my mid-thirties, so I should think so too.

Sianna tear off the las ah the wrapping paper. She open the box an shriek when she see diamonds in her earrings. They cost a bomb from a friend of a friend who had a Hatton Gardens link, so I hope they don't break or nuttin. Tarryn begs a look. I give Sianna another hug, which she returns with more enthusiasm, den go in the kitchen to make ackee, saltfish an fry dumplin, everyone's favourite breakfast.

It must be around twelve or suttin when Simon Bassey reach. I open the door to him, tryin to be nice an dat, failin miserably. My spirit jus don't tek the brer, you know what I'm sayin? He jars me up the wrong way. Not dat any of the gyal care what I think. He's got the sweet-boy look, yuh know dem way deh? Tall, light-skinned, hazel eyes, fresh barbershop trim wid the beard join up wid im sideburns, like nuff ah the mans round ere. Ah name brand yout, dey always call im Simon Bassey, never jus Simon. Like I say, I never really check fuh im but Tarryn an Sianna always go on bout how's he's choong, drives a nice ride, stupidness like dat. I don't really care if he pushes a Beamer or a Mountain Bike, as long as he treat my daughter good. At least I don't hafta hear sinister stories about what he done to get the ride, the garms, an pay his hostel rent. Simon Bassey's a good guy from what dey say on road. Co-owns a barbershop on the Bella an studies stylin every hour God send dey tell me.

I let him in, tryin not to watch the smile on im face as he pass. He's smirkin like he float inside my yard on thin air an expec me to be impressed.

– Yes, Kay!

– Y'all right, Simon Bassey? I say. He's lookin me in the eye, lettin his gold tooth show. I look away.

– You look criss today, believe . . .

As pretty as he stay I don't give ah inch. Sianna would kill me, she's well jealous bout him already, an she done tell me nuff ah dem little man-bwoys like to talk after me, sayin I'm sexy fuh a mum an all dat, like dey could do me anyting. I don't say jack. I jus follow him thru to the livin room where the girls are sat boxin warm dumplings an watchin cable TV. All mornin dey been like dat, but dey jump like soldier as soon as Simon Bassey walk tru the door. Tarryn run out the room talkin bout how she don't look good. I watch Simon to see if he take a look at her big bumper as she go, cos Tarryn's arse in dem leggins are like two watermelon in a cotton sack, but he musta know I was watchin cos he just hug up my daughter the way he should. I keep my eye on im still. A sweet bwoy like dat wit nuff gyal on his case is gonna fall to temptation someday or another, I tell myself. I jus hafta be dere fuh Sianna when he does.

– Hi, baby. How are you?

Sianna's all over Simon Bassey as soon as he walks tru the door. I feel say I taught her better dan dat, but it look like she forget everyting I say bout man an how dem loose respec fuh you if yuh gi dem too much when she hear is car keys jingle like dinna bell. He fling himself on the couch as if he loss the use ah is legs, an sit wit dem spread wide open, which always winds me up. Why do men do dat? Dey tryin to make us tink dey tings dat big? Before he even kiss my daughter Simon Bassey draw for his Rizla an cigarette an Tarryn come back wearin tight-fittin jeans an a T-shirt. I can't watch anymore ah the young people foolishness. I leave an go to my bedroom to phone Marcia.

We drink an smoke an smoke an drink till the livin room look like the view from my plane window when me an Sianna went JA las year. Dat was her birthday present, but I hafta admit it was kinda my present too. The land ah me Gran Gran an my mudda, God rest their souls. We did rave from sundown to sunup, I tell yuh. It was the best holiday ah my life.

I cook a big dinner, cos we was too full fuh lunch, an a good few friend ah Sianna pass thru an eat. By the time I start get dress to leave out my house, I was well tipsy. Marcia pass to keep me company wid so many young people about. We nick a bottle of Archer's an take it upstairs so we can chat by ourselves while I get ready to rave.

Portobello weren't ready fuh us when we hit road, believe! Dere mussa bin eight of us at least, pissed an makin bere noise. Simon Bassey had couple bredrin's wiv him, one cute guy wit a name like a watch I could never remember, an a marga bwoy wid braids. I was tryin not to stare at Cutie by den, cos he was lookin at me hard an the drink was makin me kinda randy. We talk on the way towards Mau Mau, where we startin off our night, an I find im different to mos ah dem loud-mout youts. Confident, but calm. Mature. I like dat.

We reach the place I get the firs round in, two bottle ah champagne fuh everyone, even though I can barely afford it, but it's my daughter's eighteenth so I ain rampin fuh no one. We toast Sianna's good health, den drink an laugh an buss joke. When the bottle done Simon call fuh anotha two. Tru it's a Saturday nite the music was on loud. I went to the barman an tell him it's my daughter born day, do he ave any dancehall? He was a stush-lookin black guy in a rip white shirt wid is hair dye blond in picky locks, but he say yeah, sure, an the next ting yuh know they bussin some Capleton an Elephant Man thru the big speakers. The bubbly mussa get to all ah us girls by dat time, cos soon we all up on a lickle stage dey ave, shakin our booties an gettin down. The posh people in the place smile dem funny smile an try not to look, even though I see some man can't tek dey eyes from us. Who would? Four sexy young women dancin like no one else in the place, people muss look! The bartender crank up the music while I catch Simon Bassey's eye. He's smirkin again. I jus turn my back on im an wind down low wid my daughter, till we laugh hard an hug.

When we go back to the table, Cutie move from where he was sittin an come sit nex to me.

– I like how yuh move, he tell me.

– How old are you? I ask.

– Twenny-eight, he say.

– Why yuh lyin!? I bawl, but the music an chat so loud no one can hear what we sayin.

– Swear down, Cutie says, lookin serious. An cute.

– Suh why yuh neva come join us on the dance-floor?

I hafta say right now, dat was the drink. I never woulda gone on so bad if I neva drunk so much, but I was startin to think he did act twenty-eight, an when I look over at Sianna to see if she notice us she was laughin wid Marcia an her bredrins same way. The only one clockin what was goin on was Simon Bassey, innit? He was starin over, still smirkin, sippin champagne wid ah arm throw back on the seat behind Sianna's head. I kiss my teeth inside my head an ignore im.

– Sometimes I jus like to watch, Cutie was sayin, though I was barely concentratin an only jus hear im. But if I could get a dance wid you later, dat would be criss still.

– Depends innit? Play yuh cards right an the answer's yes, I say, den I lef im an squeeze over to where Marcia was sittin, cos I could see she notice us talkin wit our heads low. She start frown. When I push her thigh an say budge up with a big smile she neva even smile back. I ignore her, push a little harder for more room, raise my hand an call fuh nex round.

We finish off dat one, beers fuh the man an cocktails fuh the girls, den we leave an cross the road to the Market Bar. Me an Marcia go to the bar an get more drinks.

– Wha's goin on wid you an Simon Bassey's bredrin? she say, as soon as she finish order.

– How yuh mean?

I'm tryin to buy time an she know it.

– You two seem kinna cosy in the corner all of ah sudden.

– Nah, we was jus talkin innit? He's a sensible brer, I like the way he drop it.

– An good lookin too.

I turn away, starin out the window at Portobello Road. It's dark by den, but you can still see the shadow of people walkin up an down. The market lights string up from lamposts, swingin wit the wind.

– He's all right.

Marcia laughs.

– You know I know your type, right? The bartender comes back wid overflowin pints an cocktails dat look like poisonous substance. Marcia pays. – I also know he's twenny-one.

I'm not supposed to be interested, so I sip from my cloudy margarita.

– Young tings, I say.

– You bear dat in mind, Marcia replies, gatherin up the glasses. I help her an we go back to the group.

Sianna seems to be havin a great time. She's tipsy, not drunk, an every few minutes she head outside wid Simon Bassey, Cutie an Tarryn, come back smellin ah weed. I wanna go out wid dem but don't wanna bait dem up, so I roll one up under the table an go by myself. A few minutes later Cutie join me. I pass my spliff an look at him hard as he's smokin. He don't seem twenny-one. He's got the join-up beard an everyting. It suit im. A few cars beep me as dey pass the corner an I wave, blow kisses. Cutie's starin at me.

– You know everyone don't you?

He looks a little lean now.

– Dat's jus Unity, Iyasha an dem . . . Yuh don't know dem?

– Dese ain my bits. I'm from sout innit?

– *Ah*, I say. All the better fuh keepin tings on the down low. Cutie looks at me an it's like he can tell what I'm thinkin. We stan up smilin at each other.

Marcia come out ah the pub an wipe the smile from my face. She don't look pleased, especially when I dash the tail of my spliff on the pavement, squash it wid my foot. She looks hurt at dat, like she come outside fuh nuttin. Serve her right.

So we're in Neighbourhood an they're playin R&B wid a bit ah hip-hop, which I like, an Cutie's really goin fuh it. He keps comin up an tryin to wine wit me in front of everyone, an I keep tellin im to hold it down, but it's like he can't. I'm pretty sure someone from our gatherin woulda noticed, but they all seem to have gone separate ways. The bright lights are spinnin, my feet keep me spinnin, an most of all my head is spinnin, but nothin I can see is really dat clear. The only ting dat makes any sense is Cutie's face, which is right in front of me, an his hands, which keep reachin fuh my waist. An right about den I'm stuck firm between my *wants* and my *needs*. My wants say I should whisper in is ear, tell im to meet me back at mines in fifteen minutes, leave widout sayin jack to no one an wait fuh him in my shortest bit ah negligee . . . But my needs say if I even wink in is direction Marcia's gonna see, or worse still Simon Bassey or Sianna's gonna see, an dat'll be it, everyone'll say I'm a slapper an my daughter will hate me fuh ruinin her day forever an ever, Amen.

Ting is, I'm gaggin for it. It's bin a long time, right? Since Sianna's dad I only had one close boyfriend, an we ended three years ago. After him, no one. Fuh three years. I was protectin her, wasn't I? Criss little thing like her, you hear all sorts about step-fathers. Abuse an all dat drama. I didn't want to take the risk of anythin happenin to Sianna, or anyone gettin between me an her, tryin to be number one in my life. I decided I'd wait till she grew up, work on the relationship dat matters. But it's hard goin. Bloody well hard.

I'm movin my feet, so caught up wid *should I* or *shouldn't I*, I start feel queasy again. My head begins to pound. I pull myself outta Cutie's clutches, say I'm goin to the loo. Which is the truth, yuh nuh. All the way I stumble tru people, an I swear I see Simon Bassey stan up like some watchdog, eyes all big an menacin, teeth showin, watchin me go. God knows where Marcia was. I try ignore im an keep headin to the ladies. I hit the door so hard it slam against the wall an all the young girls turn from the mirror to watch me come in.

I bang into the cubicle, pull up my skirt, drop my panties an sit. It seems like I'm dere forever waitin fuh my bladder to empty. While I'm listenin to the voices chatter, the shuffle through handbags an the occasional loud sniff, I put a hand on my head an moan. I think about what I'm doin wit Cutie an I feel like shit. I wanna sit dere forever, not come out an face anyone.

It was all so stoopid. Wasn't I supposed to be caterin to my needs, not my wants? Spendin the anniversary of the most special, remarkable time in my life wit the one person I share it wit?

I wipe, flush, get out an look in the mirror as I wash my hands. Get yuh mind right, Kaylene, I tell myself, concentrate on what's most important. I try not to notice how big an round my eyes are because it makes me look pretty in ah aging kind ah way. I fix my make-up as best as I can an try smile at my reflection. All I tell myself is I need to find Sianna, tell her I love her. It seems the most important ting in the world. I love her an I think the worl ah her. Dat's it.

I come outta the ladies wit dat on my mind – find Sianna an stick wid her fuh the rest ah the nite, neva mind how embarrass she might get. An part ah me know I was lookin fuh her to stop myself doin someting I would regret come sunup, like wakin up with Cutie in my bed while his bredrin's in Sianna's, but I push it away wit the thought I ain seen her since we reach Neighbourhood. I look everywhere. The VIP section, the bar, the area by the stage, though I try keep away from the spot where I see Cutie dancin wit Marcia an a few ah Tarryn bredrins; when he turn my way I duck down in the crowd an walk all the way to the main entrance ben over. I go upstairs an look for Sianna on the balcony, but she not dere either.

Simon Bassey is, lookin out over the crowd wit a plastic bottle ah Stella in is hand. He gives me the smirk as I come closer.

– Yuh see Sianna? I ask.

– She went toilet wid Tarryn. He's starin like a

hungry man looking at prime steak. I wanna bounce his plastic Stella bottle from his head.

– So what, yuh like my bredrin Zeiko?

So *dat's* his name I think to myself. I knew it sound like a watch. Black people an names eh? We're well funny wi dat.

– He's a young ting, I say, like you.

I walk off, leavin him smirkin like the Cat from Alice in Wonderland. On the way I'm not thinkin about him though. I'm thinkin about the fact he say Sianna an Tarryn go ladies together. Cos dey didn't. I was dere. I would see or hear dem, I know I would.

I go back to the dancefloor an worm my way tru the crowd until I finally see Tarryn. She find a spot in the VIP section talkin to some tick man in a black T-Shirt an trousers. He ave a walkietalkie on is hip. Dey heads so close dey look like dey might kiss. She laughin. So is he, not as hard. Dey wrap up in demselves, each other is all dem can see. I step pass. All my tipsy, queasy feelin gone, I'm alert now, together an sure. Dere's a small door at the side ah the stage where the DJ playin. I pass Tarryn an her new man, move towards it. The door say STAFF ONLY. I push wit one hand. It open easy. I go in.

When it close I'm on the other side at the bottom of a small stairwell where the music less loud. I smell weed again, strong too. I step forward, wantin to call Sianna until I hear noises. A deep-voice man panting, a girl's high-pitch moan chantin. I don't want to carry on but my feet move me furtha until I get to the bottom ah the stairs, which go up on my right-han side. I turn an look, slow. Like I already know. I see the man's black trousers down by his black shoes, his ankles. Black socks. Big, hairy legs. A brown, firm butt movin slow. The black jacket wit the name ah the security firm stitch on the back. Long gleamin brown legs on either side ah his. Twitchin as the security guy start go faster, an she cry out an slam her han on the wall like she wanna tump it down, an it's den I know say it's her because I see the ring on her finger, white gold wit a big ruby in the center cos the man who sold me it said ruby is the stone of love, an I close my eyes cos it sound like he's hurtin her even though he's not, I know he's not because Sianna say so, she say *it's so good*, an *don't stop please*. I turn an run out the door, slam it open, push thru the dancin people, pass Tarryn an her new man, ignorin dem lookin up at me, shocked, ignorin the people as dey cuss me, ignorin the music the lights an the drink spillin on my garms, I jus run as fast as I can even though I can't escape the bass, the noise, the sound of Sianna's voice in my head.

Underground

She was staring. At me. Hands clasped tightly, head tilted to one side, forehead carved with the slight hint of a frown. Her face thin and pale with cold, her eyes wide and circular. I tried to keep my mind on what I was doing, why I was there, but it was almost as though, with my gaze cast at the flowers and stone and the tangled grass that sprung from damp earth, I could feel the tug of some invisible force wrench at me until my eyes were lifting, raising my head, finding her again. Then I would experience a sharp pain in my gut – nerves or something similar – and I would grow hot, embarrassed, like a child caught in the act of performing some wrong. My head would fall, my gaze return to the trinity of objects beneath my feet, knowing she had seen me noticing her.

I knelt in the grass hoping that would obscure me from her vision. Or her from mine. The knees of my jeans became saturated with fallen rain, but I didn't care. I bent my head and began to pray, murmuring beneath my breath, closing my eyes and picturing my mother, wherever she may have been. Time passed. I opened my eyes, face-to-face with the inscription etched into black-and-grey-speckled stone: *In Loving Memory of Altina Solomon: Mother, Sister and, most of all, friend – 1952–2004*. There was more to say about my mother, had my family or I possessed the money to say it. Funerals were costly things, headstones and inscriptions even more so. A broken pillar or down-turned torch, like some of the older gravestones, might have symbolised what she meant with greater clarity, yet that single-sentence epitaph was all we could afford.

I got to my feet, wiping stray grass from my knees and there she was. Fingers overlapping, dark eyes unblinking, staring at my face. A shard of my former tension ran through me, and then I felt outrage, anger for having been disturbed. I stepped towards the woman, trampling long grass flat beneath my heavy boots. I felt my hands form fists by my thighs.

Her fingers unravelled, leapt towards her face. Covered her mouth in shock. She stepped backwards, away from me. A small noise escaped her lips, a sharp note that floated across the space between us, although I heard the sound in my mind, rather than my ears. The woman's eyes grew larger, darker as I watched, stunned and unable to fathom what was happening. They stopped me in my tracks, while everything around me – the grass, the gravestones, the looming trunks of trees – seemed to fall away into nothing.

The dark shadows cast by leaves were gone. White light reflected from cloud-filled skies bathed us in sunshine. Behind the woman, a group of men wearing flat caps, shirts and britches were standing beside a deep pit, leaning on spades, talking. Beside the pit were a number of plain-wood coffins, stacked on top of one another like logs for the fire. Thrown, I looked around, breaking my stare from the blackened expanse of the woman's eyes. In the distance, though I wasn't quite sure at the time, I swore I could see the faint outline of a horse and carriage.

Then we were back beneath the shadow of leafy trees, my head reeling and the thump of a migraine beating at my temples. I slipped on wet grass, almost falling onto the stone, and when I looked up she was still watching, her dark eyes slightly less fearful. I was on my knees again, my hands buried in long grass, propping myself up, breathing heavy. I heard the rustle of her approach, and for a long while I could not bear to look. It was only when I noticed the damp hem of her dress, the frayed tan material and tightly stitched lighter patches, that I realised how out of place her clothing was. Mouth open, I looked the woman up and down, partly hoping she was an illusion conjured by my own isolated, crazed mind.

It was a simple dress, a one-piece garment that fell past her ankles, although I could see a white petticoat beneath. The sleeves reached as far as her elbows and the neckline was low, slightly exposing a full cleavage. The front of her dress was criss-crossed with black ribbon. She wore a white piece of cloth to cover her head, with another black ribbon wrapped around it to keep the cloth in place. I'd seen enough history books to recognise that this woman, and her clothing, were not of our time. I remembered the men's flat caps and britches, the rhythmic sound of horse hooves. A shiver exploded throughout my entire body.

The strangely dressed woman was standing over me. Her curious frown returned. She peered at my trembling body as though I'd asked a question in a foreign language. I tried to breathe more fluidly, and stumbled to my feet, the world tumbling and turning around me. Once I was standing and looking into her face, I found myself drawn in by those amazing eyes, so black they seemed like large pupils. I could see my own face reflected back at me. I couldn't move.

A hand caressed my cheek. Her fingers were as cold as the gravestones that sprouted from the earth, but I didn't have the power to flinch, even if I wanted to.

Ashampo?

She had spoken, but once again the sound avoided my ears. The strange, although familiar, word occurred in my head like a thought I had formed myself. Still, the voice was not mine.

John?

This time I was surer that she was speaking to me, and the question in her eyes was obvious. I shook my head, looking away at a dusty cemetery worker strolling along the pathway where moments ago I had seen the illusion of a horse and carriage. The worker ignored us both, whistling as he walked. She turned my head with a cold, gentle finger, until I was looking at her again.

Yes. You are John. You recognise me no longer?

I wasn't sure how to respond. I could only stare into that reflective darkness, my mind reverberating *No, No, No,* until I realised my answer was not sufficient. I steeled my thoughts and forced myself to focus on each individual word.

I am not John. My name is Joshua.

She smiled, severe expression breaking like an explosion of birds taking flight. She looked young and beautiful and her dark eyes sparkled.

It has been too long. You have forgotten. I forgive you.

Then she was tugging my hand with frozen fingers, leading me from my mother's gravestone, across the grass and onto the rain-soaked path with no idea where I was being taken, only that I should follow without protest. Something in her eyes, her manner, her *being* told me I could trust her. It sounds ludicrous, but I can't say any more than that.

We walked hand-in-hand amongst the forest of stone, the overhanging branches of ancient trees and the heavy silence of the cemetery without another word, spoken or otherwise. Past lofty mausoleums tinted green with moss and crawling weeds. Between all manner of grieving angels, their wings spread ready to take flight, or folded neatly behind them with a finger pointed upwards, indicating where the escaped spirit may have fled. I gripped the cold fingers and let myself be led. I saw a handful of people on that short walk; none recognised the woman, or even noticed she was there.

We reached a lonely place that seemed quieter than my mother's burial site, which was not far from the Garden of Remembrance on the cemetery's west side. Here, there were leaning headstones, grass and weeds as high as the average man's waist, a crumbling Colonnade. It was a large, dilapidated building that stood on a slight incline, thick stone columns erected every five feet. I imagined it might have been grand and spectacular decades ago, but those glory days had long faded. Beyond the cemetery walls, the rear windows of a huge building I happened to know was a youth hostel overlooked the grounds. Not far from where we were walking, the Colonnade's only keeper, a rusty black-and-orange cat, sat curled on a grave-stone. It squinted at my companion and yawned.

We trampled through tall grass, over the tombs of the dead until we had climbed onto the raised concrete of the Colonnade. Here, the woman left me to bend before a trio of flagstones, looking as though she might attempt to shift them with her bare hands. I approached to help, only for her to wave me away. I stood to one side, reading inscriptions on the weathered memorial tablets, listening to the drip of water on stone. When I looked again, she'd lifted every one of the flagstones herself. Beneath her feet there was a dark window of nothingness that almost seemed solid. The woman grabbed my hand, tugged me towards the window. I pulled back, my hypnotic spell broken, realising what she wanted. When I shook my head as violently as she had moments before, she smiled again, took my face in both hands, pushed hers close until I could feel light breath against my nose and lips. It was as cold as the touch of her fingers, and smelt like a cool breeze. It was soothing. I closed my eyes.

Home, I heard inside my head, as she turned to look at the black window, indicating the rusting spiral stairs. This time, when she tugged at my hand, I offered no resistance.

It was as dark as death itself in the depths of what I realised was a catacomb, and yet I found I could see. The air was stale and unused, and smelt of damp wood, although I breathed easily. Water dripped from the roof. I could hear the scratch and squeak of unseen animals. Coffins were embedded in the walls behind rusting steel-fenced compartments, though I turned my head, not wanting to dwell on the sight. My hand gripped in her ice-cold fingers, she took me deeper into the catacomb, which was as large as a church hall, into a room where there were no coffins, only a simple low-slung iron bed, a gas lamp, an elaborate wooden desk and mirror, a wardrobe with open warped doors and no clothes. In the centre of the small room more flagstones had been removed. There was a hole, the bone-white remains of a fire. The woman guided me to the bed, where I sat, looking at my sparse surroundings. It was a dank and hellish place and I had no fear, but I also had no idea why I was there.

She stood before me, staring with those opaz eyes. It was embarrassing, but there was nowhere else to look. Her thin face was earnest, and although she was too dishevelled and shrouded by pain to be beautiful, her looks remained bewitching. I had a sense that had she been alive in any real sense of the word, the pumping of her heart would have brought colour to her features that would attract any man, in any time. The woman's eyes filled with tears. I felt a hot burn in my cheeks as I realised she might well have heard my thoughts. I reached a hand towards her, which she took and placed on her cold cheek, her chest. As I had guessed, her heart was still.

Ruth, I heard. *They called me Ruth.*

I nodded to show I understood. She released my hand and pointed at me.

John. Yes?

I had no more idea whether I was really that person than she it seemed, but I had decided I would accept it as fact, as I had accepted everything else. Ruth smiled, then without another word crossed both hands, clasped the shoulders of her tattered brown dress, and pulled it from her body.

Beneath the clothing, she was naked. Her dark body shone, though I couldn't tell where the light came from. As she turned to hang the dress in her wooden wardrobe, I caught sight of long, angry scars across her back, running from shoulder to hip; so many that they overlapped over and over, deep weals in her flesh that would never heal. The wounds reminded me of torn brown paper. I couldn't help myself; by the time she was facing me, my eyes had already leaked tears onto my jeans. Ruth stepped towards the bed, sat beside me, cradled my head in her hands. She rocked me as though I had been the victim, back and forth, and although in some way I knew I was, I couldn't quite work out how. I caressed her in return, fingers skimming dry, untended skin. On her shoulder I found the brand, a blackened, raised portion of flesh bearing two letters, **RC**. Without knowing whether she would allow such a thing I found myself kissing Ruth on that scarred flesh, hoping to soothe her pain with my lips, erase what I'd found.

The dreams, when they came, were terrifying. I saw Ruth at work in the fields, sweating beneath a Windward sun only to look up and turn her body to receive the lash of a whip from a red-faced man on horseback. Blood seeping through thin clothing like an ink stain. I saw her asleep in a meagre hut, light from the full moon as the hut door opened, a shadowed figure that crawled onto her body and held her mouth closed with a rough hand as she fought and kicked. Some nights there was childbirth, a cane-coloured baby snatched as soon as the umbilical was severed, Ruth knocking at the back door of the big house only to be turned away by an elderly African with sorrowful blue eyes. I felt her misery as she stood in a row of captives by a dockside and opened her mouth so a young blond man, too hot in his foreign attire, could inspect her teeth.

After four nights the dreams were of a crossing, chained within the bowels of the ship, rocking against Africans from tribes she could not understand, speaking several broken European languages. Shivering as she stood on a London dock and then a huge wooden stage in the city centre before hundreds of well-dressed buyers and sellers, chained with her countrymen and women as a Barker with a long stick pointed. Ruth being taken away on the back of a horse-drawn cart to a mansion house in the centre of a large field, where there were others dressed in clothes that had once been fine. I felt Ruth's cautious delight when she came into the kitchen, scrubbed and ready to work, only to notice a man that could have been my twin – John – already smiling.

At first I was so overwhelmed by the visions I could barely ask questions. I had become a creature of nocturnal habits, resting during daylight, climbing the spiral stairs to breathe fresh air at night. Ruth produced food from somewhere; vegetables and meats she'd heat on the tiny fire in her darkened room, sometimes even fresh fruit. I sat on the cold flagstones of the Colonnade waiting for her to cook our meal, for it was too smoky for me in the catacombs. When she came topside with tin plates and cutlery in hand, we would eat and look over the still grounds of the cemetery. I felt serene, at home for the first time in my life, for I was not a man comfortable with the world in which I lived. I guessed I wasn't the only one. Others roamed amongst the crowded headstones at night. I could hear low voices, the rustle of movement too loud for any animal, sometimes even the light of a match or torch. Ruth seemed unfazed by our nocturnal neighbours. I tried to relax and force myself to feel the same.

One night, sitting outside in the dark after dinner, there was that strange flash in my head, the heavy thump at my temples and blurred vision. When I blinked it was suddenly daylight. The cemetery was transformed. The marble stones and columns of the Colonnade were gleaming, the weeds and long grass gone. The horses and carriages were back, but this time many of them dotted the landscape. There were far less trees, which provided an unobscured expanse of low-cut grass, the sporadic white of tombstones and rich farmland beyond the cemetery walls. I could see family groups in Victorian clothing, the men in top hats and tails, the women in elaborately tailored dresses with dainty umbrellas in hand. They walked the pathways, inspecting gravestones and memorial tablets with great interest.

The thump in my head became a migraine. Soon,

the world grew dark again. When I came to I was back inside the stifled depths of the catacomb, lying on the tiny iron bed. Once again, I had to marvel at Ruth's strength. I winced from pain, watching her watch me. I remembered my first vision, of men in flat caps standing by the crumbling hole of a mass grave, leaning on shovels.

How did I die?

Ruth turned away.

Please. I must know.

Still she would not turn towards me, even as she spoke.

The doctor could not say. He thought it may have been your heart, but he was not sure. I could not afford the best.

I lay back, silent.

One day you were alive, the next they put you in the ground. When it was my time, I returned. I do not know why.

I sat up and held her hand. She was shaking.

Don't question what has happened. It could leave you, I told her. She faced me, a tiny smile on her lips, stroking my cheek.

You always used such wise words. That is what I missed most.

We hugged then, her icy body tight against mine.

Now there were two within the catacombs, it was only a matter of time before we were discovered. By the sixth night I noticed voices and torchlight drawing close. When I looked at Ruth she said nothing, but I could see the glow of the yellow beams reflected in her dark eyes. She shuffled, uncomfortable as the voices got louder, and when I tried to ask whether we were in danger she only shook her head and looked away. For the next two days I waited for my dreams to tell me what might happen next. Although they were silent, I knew our time in the Colonnade was short.

We hadn't been sleeping long, wrapped amongst one another like the weeds that embraced tombstones, when I heard the static scrape of flagstones. I jumped awake, as I had been on the edge of slumber, only to see that Ruth had already raised her head, listening. She put a finger to her frosted lips, grabbed my hand and led me from her tiny room. As we were on the far side of the Colonnade and our visitors were moving by torchlight, it would take them time to reach our room. Ducking so the wild, jerking beams wouldn't catch us, we moved quickly towards the far end of the catacombs where I could already see another spiralling set of stairs. Ruth climbed first, letting go of my hand to push at the flagstones. I looked across the huge, dark space, watching silhouettes inspect the incarcerated coffins and grunt at each other, then inexplicably begin to smash and tear at the wood. Ruth gave a huge grunt, struggling with the flagstone above her; when it toppled aside with a crash, the torch beams froze, flew erratically, pointed at the stairs, at us. Moonlight spotlit our position. Cool air caressed my upturned face. Before I could fully appreciate that fact, there were shouts and running footsteps. I felt a cold grip on my hand and I was wrenched upwards, feet clattering on rusty iron.

Topside, Ruth tugged me up to join her one-handed, easily. It was the first time I had witnessed just how strong she was, though I barely had time to take it in. She was pushing me from the Colonnade, ordering me to run into the long grass before she took off herself, gathering her undergarments in a fist. The sharp edges of tombstones scraped at my heels, yet I hardly felt them. The voices of the men stirred me on and I followed Ruth to the nearest path where the going was easier and soles of our bare feet rang out in harsh explosions that filled the night. She seemed unsure where to head, so I pumped my legs harder and took the lead. I'm not sure how long we were chased, as my noisy heart drowned their progress, but I found a place where the cemetery walls had crumbled and were undergoing repair. We climbed fallen brick and stone until we reached the other side, stumbling onto Harrow Road. There, we paused, I with my hands on my knees panting hard, Ruth straight as a ruler, chest hardly moving, as though she'd taken a midnight stroll. It took a moment longer for me to catch my breath; when I did, it was to witness the crazed look of wonder in Ruth's eyes as she tracked cars, vans and buses, reflected by drivers' faces as they craned their necks to see what the hell we might be doing on the Harrow road, half-naked in the early morning. Crack heads was their summation, no doubt.

There was nowhere else to go but my flat, a one-bedroom housing-association residence not far from Kensal Green station. Ruth was silent all the way, gazing at the world around her. Over a few hundred yards our roles were reversed. When a dog barked she clutched my elbow; when a motorbike roared she nearly set off running again. I spent the entire walk crooning beneath my breath, holding her by the arm, telling her we were all right now.

I'd left my keys in the catacomb, though I was pretty absentminded and always kept a spare under a neighbour's plant pot in our shared front garden. When we entered the flat, feet kicking at the mound of letters, it all seemed too much for Ruth to take. She fell against me, superhuman strength gone, and I had to fairly carry her up the stairs to my front door. Once inside, she lurched from room to room like a blind person in new surroundings, fingers splayed, touching everything. She caressed the television like a long-lost family member. Jumped when I lit the gas cooker. Gazed at my Blacksploitation poster of Pam Greer with a look of confusion, made a similar expression when she found my PC. When I switched on the television she screamed as though she had seen an apparition, backed away until she fell onto my sofa, and wouldn't move. She stayed there for the next half hour, sometimes getting up and touching the screen, the rest of the time sitting on the sofa and laughing. She only looked at me once, with the expression of a child given a new toy; after that I was ignored. I didn't mind. It gave me the mental space to look through my letters, become reacquainted with my living space. I walked into my neat, well-ordered bedroom and sat on my bed, deep in thought.

I had never lived with anyone besides my mother. Since she died there had only been my aunt, who lived in Watford and I saw on rare occasions. I'd studied nineteenth-century literature in hope of becoming proficient, but jobs in academia were rare, and other, more dynamic tutors had taken the posts, I guessed. I worked part-time in the local library and claimed housing benefit to take up the financial slack. I'd always been a bit of a loner, made precious few friends. Now I had invited a woman who could most accurately be described as a spectre to live with me. The possibility of a negative outcome was overwhelming.

I set about my room, getting rid of anything Ruth might somehow deem offensive; the scant collection of girlie magazines I'd bought and instantly regretted; a hip-hop CD my aunt had given me; a copy of Joseph Conrad's *Heart of Darkness*. When I was satisfied everything was in order, I squared my shoulders and took a deep breath until my chest was full. I exhaled and left the room to offer Ruth a cup of tea.

Re-Entry

Outside the underground station, everything and nothing like the Ladbroke Grove of his memories, Craig realised he hadn't told Drake about the beard. He sighed beneath his breath, something else he'd done wrong. It had taken a while to get into Victoria, partly because he had errands to run, partly because that forced him to catch a later train, mostly, he admitted as he circled on one spot, because he'd been putting the whole thing off, using the distractions as an excuse, a deeper part of him scared what he might find. Laura thought it was a good idea, saying she could look after Toby and Jake well enough, although he felt guilty about that too. At the station, leaving them, he couldn't help but note the tiredness in her eyes and the un-brushed hair that fell to her shoulders, limp as string.

Orange sodium made city faces look sickly; he'd always thought that. Above his head the stream of cars on the Westway calmed him. That hadn't changed, probably never would. The row of shops across the street was a strange mixture of things that hadn't been and always had. The bright lights of the estate agents, new; the gloomy façade of the former Lazerdrome, old. The shop that sold custom refrigerators, old. The post office, well old. The dentist's, refurbished but old still, likewise the charity shop and bakery. He bounced on his toes, fingers clenched in his pockets, until he thought that might make him look too out-of-place, too foreign. Then he took another look at the pedestrians and knew, somehow, that didn't matter anymore.

A familiar face, walking past the empty Lazerdrome on the opposite side of the road. Craig smiling in recognition, raising a hand until he noticed the stumbling gait, the fixed look in the eyes and zoomed in on the rest. Skin the colour of paving slabs, protruding cheekbones, pedestrians sidestepping. He watched the skeletal man walk beneath the motorway and rumble of train tracks, heading up Ladbroke Grove for God alone knew where, Craig not even wanting to guess.

He turned just in time to see Drake attempt to sneak up on him, which never worked even when they were kids, Craig relieved to see his full, weighty frame and face, bright eyes, clean clothes, a casual black jacket and jeans way more fashionable than his. A green-striped polo shirt and crisp Nikes with a grass-coloured swoosh, the Lakers cap on his head. They hugged tight, Craig surprised after all.

'Damn, bruv,' Drake said, voice muffled. 'Damn.'

'How are you?' he mumbled, glad when Drake didn't answer, knowing his penchant for rhetorical questions. They let each other go. Drake stepped back and looked him over like a proud grandparent.

'Man's got a beard an *everyting* . . .'

'I didn't think you'd recognise me.' Looking at the shadow of the Lazerdrome as he said it.

'How'm I not gonna recognise you, man looks the same.'

'Yeah?'

'It's only the beard.'

'Safe . . .' Stroking thick hair beneath his chin, feeling the weight of that one word on his tongue. 'And you, you still look twenty-odd.'

'I wish . . .' Drake was beaming. 'Come we go . . . Any place you're feelin?'

They began to walk, the wrong way for the first location conjured from memory but he didn't care, he felt so good, nerves gone.

'Tabs?'

'Come we go Inn On the Green, yeah?'

'Where's *that*?'

'The old pool hall? Over Portobello fitness centre, by the Green?'

'Yes . . .*Yeah* . . . Sounds good . . .'

They crossed the road and took a first hard right, following the trail of the underpass, Craig expecting to see more familiar faces but recognising no one. It was difficult not feel cheated, especially when Drake raised his hand and nodded every few steps or so, talking rapidly about that year's Carnival even as Craig smelt it in the air, a leftover funk of spilt alcohol and uneaten food he remembered for the first time.

Then they were turning through metal doors, up stairs and into a bar where the lights were bright and the place was full of people, and it was like a surprise party arranged for his benefit; only it wasn't, they were just *there*; his old youth worker and her husband who'd both known him since he was fourteen, had first taught him to use computers and helped him fill out college applications. The rapper he'd seen perform in the parks all those years ago, the local who knew everyone and got the rounds in, the sexy girl from school, older with two kids, still wearing the smile that had danced above his teenage head at night. The musician, the actor, the dealer that offered him pills for nothing, all the faces he'd known. He smiled in every direction, glad he'd listened to Laura and made the long overdue phone call in return.

They sat on the balcony overlooking Portobello Green, erect pints bubbling on a precarious table with legs as weak as a foal. Inside, his pack of well-wishers fanned across the bar like a magician's hand of cards, backs turned so he couldn't read faces. Drake was still smiling, his grin much the same, perfect apart from a raincloud-grey tooth. Craig eased back in his chair, testing for give, relaxing as it took his weight. He reached for his pint, knocked back gulps.

'So what's gwaanin, man?'

He shrugged.

'Just doing what I have to, you know.'

'Your wife sounds lovely.'

'Yeah thanks . . .' Another gulp, swallow. 'Yours too . . .'

'Yeah, you know . . .' Drake turning side on, eyes cast over the Green. 'How long you bin married?'

'Five years.'

'Enjoy bein a paps?'

'Best feeling in the world.'

Nodding, reassuring each other.

'Got three boys myself, little terrors. You remember Kaylan, right, my oldest?'

'Yeah course, from when I used to babysit. How is he?

'Seventeen.' Drake gauging his reaction. 'Man's beard look like yours.'

'You're kidding.'

'Swear down.' Drake took a sip of his own pint, gasped and grinned wider. 'You have to meet em all. His brothers are twelve and ten. They're good kids, bruv, believe.'

'I do.'

He noticed Drake's leg bouncing under the table. Once sighted, it was difficult to take his eyes away. It made him suddenly nervous.

'I can't believe Kaylan's seventeen. What happened to the time?'

'We're old now, bruv, that's what happened. Dem yout's live a different world, dealin wid shit you wouldn't believe.'

'Makes me glad to be down in Lewes,' he said, instantly regretting it. A flash of surprise darkened Drake's features. Craig found it hard to forget once the light was back.

'How's business treating you?'

Not meeting his eye, scaring him further.

'Oh good, good . . .'

'Saw that new ting, *Vintage Racers* . . . The boys were killin me for it . . . Forty pound a piece, blud, what's goin on wid dat?'

'I know . . .'

'Tried to drive like dat on the way home, thought I'd impress the kids. Got tugged goin down Nottin Hill.'

'Serious?'

'They were. Gave me two points, six-month ban.'

'*Fuck.*'

'Just my luck innit?' Drake had the good grace to look amused, even if he wasn't ashamed. 'So what, bruv, you can't bring man in?'

'Well . . .' Feeling his heart plummet, thinking *already*, even though he knew what Laura would say considering he always gave away games; sometimes freebies for Toby, sometimes for his friends, a lot of the time for the fathers of Toby's friends. He felt bad once again, irritated by his guilt. 'I suppose I could put something in the post . . .'

'Yeah . . . That would be cool . . .' Drake turning his head from left to right, scanning full tables like a Cold War spy, Craig guessing the real reason for his call, remembering why he'd been so scared when Laura passed on his message, knowing why he hadn't picked up the phone until she pestered for days on end. It was the foreseen look in Drake's eye that stopped him, as if they were colleagues involved in conspiracy. All the way from Lewes to London he'd wished things might have changed, but they never did in places like these, just kept the wheels turning and the people running in place, panting with the effort of staying upright.

'What's on your mind, Drake?'

He knew he'd misjudged his tone when he saw Drake falter, his shield of confidence dented, thrusting him back a measured step.

'Know me too well still, innit bruv . . .'

Craig's laugh was bitter, the taste sharp in his mouth.

'It's all right, it's all right . . .' Drake was saying, avoiding his eye. 'I was thinkin maybe I had a little idea you could use . . . We could work on it together, you know, me an you . . . I was watchin the youts play GTA and I was like, yeah man, dere ain nuttin representin *dem* you know . . . So you could ave like, a game set in the ends where mans is on the estate, an he's gotta shot tings on the other side a town right, like in a nex code where man like him's not supposed to go, but it's bait cos dem man don't like it yeah; den feds are on his case, and the olders don't like what man's dealin wid so he's gotta dodge alla dem man and get the work to dis nex ends on the ovva side a town . . . An while he does he's got side missions innit, his girl, his mum, beef his boys get him into . . . I ain really thought it out proper, but I jus wanted to run it by you, see what man thinks . . .'

And the worst thing about the whole conversation, the thing that stung him most, wasn't his thoughts that it was the worst pitch he'd heard in all his years of developing; or that he didn't understand fifty percent of what Drake was saying because the slang had changed, of course it had; but despite his disgust, driven by his guilt, he found himself nodding in all the right places, saying how good the idea was, that it was something he could use, even as he mentally dismissed his awful-sounding game, the visit home, the dialling of Drake's number, even the possibility of seeing his former best friend again.

They were back on the streets, a bitter wind blowing through winter clothing, copper leaves chasing at their feet like a dog trying to catch its own tail, Drake walking head down, talking fast. Craig didn't know why he'd agreed when he felt so bad, melancholy sucking the words right out of him, seemingly transposing them into Drake's mouth, making his jaws flap and sentences tumble onto the pavement before them. There was no reason to follow, no need, and yet Craig took right turns and lefts, sighting flats that had previously been squats and crack houses, but were now penthouse apartments, studios, gated communities. Drake bowed his head and led him further off the main road, away from sirens and take-aways until they entered the estate he remembered, chalky walls and penitentiary landings, raw wind howling through long corridors, pushing from behind as if forcing him not to lag no matter how much he wanted to, making him walk faster.

Drake took a key from his pocket just before he reached a battered red door. His full grin was back, grey tooth visible, Craig noticing that the colour matched the estate block, hating his own observation. His friend was winking as he unlocked the door.

'Let's have a drink an celebrate, blud . . . We're gonna make history – me an you, like old times . . .'

He tried not to wince as Drake ushered him in, which caused him to grimace instead. The musty smell of contained air flavoured by an odour of old household items. Weed smoke greeting him at the door. Drake sauntered through the house flicking light switches, stumbling over blackened trainers and broken toys. There was no one in the kitchen, but his sons were in the bedroom worshipping before the alter of yet another *Super Mario* adaptation, gazing at the screen, pads in hand. The oldest, Kaylan, was a man before his time, sporting hulking muscles and tattoos to go with his Islamic-style beard. The younger children were skinny in comparison, flat-eyed and sullen.

'Yes, my youts!'

Grunts and groans, flouting their father's presence.

'Sit up when I'm chattin to you! Dis ere's Craig, yuh know, the one I was showin you about? Makes dem games you lot are always playing.'

No one even looked in his direction.

'What's wrong wiv you, man, say hello nuh? Ain you lot got no manners?'

Longer grunts and groans.

'I give up, man, I tell yuh.' Drake turning on his heel, bumping into Craig, almost sending him flying. 'Sorry, blud; let's go meet Karen.'

He flattened himself against the wall and let Drake lead again, wandering into the living room. There was time to look at the pictures in the corridor; Drake's Grandmother Irene, who'd brought up him and his siblings, an older brother and younger sister Craig remembered, probably too well. The siblings themselves, Jonathan, who'd done manslaughter time, and Christie, who'd come on to him when they were teens and stopped speaking to him when he'd turned her down. He stood staring into their pixelated faces, recalling all the things he'd pushed into that locked room of his mind, before he heard Drake's voice call over the bass thunder of a television.

'Sorry, just checkin out your photos,' he said, following.

A woman he guessed was Karen sat frozen in the midst of a miniature forest of bottles, some empty, some not, most containing alcohol. She had a thin sheet of Rizla in hand while a girlfriend next to her broke weed above cigarette paper. There were a few men too, lounging with legs spread, ignoring him, drinking amber liquid from cups adorned with purple and orange spots, watching the huge screen hung on a far wall; MTV Base, Craig reckoned from his quick glance. It was very loud. Drake was stood by his partner's chair, swaying to the beat, smiling.

'Craig, this is my fiancée Karen; Karen, my best friend Craig, yeah?'

'Please to meet you,' she told him. Her grip was light, featherweight, and her skin dark. He thought of Laura, freckles and red spots left by the imprint of his fingers.

'Yes, and you,' he said, feeling eyes on him.

'Sit down, please,' Karen continued, licking and rolling her joint. Her eyes were large and confident. 'Make yourself at home.'

'Well, actually, I was just leaving.'

He imagined he could hear the room exhale. Relief. This had been expected. Hoped for, except by his host and hostess.

'Yuh not stayin, bruv?'

'I gotta train to catch; sorry, mate.'

Craig held out a hand. It hung, stiff as a broken branch.

'That's a shame,' Karen said, not looking at him. Her voice was level.

'I thought you was staying,' Drake muttered, reaching for Craig's hand and grasping the fingers as though he'd been forced into a pact against his own will.

* * *

He walked to the train station alone, fists clenched deep in his pockets. Once in a while he wiped his damp cheeks and told himself the wind was blowing stronger now the sun had gone. It had to be.

Miami Heat

Anyone could tell life had been cruel before I got to the airport, and it didn't change once I got there. I stepped from the cab and ran inside the terminal, dodging fellow travellers on the conveyor belt, dragging my suitcase on wheels like some reluctant pet, face flushed, hair all over the place, sweating beneath my thick winter jacket. Nothing had gone according to plan. Eden was still calling over that cat business. The traffic on the motorway had been particularly bad due to some calamity or other, and it had taken much longer to reach Gatwick than either I, or my cabbie, had envisaged. Then there was the thing with Mother. While I was away she would be going into surgery, just a keyhole operation on her knee but I was worried all the same. After reading about Kanye West's mother passing away during routine plastic surgery, I'd been very nervous about Mother's forthcoming operation. She was fine about it, but Mother tended to be fine about everything, I'd learnt that from an early age. Once, when I was seven years old, I'd been playing *American Gladiators* on a low brick wall. I hopped and spun, blocked and parried, while Mother talked with a friend she'd met and somehow, though it must have been inevitable I know that now, I slipped and fell, bashing my ribs against the corner of the wall, crumpling into an already bawling heap on the pavement. Mother took one look and without missing a beat said, 'I suppose she'll try a lower wall next time,' then she turned and kept on talking like nothing had happened. When I'd cried myself hoarse and alarmed enough passing shoppers, I got to my feet, dusted myself off and stood beside her expelling random sniffles. Mother ignored me. She was still the most pragmatic woman I'd ever met.

My penchant for ungainliness was like a trusty sidekick; it hadn't left me, and had actually got worse as I aged. It grew especially bad around the time of my period, due in the next two to three days. Every month I became a magnet for mishap. That morning was no exception. Trying to dodge all the obstacles on the conveyor belt I took one too many chances. My suitcase on wheels got caught on some unknown object, almost at the same time as I tripped on a child's miniature pushchair. I don't know what happened next, just that I found myself face down, arms outstretched, rolling along the conveyor belt like some household item in a supermarket. How embarrassing. What made it worse was not the point when my chin hit the metal at the end of that human treadmill, or when my suitcase on wheels caught me up and rammed into the soles of my feet, causing a pile up similar to the one that had made me late in the first place, but when a kid walking with his family a couple of feet away pointed me out and went 'Ha, ha,' like that annoying little brat from *The Simpsons*. Oh, how I wanted to tear his podgy limbs from his fat body and beat him until he screamed. The boy's father told him off but I could see he was trying not to laugh too. I got to my feet, fended off the smirked concerns of my fellow travellers, collected myself as best as I could and limped to the check-in desk.

I only remembered how much I hate Gatwick Airport when I saw the queue. It always reminds me of a budget Heathrow. There was no way I would have chosen to fly from there myself and it was actually quicker to drive to Heathrow from Brixton, but my tickets had been booked by the record company, who had a deal with Virgin, so there was nothing I could do. My phone began to ring. Angry, I took it out and looked at the screen. Eden again. I got in line, preparing to wait, switching it off. I wasn't having that conversation around that many people. I actually didn't want to have it at all.

So there I was, standing in line, checking my watch every five minutes. My chin felt painful. I knew I wasn't bleeding because I'd checked, but still. I wondered whether I could sue. Wished it had happened in Miami, where I could. The monotony of the queue system must have really got to me because I began to feel this hard object repeatedly strike my Achilles tendon and when I raised my head there was a wide space between myself and the person in front. Over my shoulder I saw a woman, tall and thin, maybe early fifties. She had greying hair, an angular face, wide glasses, thin lips and no smile. She was still pushing her airport trolley into the back of my legs.

'Excuse me,' the woman said, eyeballing me like a mortal enemy. 'Excuse me, do you mind moving up?'

I shot her my dirtiest look, kissed my teeth and moved.

Two steps later a Virgin representative approached. 'Going to Miami, madam?'

'I am,' I heard from behind me. It was that blasted woman. When I looked around she had reinforcements: a huge guy, well over six feet, towering over everyone in range.

They muscled their way past me. Before I knew it they were conversing with the Virgin rep and I had been elbowed to the side. I fumed, although I knew it would do me no good, waiting for them to be led to an empty desk. The woman looked back at me in triumph. I was so angry I wanted to punch her face in.

I have to say at this point, I'm not normally violent. It was the strain of the last few weeks and the stress of the morning that pushed me there. And Morticia of the check-in queue was rude beyond belief, there was no doubt about that. I watched her and her boyfriend laugh with the woman behind the desk as though they were so friendly, so much fun, and I honestly wanted to puke. No wonder Morticia had been willing to throw her weight around. She had Lurch's weight to protect her.

Eventually I was hurried to the check-in desk where everything went smoothly. I queued at the security gates and went through the whole water, cosmetics thing – although I read somewhere it's impossible to blow up a plane using bottled water, and as soon as you get to Duty Free the shops are selling Evian and the like at double the normal price, so there's something going on for sure. I milled around looking in the windows of the clothing stores, but like I said before I find Gatwick pretty dry. I had a Latte and a blueberry muffin, switched on my phone and decided to call Mother.

I'm paraphrasing, but the conversation went something like this:

ME: Hey, Mum, how's it going?

MOTHER: Where are you?

ME: Here. At the airport. I just arrived.

MOTHER: Oh. What's happened, why are you calling?

ME: Because I'm *here*.

MOTHER: –

ME: I wanted to say goodbye?

MOTHER: Oh! Oh, yes of course!

ME: –

MOTHER: So, goodbye then, have a good trip, get yourself some sun.

(She always says that, as though sun is something you can purchase in Duty Free and place in a pretty little bag with a bow.)

ME: How's the cat?

MOTHER: The same as when you left. I must say, I still think she has issues.

ME: *Muuum* . . .

MOTHER: I know you don't want to hear it, but it's as plain as the nose on your face . . .

ME: Please don't speak in clichés, Mum, you know I hate it.

MOTHER: Never mind me, you need to take your cat to a good shrink; I've read about them in the paper. Go to Notting Hill, I bet they have them there. Your cat has sexual problems, Seren. You must face up to that.

ME: Mum, not again . . .

MOTHER: I'm hardly surprised anyway, living in that house of yours.

ME: OK, Mum? I think they're boarding now. I have to go.

MOTHER: OK, dear. Have a good trip; don't forget to get yourself some sun.

ME: Will do! Good luck with the operation! I'll call!

Mother made an irritated noise and rang off. I sat looking at the phone, trying to ignore my stinging chin, wondering if things would ever change. Conversations with Mother always went like that. I'd start off hopeful and immediately find myself perplexed, only to end the call thinking I shouldn't have bothered. Don't get me wrong, I love Mother and she loves me, but you could hardly say we understood each other. Sometimes, especially when I went for Sunday dinner with Eden, I'd catch Mother looking at me as though she was trying to work out what had happened, how we'd got thrown together on this extravagant ride called life. I never spoke about it because I knew I did the same thing. I suppose, with hindsight, she felt that she'd chosen the perfect name for me, Serendipity. Mother and I had nothing in common. Only a meaningless quirk of fate could explain how we'd ended up related.

We were really called for boarding a few minutes' later. I was edging sideways down the aisle, saying 'excuse me' every five minutes, waiting while some guy fiddled with his bags by the overhead lockers. My seat was at the rear of the plane so I had to do that a lot. Halfway there I saw Morticia and Lurch sitting in the emergency-exit seats – the ones that cost fifty pounds extra for the privilege of stretching your legs – laughing with one of the flight attendants, a blonde with frizzy hair and an Essex accent. They made me fume and I didn't even know why. I performed my crab-walk at an even faster rate.

I found my place, the middle section next to the aisle, which was as good as I was getting for free. I stowed my bags above and under my seat and strapped myself in with the latest copy of *Blues & Soul*. It wasn't the greatest issue ever produced, but there were a couple of reviews and an interview with Peven Everett penned by yours truly. I tend never to get tired of reading my own work and seeing my name in print. Sometimes I'd be lying in bed on a Sunday morning with an edition of *Echoes* or the *New Nation*, or if I had a lucky month, *The Independent* or *The Guardian*, when Eden would come into the room and say, 'Reading yourself again?' I would have taken offence except that she was usually smiling when she said it, and she would sometimes lie on the bed, congratulating me on a point I'd made, or just the simple miracle of getting a piece in the broadsheets.

I'd been a freelance music journalist most of my adult life. It was the only thing I'd ever wanted to do, spurred on by the Nelson George biography of Michael Jackson I'd devoured when I was twelve. I still wasn't sure what had cemented that final decision, which passage or chapter I'd read that turned the switch in my head; only that I remembered closing the book and going into the back garden of my mother's house, where the sun was shining in the cloudless sky and the buzz of insects and bees was loud, and the underground trains at the bottom of my garden trundled past with laborious power. Heat was heavy on my face. I recall looking up at the sky, not directly at the sun because that was just stupid, Mother told me as much, but up into the pale, expansive blue. I remember taking a deep breath in and another out feeling content, just so. I lay on the grass and imagined what I would have written if I had met Michael Jackson. And that was it I suppose. My path was set.

Nowadays, I wrote copy for a music-promotions firm in town to pay rent and fit freelance articles in when I could. It wasn't exactly the career I'd imagined while laying on my back casting dreams into the clear sky, but it was close enough to give me vague moments of satisfaction, a flimsy sense of security and more CDs and records than I could ever listen to.

I spotted a guy a few rows in front of me. He was short with a balding head and thick glasses. Rodney Weintraub. I should have known the flight would be packed with journos. Rodney had written a few articles for the *Observer Music Monthly*, *The Independent*'s music section and American journals like *Vibe*, *XXL* and *The Source*. He was English as they come and had been known to upset musicians of colour on occasion; mostly, he kept to himself. The majority of his work possessed that rare amalgamation of wisdom and quality writing I was eternally striving for, echoing the likes of the greats: Greg Tate, Carol Cooper, Sacha Jenkins, Harry Allen. I watched him place his bags in the overhead locker and find his seat with the calm assurance of a man who knew how to bend the world to meet his needs. I wished I could be that confident. I wondered how many people sitting in what was really just a hollowed bullet realised they were in the presence of what amounted to music-journo royalty.

The plane started to shudder. The flight attendants began their emergency display. I bowed my head and continued to read myself with a tiny smile of pleasure.

I'd been hired by the record company to fly to Miami in order to write up an interview on The Cheeba Monks, a C-list LA-based rap group who had been stirring up the underground scene for five years. The Monks were a trio of two MCs and a DJ, the archetypal hip-hop hippies who smoked weed, made jazz-influenced music and chanted mellow lyrics no one understood. I liked what I'd heard of their latest album, *Blunts n Blessings*, although I had no idea what direction to take the interview in. The bios I'd seen online were so vague they were almost unhelpful. Trying to piece together an idea of the Monks from their music was like attempting to complete a still life of Jackson Pollock using his paintings as the only guide.

During my time in Miami I would also be attending the twenty-second IDMA, the International Dance Music Awards, hosted by the Winter Music Conference. According to the website I'd been excitedly scanning for weeks, the WMC was regarded as 'the singular networking event for the dance-music industry, attracting delegates from sixty-two countries'. Amongst the topics up for debate were the technological changes the industry was undergoing in the form of CDRs and MP3s, new inroads for music development and hundreds of seminars on artist management, marketing, distribution, radio promotion. After dark the WMC really came alive, with hundreds of venues opening their doors for superstar DJs of every genre and nationality, spinning tunes every night for six days. The event would culminate with the Ultra Music Festival, the largest US music festival of its kind.

Eden was disappointed I hadn't managed to swing her a plane ticket when I'd been booked a few months back, but in light of what had happened I was glad. The bust up occurred a fortnight ago. I managed to change my ticket so I could stay on a week after the WMC and explore the Miami scene. I was looking forward to sunshine, nightlife and sexy women now I was single, and couldn't stop singing Will Smith's 'Welcome to Miami' under my breath when no one was in earshot. London in March wasn't exactly hell on earth, but it wasn't paradise. It was good to be heading for a land of white-sand beaches, a warm ocean and fantastic seafood.

I reclined my seat, put on my headphones and waited for the movies.

The flight went by without incident. We were herded through US Customs and out the other side, blinking at the placards. I'd been told I was going to be picked up so I wasn't looking forward to seeing some greasy-looking guy broadcasting my name to all and sundry; even so, I was slightly disappointed when I spotted a biscuit-thin blonde holding a handwritten sign. Maybe next time. I approached, unsure whether either of us was the person the other was looking for. She beamed even wider when she saw me, jumped up and down like a cheerleader.

'Serendipity? Serendipity Henry?'

I cursed the Jamaican stubbornness that caused Mother to give me such a God-awful name, thinking for the millionenth time that she could have at least changed my surname. Then I smiled, trying to be on my best behaviour.

'Yes, you can call me Seren if that's easier.'

'Oh, gosh no. Serendipity is wonderful. I love your name! I'm Mercutio, lovely to meet you!'

Perfect, I thought to myself, just perfect. I would have to be met by some ditzy blonde who'd been cursed with a moniker worse than mine. I made a mental promise not to throttle her if she kept screeching my name like a cartoon parrot.

'Mercutio . . . Interesting. From *Romeo and Juliet?*'

'Yeah!'

I wondered whether her face would collapse if she ever stopped smiling.

'But isn't that a man's name?'

'Yeah but you know, my parents were like, major Shakespeare buffs and they just love that play! Isn't that wonderful?'

My God, I thought. Her entire family was stupid.

'So, are you called anything for short?'

Mercutio turned the thought over. I could practically see a line of expanding bubbles emanate from her head.

'Well, the guys at school call me Cuchi . . .'

Disbelief silenced me. Mercutio began to jump up and down again.

'Hey, here come the others . . .'

There were four. The main man, Rodney Weintraub, a stocky black guy known on the scene as Text; an Indian guy I'd never met; and, last but definitely least, Morticia and Lurch. I should have bloody well known. We tried to ignore each other pointedly enough when the introductions were made. As a result, everyone guessed something was wrong. Turning my back on the pair I touched fists with Text, swapped a friendly handshake with the Indian journo, called Sailesh, and practically genuflected before Rodney, blurting out that I'd read all his work. We dragged our luggage to the car park, me trotting by Rodney's side leaking words like a faulty tap while he nodded as though listening to a beat in slow time and Morticia and Lurch smirked. Yes, I had been told their real names – but they were Morticia and Lurch to me so I soon forgot them. And, no, I didn't look at them after that, so I have no idea whether they were really smirking or not, but they looked like the type of people who would.

Miami heat struck as soon as we escaped the air-conditioned terminal. I'd taken off my thick winter jacket and placed it on my suitcase, but I still had on a jumper, and I immediately began to sweat. Not that I was complaining. The sun on my face was like a blessing from God, and it felt even better when Rodney said he'd read my Peven Everett interview and thought it was the best coverage of the artist he'd seen. I was so flattered I didn't notice everyone opt for the back seats of Mercutio's Space Cruiser, which left me sitting up front with the hollow bombshell, cursing my lack of observational skills. I slammed the door behind me, resigned.

Mercutio had enough sense to tell we were all shattered. She maintained a comfortable silence and even slipped a great ambient CD into the deck, which was chilled enough to match the slow, rush-hour vibe of the Miami streets. Text and Sailesh began to talk shop. Morticia and Lurch talked food and designer stores. Rodney nodded to the music while I looked out of the window. Everything was like a scene from a movie.

Mercutio told us the hotel wasn't far from the airport, pointing out sights. My phone rang at least five times. I switched it off. Eden was relentless when she wanted to be, a trait she shared with Mother. After the final call Rodney tapped my shoulder and said I was obviously a popular woman, slipping me his card like a waiter depositing the bill. I smuggled it into my pocket with equal nonchalance, even though I was elated.

The record company had spent money on the hotel, no doubt. It was at least four stars and amazing. Huge glass windows, porters in top hats and tails, taxis lined outside the lobby. Hulking men in hoodies and basketball vests. Mercutio got us checked in, handing us our room keys and press packs. There would be dinner at seven in the hotel restaurant and free tickets to a club, although no one was obliged to attend. Either way, we were all to meet in the lobby the following morning at nine. She wished us a pleasant stay and left with her short summer dress clinging to flawless thighs.

I gave her a quick once over. It was amazing how a person changed in your eyes once you'd warmed to her.

Rodney, Sailesh and Text were talking drinks in the hotel bar. Morticia and Lurch had already gone to their room to make stiff, passionless monster-love, I guessed. I begged off and went to my own on the fifteenth floor to unpack and grab some downtime. I still hadn't thought of enough questions for my interview, scheduled for one the following afternoon. There were three days of the conference, which happened to run over the weekend. My interview would take place during the workshop part of the day according to the schedule I found in my press pack. That would give me the chance to attend seminars, network and generally have a good time.

I showered and put on the hotel dressing gown, looked out of wide windows. Miami spread below me as though it had been flattened with a butter knife. There wasn't a hill or raised area to be seen. I contemplated sending Mother a text to let her know I'd arrived, until I lay on the massive bed and switched on the cable. Promising myself five minutes rest, I closed my eyes and didn't wake until morning.

I rose early, texted Mother, scribbled questions, then went downstairs and met Text, Rodney and Sailesh for breakfast. The boys had been dancing and gone on to a strip club. There had been drinking and the shaking of hindquarters, even a bit of snorting. I laughed along with their jokes and banter, mostly enjoying my pancake breakfast. When I finished Morticia and Lurch were shovelling food a few tables away. They were keeping to themselves, which was fine with me.

We met Mercutio in the lobby just before nine. She was wearing skin-tight jean shorts, Timberlands and a torn frat T-shirt that only just reached her ribcage. A number of guys in the reception area were checking her out, but she seemed not to notice. After hugs and kisses for all, Mercutio guided us outside. I suppose the guys must have been too tired to fully appreciate her the day before, because there was nearly a fistfight between Text and Sailesh over who would sit in passenger seat. Mercutio giggled and told them to stop. Rodney was already climbing into the back seats. I joined him, as did Morticia and Lurch, who pointedly turned away. Sailesh eventually got in the back looking pissed. I started a conversation between myself, Sailesh and Rodney just to take his mind from Text, who was already yapping.

The conference was at the Miami Beach Resort, not far from our hotel. The morning's events, live DJ sets, were underway in the lobby. People were standing in a thin but growing crowd watching the DJs. Some already had drinks in hand. I swore I could smell drugs being smoked, which made it my type of party. Mercutio left us to mingle and do her own thing. I hung out with Text and Sailesh; they were more like my age and I felt I knew them quite well and Rodney seemed to have disappeared. At midday we scooted to the poolside to watch the scratch DJ battles. We whooped and screamed at the sight of grown men making funny noises with the aid of a turntable, a record and household objects such as sinks, wooden chairs or televisions. I was so enthralled Sailesh had to tell me he was leaving before I remembered I had an interview too. I wasn't sure what was wrong. I was rarely scatty at work. I hotfooted it into the building and checked my press pack to see which hotel room I was in.

It was only in the lift, heading for the eleventh floor and searching through my little bag, that I realised I'd forgotten my iPod. Which meant it was on the bedside cabinet back at my hotel. No iPod meant no digital recording, since I usually connected the MP3 player to a small microphone and used it to tape interviews. Though I hated to transcribe I hated longhand even more. I cursed myself all the way to the eleventh floor and would have kicked the lift walls, but was scared of being seen by cameras. In the hallway, walking towards room one thousand and thirty-four, I bowed my head and greeted the Monks' PR, another smiley college girl, in a monosyllabic grunt.

There were three journos before me so I had to wait; mercifully they were all self-centred enough to completely ignore me and concentrate on their notes, which I would have done if I had any. I looked at my scribbled questions. They were hardly in-depth, although decent enough. The most difficult part would be capturing all the rapid-fire answers I was likely to receive.

It was my turn sooner than I wished. Morose and anticipating failure, I crept into the hotel room to find the Cheeba Monks lounged in various positions: one on the bed, one on the small chaise longue, another on a sofa in the corner. There was a huge burgundy leather chair with diamond-shaped stitching placed dead in the centre of the room. Three thirty-something African-American men, each of whom seemed five years younger than their actual ages, looked up from rolling blunts (of course) and chatting idly to each other as though I was Alice tumbling into the middle of their tea party.

'S'up, shawty?' said the Monk on the bed, known to his fans as Brieze Block. Tall, skinny and fudge-skinned, Brieze was the producer and DJ.

'It's dat England writer, the London sister . . .' said Prime, top-gunning MC and, personally, my favourite. Prime was dark and kind of tubby, like a cute younger brother. He had ice in his ears and thick waves in his hair.

'Oh fuh real? You from the UK, shawty? They really make em dat fine over there?' Vocalo, Brieze Block's younger cousin leered. He was a renowned player, partly because it was practically all he rhymed about besides weed, and partly because he was model pretty without the charm of his rhyme partner. The Monks started to laugh and slap palms while I blushed, trying to sit without tangling myself in my bag, smiling to show I was a good sport but not enough to give them any ideas.

'I know you've been to London – I saw you perform at Jazz Café – so don't give me the "I-never-knew-there-were-black-people-in-England" routine . . .'

I thought I'd given them food for thought, but it only made them laugh harder.

'My bad, my bad, you cawght us an shit . . . We

been to London a few times, true . . .' Prime chuckled, running the blunt beneath his nose.

'London cats usually get offended if we tell em we thought England was fulla Caucasians . . . We was . . . what you guys call it? Pullin yuh leg, dat's all . . .'

'Ah, you guys . . .' I groaned, playing the whole thing out for the sake of bonding. Hopefully if I bantered successfully enough they wouldn't notice my lack of tape.

It worked. I quickly found that if I flirted while acting like the older friend of their older sister, the one they could admire but couldn't possibly have, things worked out fine. Knowing their back catalogue down to the white-label forty-fives impressed them a fair bit and I even took a pot shot, wishing Prime's son a happy Easter, which made him smile and look serious whenever I spoke. I'd often believed myself the queen of the follow up question and I more than proved it that afternoon, recalling songs and disputes with other rappers with fond nostalgia (of course, I only mentioned the battles they'd won). The Monks were pretty coherent until they smoked that blunt, then it was slurred words and mumbled phrases I had to strain to pick up. I'd been granted half an hour. I knew we'd go over at that rate of conversation, which was great for my stilted longhand. There was nobody behind me while I'd waited in the corridor and I guessed no one was booked. When Brieze talked about the disparity between when they'd got started in the game and the present, I couldn't help thinking about the rumours I'd heard concerning their first manager, IPB from the rap group Itchi Krax.

'So, are you guys still in contact with IPB at all? He managed you for like, three years right? Do you and the Krax hang out at all, I know you were tight way back . . .'

Prime was suddenly quiet, and stopped looking at me with pleasure-filled, slightly leery eyes. He stared at the king-sized duvet as if entranced by its patterns. Brieze was giving me a glare that would have sent a chill through Medusa, and Vocalo seemed partly embarrassed, partly sympathetic, as though he knew what my big mouth had got me into but was powerless to save me.

'Why you have to bring dat nigga up? That's old shit . . .' Brieze spat, eyeballing me. I didn't know what to say next and it showed.

'Well . . . I was just wondering . . .' I smiled, trying to retie our former bond. 'Hey, isn't IPB white?'

'So?'

That was from Prime. Stupidly, I didn't get the message.

'Well, you said why did I have to bring that n . . . That *negro* up, but as IPB is Caucasian I really don't see . . .'

I trailed off when I saw their faces. My follow up question would have been how did they feel using the 'N' word when they performed in front of their majority white fan-base, but it was pretty clear the interview was over. I switched topics and asked a few more questions about *Blunts n Blessings* to test the water. When they pointedly refused to answer I wasted no time gathering my notepad, pen and bag. I'd visited the land of All Clammed Up before. Wishing the

Monks luck with the album, I left. As I walked out of the door I thought I heard Brieze Block mumbling about 'Some punk-ass sell-out from some punk-ass country playing like a journalist when she didn't even have a tape recorder.' I'd never left an interview feeling so low.

I assured their PR the interview had gone great even though she could tell by my face it hadn't, went downstairs to the Scratch DJ battle and flopped in front of the bar. I ordered a large Mojito, and knocked it back, then quickly ordered another, telling the barman he should throw in an extra shot of Bacardi on the house. Surprisingly enough, he complied. It must have been the accent. I drank that and ordered another. When he asked me where I was from I told him Australia and moved on.

Text and Mercutio were in the lobby, all smiles, dancing to the DJ set. I gave it less than twenty-four hours before they were in the sack. Sailesh was probably doing interviews and Rodney was still missing in action. I tried to let myself go and dance, but I felt out of place. I checked my phone. Mother hadn't replied to my text message. Eden had called three times. I didn't know why she was being so persistent. We were supposed to be finished. I felt a tap on my shoulder. Rodney.

'How's it going?' he grinned, old fashioned Sony tape recorder hanging from one shoulder, a Tequila Sunrise in hand.

'Crap,' I responded. 'Really crap.'

'What's up?'

I told him about the Monks interview, my promising

start and dismal conclusion. He thought it was funny.

'That kind of thing happens . . .'

'Yeah, I know . . .'

'What can you do? You've got enough notes for the write-up, haven't you?'

'Yeah . . .'

I actually did.

'Stop being negative will you? You've done your job, now how about enjoying yourself? You're in Miami for God's sake . . .'

I figured he was right. Rodney dragged me over to where Text and Mercutio were dancing and for the rest of the afternoon that was where we stayed. Sometimes he would grab both my hands and swing them from side to side, which could have been embarrassing, but for an old guy he was quite a mover. After an hour or so Sailesh and a stunning Cuban music journo he'd met joined us. She was called Isabel and was way too gorgeous for him. Text kept looking from Isabel to Mercutio like a cat caught between the cream and the fish meat. Sailesh was too busy with his Cuban *mami* to notice, thank God.

We grew hungry, so our little group left. Mercutio took us to a small Mexican place that looked pretty authentic. She seemed to know the owners and when she spoke Spanish, Text began to smile again. I was equally impressed. Isabel approached her and before we could say *chimichanga* the women were deep in conversation. We grabbed a table and ordered. I speak a little Spanish, not much, just stuff I picked up in school. I sat with the women and tried to join in. Rodney, Text and Sailesh seemed happy enough to talk about manly things at the other end of the table. That was fine with us girls.

After we ate, we went back to the conference to catch the first night of the Ultra Music festival. Techno was the order of the day, just the right music for dancing without thinking. We stayed at the Miami Beach Resort until Rodney said he knew a club where Fabio, the UK drum 'n' bass DJ, was due to play. Our little group was instantly sold. Mercutio drove us back to the hotel to shower and change. She was going to go home and do the same but I had enough outfits for her and Isabel too, and we were all roughly the same height and shape. We tramped up to my hotel room and got ready together. I was pretty high on the drink and a line we'd snorted in the girl's room, so I was ready for anything.

Fabio took me back to the days of two-stepping in some hole-in-the-wall venue where sweat dripped from walls and dark melodic music rattled my rib cage. Mercutio had a baggie of glittering MDMA powder, which gave me an instant hit as soon as I put it on my tongue. I was bouncing hard enough to touch the ceiling for the rest of the night. Feverishly, I got the rounds in. The drugs must have given Sailesh confidence, because he was dancing close with Isabel and Mercutio, and they were looking at him as though he was the only man in the room. Text tried to move his solid feet a few metres away. He was sweating and looked too far gone to even notice. I danced with Rodney, trying to forget about the botched interview, mother's operation, breaking up with Eden, my allegedly mixed-up cat. I let the music wash my negative thoughts away.

We left in the early hours. I had no idea what DJ was playing, neither did I care. We jumped into Mercutio's cruiser and were ready to go until we saw that she was too high to drive. After a great deal of deliberating I decided to take the wheel. Mercutio climbed into the back with Sailesh and their new-found friend. Text fell asleep on one of the lone seats while Rodney sat up front. I'd never driven on the right but I thought I'd give it a go. The air was warm, with little breeze. Mercutio directed us to South Beach where we parked and ate hot dogs. We took a moonlit stroll, the perfect end to our night, and then it was back to the hotel.

I'm not sure what happened when we got there. Everyone seemed to disappear. Rodney was the only one left, looking at the lights with lacklustre eyes. He told me he'd walk me to my room.

Outside my door I fumbled in my bag for the keycard, waving in triumph once I found it. I slipped the card into the lock, opened up. I kissed Rodney on both cheeks.

'Thanks for looking after me tonight, Rodney. I really appreciate it. I feel miles better.'

'A pleasure,' he said, beaming a toothy smile, no doubt enhanced by the drugs.

'Good night.'

I caught a glimpse of his frown. Felt a quick moment of dread.

'Wait.'

Something told me to play like I'd not heard. I should have listened to myself. Scared of what might happen, I turned to face him.

'Yes, Rodney?'

'I thought–'

My horror multiplied. I should have known. 'Thought what?' Trying to make my smile sweet. Hoping he'd let it go.

'That we'd spend the night together.'

'Rodney–'

'I fancy the pants off you, Seren.'

I tried not to shudder at the thought.

'Rodney. I'm gay.'

His bushy eyebrows twitched. 'I take it you don't mean you're ecstatic to hear that?'

I smiled at the carpet. 'No, Rodney. I don't.'

'Do Text and Sailesh know?'

'Everyone does. I thought you did too.'

Rodney went bright red. I really felt bad, even though all I wanted to do was sleep.

'I'm sorry . . .'

'Yeah, well you should be, you little cock tease . . .'

That hit me like the MDMA. I let his words sink in.

'Goodnight.' I shut the door, turned the lock. There was a bang; he must have hit it with his palm. I crouched down with my ear against the wood and listened to Rodney walk away. My phone began to ring. I looked at the screen. Guess who.

It must have been early Sunday morning back home. Eden would be lazing in bed with two slices of hard-dough toast in a T-shirt and knickers, watching kids' shows. We used to watch them together.

I shut off the phone and dragged myself to bed. Lying spread-eagled, I closed my eyes.

* * *

The next morning I forced myself into the shower even though I felt like shit. My belly was calling for breakfast. I'd eat and go back to bed.

When I got to the restaurant it was no surprise that Rodney was the first person I saw. He was sitting at a far away table with Morticia and Lurch. As I crossed the room they all turned and gave me the dirtiest looks I have ever seen. That threw me. Rodney I could understand, but what business was it of theirs? I put their behaviour down to homophobia. While I would never say it was rife in the Black community, I have to admit, I did come up against pockets of random ignorance. Even Mother had a hard time coming to terms with my sexuality and she was pretty liberal for her generation. I was going to stick up my middle finger but I decided to act with dignity. I sauntered to the table where Text and Sailesh sat. Text was holding his head, picking at scrambled eggs. Sailesh had the relaxed look of the cat that got the cream *and* the fish meat. Sitting as he was, with Isabel on one side and Mercutio on the other, I realised he probably was that feline.

'Morning, guys!'

Everyone besides Text seemed in good spirits. I sat and ordered pancakes. We tried to have a conversation that avoided the obvious, but I suppose it was inevitable.

'Where did you guys get to? We were looking for you everywhere . . .'

Isabel, Mercutio and Sailesh swapped coy looks. Text shifted in his seat, his sickness seeming to worsen. I dropped the subject.

'How'd it go for *you* last night?' Isabel said, hazel

eyes sparkling. She looked fresh, as though she'd gone to bed at nine the previous evening, not five in the morning like the rest of us.

'With *what?*'

'With Rodney,' she said, inclining her head towards the table where he was sitting. 'You two looked like you were really getting on . . .'

'I'm gay, Isabel. I like women. Nothing happened and nothing will.'

She gaped. Turned to Mercutio. They began speaking machine-gun Spanish, staring at the boys with hard eyes. Sailesh turned pale. I thought I might have encountered yet more homophobia until I picked up two words: *malo* and *mentiroso*, which roughly translate into 'wrong' and 'liar'. I didn't get it until I noticed Text and Sailesh swapping anxious glances. I remembered what Rodney had said, whether they had known I was gay. I remembered how they'd behaved in the Mexican restaurant, sitting at the other end of the table, talking with their heads low.

'Did you guys tell Rodney I had a thing for him?'

'No . . .' Text managed. He looked pretty green, I had to admit. If I hadn't been so riled I might have felt sorry for him.

'Not in so many words . . .' Sailesh concluded.

I was going to say more, and probably would have let rip once it became blatantly obvious they were both lying. Text half stood up, held his belly with one hand, opened his mouth and ejected a thick stream of vomit. It went all over his plate and the table. We jumped to our feet to get out of the way. Other diners watched, covering their noses with napkins while Text heaved.

When there was nothing left, he flopped back into his seat; mouth wet, face pale, breathing heavy. Waiters appeared, trying to clean up and lift him out of there. I stood over the mess.

'I find that quite ironic, seeing as you're two sick individuals,' I told them, feeling pride at my clever wordplay. 'Stay away from me from now on, alright?'

I know I was being a bit hard, but what can I say? I was way past angry. They looked sorry; they knew they'd acted insensitively. If it wasn't for the stress of the past few weeks I would probably have let the whole thing go. I do have a sense of humour, you know. Wallowing in the heat of my wrath I stomped away, hearing Isabel and Mercutio calling me back, watching Morticia, Lurch and Rodney watch me. This time I did give them the finger. Oh, the stupid things you do when you're all fired up.

So that was pretty much it for the WMC and me. I spent the rest of my time in my hotel room watching cable and ordering room service, taking taxis to the Miami Beach resort, wandering between workshops and seminars, dancing by myself at DJ sets. Mercutio called to check on me a few times, bless her. She even offered to take me out for dinner and drinks with Isabel, but I begged off. I was wrong about her, she's a lovely girl, and we're actually still in email contact. At the time, while I appreciated her loving nature, I decided I was better off by myself. My few days away from home were supposed to be a way to get my head together. Clubbing and taking class As wasn't going to help. What Text and Sailesh had done was for the best.

Saturday night I went dancing, which didn't go down too well. Not that the ravers weren't friendly, just that I wasn't in the mood for socialising. I ended up in a corner by myself feeling worse than when I'd arrived. I left within three hours.

Most of that Sunday was spent wrapped in a hotel dressing gown, typing up the Cheeba Monks interview, which had actually turned out pretty good. My period arrived. I took that as an omen. I called Mother to wish her luck with the surgery. She didn't have much to say, just more complaints about the cat. I cut her off and said I'd ring in the next few days. That night I opted for room service and cable even though it was the last night of the conference. I could hear people leave their rooms, the roar of cleaners' vacuums. Mercutio called again but I shut the phone off. I tried not to think about all the fun they were having, or the fact that no one had cared enough to knock on my door.

On Monday morning I packed and had my last heavenly breakfast. The restaurant was mostly empty. When I took my suitcase-on-wheels into the lobby, there were Morticia and Lurch. I pointedly ignored them again, dragged me and mine out of there and into a waiting taxi without another look. I never did find out which one was the journo.

The 'affordable South Beach hotel' I'd booked on the Internet was like an online dating nightmare – the reality looked nothing like the picture. When my taxi pulled up I repeatedly asked the driver whether he'd got the right place, until he laughed and assured me it was the Palm Tree Beach resort. Resigned, I paid and stood on the pavement, looking at my home for the next five days. Oh, how the mighty had crumbled. The entire hotel was painted pink, although the paint was flaking. The building design was fifties art deco, rounded corners, big glass windows and white metal bars that made it look like a psychedelic mental asylum. Worse still, crawling everywhere, from the building steps to the sun loungers, were hundreds of blue-rinse grannies and tortoise-skinned old men resembling an infestation of red ants. I would have turned around and gone right back, were it not for two things:

1. I couldn't afford the hotel rates anywhere else.
2. It was the nearest hotel to South Beach that had any rooms left. I knew because Eden and I had rung them all weeks ago. This had been the best we could get.

So, like two dogs joined in the street, I was screwed and stuck. I buried my displeasure and rolled up the luggage ramp, nodding hello at the elders, who stared with open-mouthed wonder. For some reason they all seemed Jewish. Maybe because they looked like the Golden Girls might have done fifteen years after the show went off-air.

The guy at the reception desk was tall and broad-shouldered, pink as an over-cooked prawn. When he opened his mouth and spoke with a broad southern accent I was instantly afraid. They'd fought to keep slavery an institution, hadn't they? If it were up to them I'd still have shackles on my wrists and ankles, some white man's brand on my skin. It took less than five minutes to realise that the man, who introduced himself as Daniel, was one of the kindest people I'd ever met. He called me *m'aam* so many times I began to look over my shoulder to see if he was talking to the blue-rinses. He insisted on carrying my luggage to my room himself, a task I'd never seen any receptionist perform. Looking around on my walk up the stairs, I concluded that was probably because porters were in short supply. Once Daniel opened the door, which obviously wasn't the most securely locked place in Miami, he offered me a safe-deposit box at no charge. I'd already seen the sign at the desk saying the boxes were thirty dollars. Twenty of that was non-refundable. I thanked the man, accepting his offer, stepped slowly inside.

Daniel left me to it, probably out of embarrassment. It was the worst hotel room I'd ever seen, much less stayed in. The walls were dark, grimy. The sheets on the single bed were grey, not with dirt, but the strain of being repeatedly washed. There was one small window with bars that looked out onto the opposite building. If the Palm Tree Beach resort had a sea view it wasn't from my room. The small wooden desk and chair was old and rickety. When I switched on the rheumy yellow light bulb, the room didn't grow any brighter. A *Yellow Pages* sat by the black dial telephone. Jesus, I hadn't seen one like that since I was a kid. I flicked through the directory and rang a few more hotels on my mobile, but it was no use; everywhere remained fully booked. I would be spending five days and four nights in the Palm Tree Beach resort. It looked more like the Heartbreak Hotel.

I put my clothes away and went down to the beach, which Daniel had claimed was five minutes away, for a walk, a think, and to be perfectly honest, to get out of that stuffy room. Down a concrete path and onto the sand. At first I was pretty excited. I'd changed into a tasteful bikini under my summer dress and I carried a beach towel wrapped around an airport novel. My iPod was tucked inside my Diesel bag. When I'd walked along the beach far enough I put my toe in the water. It was greyer than I'd anticipated and a little cold, but the sun was warm so I didn't mind. I walked further, where it was more populated. Chiselled gay men walked along the shoreline hand-in-hand. Groups of Latino families played volleyball. There were stalls selling food and trinkets, not much else. When I asked someone how far it was to South Beach he gave me a strange look and said I was standing on it. Behind me was a wall of plush hotels. The main road was four hundred yards away. I sighed and searched for some-where to lay my beach towel down, finding a spot not far from the sea.

My phone rang. Without looking, I switched it off. I scanned the beach. It was nothing like the music videos or my imagination. I could have been in Bournemouth except for all the muscled gay men. Maybe it was the time of year.

Opening my airport novel, I consoled myself with the thought that it was unlikely I'd get hit on. I lay on my back and slipped my glasses onto my nose.

* * *

The cat business had been it as far as Eden and I were concerned. She was Persian – fluffy and grey with bright blue eyes and a look of stern intolerance I loved. I'd bought her from the *Make A Home* cat sanctuary in North London. When I walked into that basement room to see hundreds of misplaced animals staring from behind thin wire cages, I burst into silent tears. The attendant passed me a tissue, saying my reaction was quite normal. Sheba, my fluffy Persian, walked up to the cage doors and sniffed my fingers, immediately began to purr. The attendant opened the cage. Ten minutes later I was still there, in the centre of the cage with Sheba on my lap, one woman and a cat making low-pitched noises of contentment.

Mother had been going on about Sheba for ages. It didn't take her long to find something wrong; only the absurd nature of her claim surprised me. A few months after I'd brought the cat to the Brixton flat I shared with Eden, Mother stood by a window watching Sheba play in the front garden with a neighbouring moggy. She looked very serious. I brought over a mug of tea and sat on the sofa. I wasn't really paying attention, so I barely heard Mother when she said: 'I know this might come as a shock, and I don't want you to get all emotional like usual, but I really think you should do something to treat your cat's affliction . . .'

All I registered at that point were the words *cat* and *affliction*. Mother worked as a receptionist at a West London veterinary clinic. She didn't know as much as she claimed; that didn't stop her acting like she did.

'Why, what's wrong?'

Mother sipped her tea and looked over the rim at

me. I hated the way she played every conversation like a melodramatic movie. 'I think you should sit down.'

'Mum, will you please stop with the clichés? You know full well I'm already sitting down.'

'I'm just asking that you brace yourself, that's all. Serendipity, I think your cat is . . . Don't take this the wrong way . . . I actually think Sheba's a bit queer . . .'

And no, Mother didn't mean she thought my cat was displaying peculiar tendencies. From that day on she never left the subject alone. Whether I was at her house, out shopping, or visiting relatives, my cat's sexual orientation was the focal point of conversation. I noticed she never said anything when Eden was around, probably because she knew how daft the whole thing sounded, and mostly because she blamed my partner's influence. As open-minded as Mother was, and claimed to be, my choice of partners was something she seemed to be waiting for me to grow out of, like my passion for hot pants and really loud Techno. It was weird because in other ways she was totally supportive. She'd been more than understanding when I'd come out a few days after my nineteenth birthday. She treated my partner like a second daughter and had even cooked Sunday dinner for Eden and her family. On paper, everything seemed fine. My friends, straight and gay alike, often held Mother up as a model of the ideal parent, yet I'd always felt weird about her motivations. This inevitably caused some distance. Mother wasn't the saint she was trying to be.

Still, her accusations stuck. I found myself watching Sheba around other cats. It was true that she seemed to turn her nose up at males, but surely that didn't mean Mother was right. I would find myself picking Sheba up, looking into her eyes, whispering encouragement whenever Eden was out of the room. If a neighbour or friend had a Tom I would get them to bring him round, or go over with Sheba and try to force them together. It never worked. At night, I would listen to the local cats making love at the bottom of my garden and pray mine was there. I don't know why, just to prove Mother wrong I suppose. I didn't care whether Sheba was gay or not, I told myself, only that Mother wasn't right.

After months passed without a pregnant belly or a litter, my worry started to grow. Mother claimed to have inspected Sheba and found abnormalities around her private parts. She wouldn't say what they were, only that I should see them for myself. I'd shouted at Mother, called her a 'wicked lady', and stormed out of her house. We hadn't spoken for almost two weeks, but it got me thinking.

That was how, four days after I'd stomped down Mother's garden path, I found myself sitting in the living room with Sheba on my lap. Mother was mad, wasn't she? Of course she was. So what harm would it cause to check her claim out? To, figuratively of course, shove the evidence in her face? Then we would be shot of this queer-cat business. Maybe she would even accept that I was gay and would remain so.

I turned Sheba onto her back. She seemed to like me stroking her tummy so it was pretty easy. I bent over and inspected her private parts with a finger. Nothing seemed untoward. I leaned further to take a closer look. I'd been down there for a few minutes when I heard a noise.

Eden was glaring at me. I jumped. My probing finger must have slipped, because next thing I knew it had gone where it shouldn't. Eden gasped. I gasped. The cat mewled.

'What d'you think you're doing?'

I shook my head, mouthed the word nothing, but it wouldn't come out. Like my finger. It wouldn't move. I tried to pull free, but I couldn't. Sheba began to mewl louder, which made the whole thing worse. I tugged harder. Eden's face went from shock to anger. She flew at me, pounding with her fists. I screamed and Sheba mewled louder, somewhat pleasurably, I noted. You might think that helped matters, but it didn't.

Some people would say Eden was the man in our relationship. I'd respond angrily; there was no need for a male role, though I could imagine how they came to that conclusion. Where I was of average height with a curvy body and small bones, Eden was tall and majestic, beautiful. She had blue-black skin, the softest I'd ever encountered. I called her my Nubian Goddess. We treated it like a private joke, even though I was quite serious. The trouble was Eden was actually as flawless as her skin and I was her tarnished diamond in the rough. The cat business wasn't the first major argument we'd had over something I'd done, even if it was our worst.

I got free of Sheba eventually. Or her from me. She ran out of the cat flap in the kitchen and didn't come back for hours. Eden and I began to argue. She was outraged she'd caught me 'fondling the cat', as she put it, and her anger grew the more we yelled back and forth, dropped the subject, sat sullen during dinner then went at it all over again. She said I was sick; she'd caught me red-handed. She'd seen documentaries about people like me. Against my intuition I told her about Mother's accusation; that only made things worse. We both had mental deficiencies, according to Eden. She'd long suspected Mother was an expert at hiding her homophobia; now she could see she was right. The next day she packed a few things and went to stay with friends in Streatham Common. I couldn't believe she'd leave me over something so ridiculous, or that she'd suspected the same things about Mother I did. I spent the next few days in tears before I got myself together and began looking for extra work to cover the rent. Luckily, my flat was owned by a local Housing Association. That didn't stop me from falling behind.

Not long afterwards Eden began calling, wanting to get back with me. I tried to forgive her like usual; this time, somehow, I could not. I wasn't even sure why. I never told Mother why Eden had left, but I did tell her she was wrong about Sheba. She sniffed and changed the subject.

My first day and night in South Beach was nothing like I'd expected. I spent a couple of hours on the beach until I grew bored. I tried swimming, but the water was too cold. I walked the streets, looking in the shops and boutiques, but it was all too tacky or expensive. I had lunch then went to my hotel room.

After spending less than twelve hours on my own I was already bored. Being a writer, I was usually fine with my own company. I'd travelled alone many times. It had never been difficult before.

I had a brief chat with Daniel, and went up to my room to read. It was my longest afternoon since secondary school. I phoned Mother, who assured me that the operation was fine and she was too, but she was just in the middle of brunch so she'd call me back. I rang off hating her and her damned nonchalance. At six p.m., I showered and changed into an evening dress and went out for dinner. There was a seafood restaurant opposite the Palm Tree. I knocked on the door when I found it closed. A small homely woman, who looked like the stereotypical mother from a fifties American sitcom, came out to tell me they'd be open in an hour. I was left wandering the main streets until then, feeling like the Littlest Hobo, watching drop tops race past. I'd never felt so desperately lonely. When I spied an Internet café I went in and checked my email, just to give myself something to do.

The seafood was nice, although bland. I ate slowly, trying to drag out time. The sitcom mother, who was polite and kind, seemed to have guessed my dilemma, because she kept checking on me, concern wrinkling her eyes. When I finished my food I opened my airport novel and drank a half bottle of wine. Most tables were empty. After I could stand it no longer I paid, walked back to the Palm Tree and was in bed by nine thirty. It took hours to sleep. I lay in the dark cursing my decision to spend more time in Miami.

For the next few days, I tried to make myself busy,

something I'd never found difficult in London. I'd sit in the Internet café drinking lattes and reading the local paper for movie listings. When I found something, I'd walk down to the cinema, often to sit in front of the dark screen a full ten minutes before the trailers. I'd eat an overpriced lunch, go down to the beach and lie in my bikini feeling stupid. Evenings were either spent chatting with Daniel, helping the blue-rinses with their luggage, or roaming Miami searching for entertainment. I was tempted to go clubbing. There were a few places on the main street, but I didn't feel like it. Sometimes I visited the designer stores, most of which were open until very late. I tried using the timer on my camera to take photos of myself, quite unsuccessfully. Eden stopped calling.

The third night I found myself wandering the main street looking for something to eat, when I passed what looked like a cinema. I'd never noticed the building. I soon realised it was probably because the establishment was a strip-and-lap-dance club, an experience I'd never had. Images of cute, nubile women twirling slow around glistening poles leapt to mind. Why not? I'd tried everything else. Without giving myself time to think, I went inside the lobby, paid the entrance fee and was stamped, walked inside.

It was very dark. I stumbled on steps just beyond the bar, where black-suited bouncers stood chatting with the girls. Huge speakers set in gloomy corners blasted music so loud I could feel my teeth rattle. The steps led down into an area of tables and chairs lit by small blue lamps. There were a few men in the club, but they were sitting on the other side of the large hall. Some looked up when I walked across the room, although most had their eyes on the stage. I didn't blame them. A number of poles were placed at eye level in varied positions. Twirling between them was a gorgeous blonde. She had tousled hair that reached the back of her thighs and a small bikini that barely covered anything. As I sat at the table nearest to her I noticed that her outfit was adorned with purple and blue sequins that complemented the table lamps. She jumped high on the pole, straddled it with her legs open and slid to the floor. I watched toned legs and arms as she spun to the bottom. I was horny. The pole dancer saw me and removed her bikini top, revealing silicone-enhanced breasts, before she stomped her way over the men, clear heels thumping. I was so busy watching I didn't even notice the waiter approach my table until he asked what I'd like to drink the second time.

Soft drinks were on the house; beers ridiculously overpriced. I decided to treat myself and ordered a Bud. The blonde was undulating against the pole as though it was a dance partner. She seemed less concerned with me than with the men, who were surreptitiously waving folded bills whenever she performed an act that met their approval. I tutted under my breath. It was too dark to see. In my imagination they were aging jocks wearing football jerseys, overweight due to a lack of exercise. I imagined them drooling all over the blonde, shoving dirty notes into her knickers, although I didn't blame her for going where the money would be. I'd come to the club with forty dollars in twenties.

She timed her performance just right, seeming to

know the song well, teasing the men enough to maintain their interest, holding back until the final few bars, when she lay on her back and pulled the bikini bottoms free, legs wide open, exposed for a second, two at the most, before the stage lights went dark. The PA informed us we'd just seen Anastasia. I clapped as hard as the men. She picked up her notes and skimpy clothing, leaving the stage naked, butt cheeks jiggling. I smiled at the waiter who brought my Bud and the bill.

R&B began to blast. The next up was Carolina, according to the PA. I sat back and took a swig of my beer, expecting another leggy blonde, curvy brunette or pale-yet-fiery redhead. The dancer that emerged was a mousy woman of average height. She looked into the lights as though petrified. The men who'd been sitting forward in their seats when Anastasia performed immediately began to drift. Others watched with bored postures I could make out, even in the dark. The woman's bikini had glittering red sequins that didn't match the blue lights of the club. She placed a hand on the pole and nodded her head, counting time. When she began to move, stepping from side to side in what I assumed was meant to be rhythm, it was all I could do to keep myself from covering my eyes.

Carolina's painful dance seemed to go on forever, amplified by the fact that no one gave any money. She writhed and wriggled around every pole on that stage. The men stayed fixed to the bar. She stripped way too early to give her audience any incentive, leaving her naked for most of her act. When the song ended and the PA announced her name again, Carolina stepped back, blank as ice. She was panting. I watched, unsure what would happen. She wasn't moving. Eventually she gave in, leaving the stage.

Another woman took Carolina's place, though I wasn't listening when the PA called her name. Mistakenly perhaps, I'd always thought of pole dancing as a kind of liberation, freeing the shackles of sexual oppression and drudgery. I'd never thought about what it might actually be like to perform for a collective of shadows. Worse still, what might happen if you didn't have the looks to capture their imagination. I watched the next dancer, a short-haired brunette, as she twirled around the poles.

'Hi there. Would you like to buy a drink?'

It was her. Carolina. Close up I could see the crow's feet at the corner of each eye, the wide, thin mouth covered with pale pink lipstick, the pasty white of her skin. She was trying to smile, lips straining with effort. I looked over her shoulder and saw the watching men. I'd probably been her last hope.

'Uh . . . I already have one . . .'

'Well, would you like to buy one for me? It's five dollars for beer, seven for wine, or if you like you could buy a bottle of champagne for twenty and I could give you a private dance in the champagne room? Whatever you prefer.'

I didn't know how to tell Carolina I didn't want to buy her a drink. We looked at each other, united by shared desperation.

'Please . . .' Her blank veneer cracked. From the corner of my eye I saw a bouncer hovering.

'Have a seat.'

She did. We stared eye to eye. Carolina gave me a huge, soulless smile.

'What time did you start?'

A slight frown, before she remembered she had to keep talking. 'Four.'

I looked at my watch. It was eight.

'And what time d'you finish?'

'Aw, I don't know about one, two.'

'Long day.'

'Yeah, but my boyfriend kicked me out so I need the money. I'm sleeping on a friend's floor until I raise a deposit.'

'I'm sorry to hear that.'

She shrugged her shoulders. They were the smallest, palest shoulders I had ever seen, covered in tiny brown freckles. I could see the bones beneath her skin.

'This dancing thing's not the most reliable career move.'

'No?'

'I used be a receptionist for an IT company but they went bust. Then I worked on South Beach at one of those surfing shops until the manager kept trying to feel me up. He was a friend of my boyfriend, can you believe that? Of course, when I told Ray, he blamed me. I think that's the real reason he threw me out. He said I wasn't bringing in any money and I was too argumentative.'

'Everything alright here?' The bouncer had reached our table without either of us noticing. When I looked into his eyes it was clear he didn't give a damn about me. On the stage, another blonde the PA called Cat replaced the short-haired brunette. The bouncer didn't give a damn about her either. He kept his level stare on Carolina.

'Fine, thanks,' I said, leaning into his line of vision. 'We're just talking.'

'Well, hurry it up,' he said to Carolina.

'Actually, could I have a beer for the lady please? Budweiser, thanks.'

He gave me the cruellest stare I'd ever encountered. 'I'll pass your order onto a waiter,' he said, leaving the table.

Carolina, who had stared at the walls the whole time, put a hand on mine. 'Thanks.'

'That's OK.'

'He's awful. Doesn't like me.'

'How can you tell?' I said, smiling. She didn't get it at first and then we both giggled. 'English humour,' I told her.

'I thought I heard an accent. Where you from?'

'London.'

She lit up when I said that.

'I'd love to go to London.'

I could feel the tightness in my smile when I looked at Carolina.

'How much did you say the champagne room was?'

That was how I found myself drawing money from the nearest ATM, walking back to the strip club and showing the doormen my UV stamp. I didn't have to look for Carolina, she found me. I passed her the bills. She went away, came back clutching a magnum and two champagne glasses. I followed her up some stairs, along a balcony that overlooked the current dancers, past the men receiving table services and on towards a closed door. It wasn't locked but she had some trouble turning the knob. I guessed it hadn't been used very often. While she fumbled I watched the table dance behind me. It was Anastasia. She was very good. Her customer was visibly excited. I turned to Carolina, wondering whether that bothered her. She led me through the doorway as though she hadn't seen anything, smiling again.

The 'champagne room' was another disappointment. It was nothing more than a balcony situated with tiny alcove spaces that gave the illusion of privacy, only to be shattered by another bouncer that stood at the far end, by the door. Carolina poured and passed me a glass. We toasted each other's health. I swallowed a bitter laugh along with the sweet fizzy wine and pretended to like it. Everything was an illusion. Only Carolina seemed real and I couldn't even be sure of that. She sat next to me, sipping fizzy wine, giving me furtive glances.

'Have you ever been up here with a woman?'

She shook her head and looked away. I had a feeling none of the dancers had.

'It's all right you know. I like girls.'

Carolina nodded without turning.

'Does that mean you'd like a private dance anyway?'

'Yes please.'

She got up, putting the bottle and her glass on the floor. I sat back in my seat. Carolina began to swing her hips from left to right and somehow they seemed to move more fluidly, although I wasn't sure whether that was really true or whether I was making excuses for her. She danced an arm's length in front of me. Came closer, turned around. Her behind was flatter than I was used to, but she did have hips. She got near enough for me to smell the baby powder and see blotches of red on her skin. She wasn't tanned like the others. I reached out a hand to touch her. The skin was surprisingly soft.

'You can't . . .' she said, looking at the bouncer.

I knew that, just like I knew there was no champagne in the champagne room, but what did I have to loose if it was an illusion? I wasn't even attracted and yet there I was. My attention seemed to excite Carolina. She got so close she was practically sitting on my lap. The bouncer began to edge forwards, suspicious. I felt myself grow hot. Burying fear, I ran a hand along her bottom. I thought I heard her moan; wasn't sure. When I looked at the bouncer he hadn't moved. Carolina came closer still, the alcove wall blocking his vision.

'Tell me what you want,' she said, turning again, her expression serious.

She leant forwards so her breasts enclosed my face. I pushed my head between them, recalled the warmth. Carolina shivered, ran a finger along my cheek.

'He was violent.'

I looked at her.

'Ray used to hit me. I know I'm better off, but I love him.'

I turned my face to the carpet. Carolina stroked my neck.

'Thank you so much. I really mean that. Thank you.'

'Don't worry about it,' I grunted. My throat was dry and I took another sip of wine. Carolina had tears in her eyes.

'I didn't even know there were black people in England . . .' she said, hesitant.

I didn't want to laugh in case she thought I was making fun of her, but I couldn't stop myself. It spurted out of me. I was worried she might be offended right up until she began to laugh too. We cracked up as the bouncer yelled time.

White Goods

I've got this tattoo on me palm, a small black spider like the one on that super hero's costume. Had it done when I was eighteen cos I was too scared to get a big one like my mate Billy Sirus. He got his whole back done, crazy bastard, a multi-coloured portrait of Poseidon rising from the sea. Looks wicked, mate; Sirus says the girls love it and I'd be a fool not to believe him. As for me, I'm just content with the spider on me palm. I promised I'd get a bigger one eventually, but I reckon me and Sirus both know that's a lie.

Funny thing is, this spider turns out to be special. It only itches when I'm about to come into luck. Most people don't believe that, but it's not for them to. Sirus does, cos he's seen it on many occasions.

It was itching then too, the day me and him were both taking time off working the stall to watch Wimbledon. Now, we wouldn't usually do that when there was money to be made, but we were both dying to see Murray play and were even hoping to catch Serena Williams against one of them saucy Russian birds, the stone-faced ones with all that flowing blonde hair. Happy days, eh? Anyway, we're both sitting in my flat watching McEnroe go on about his glory days and that tattoo on me palm just wouldn't stop itching. I was only paying it half a mind, even though it had come through in a big way over the years; I'd met birds, found money, my horse had come in first, so I wasn't dismissive about being lucky that day either. It was more like I was concentrating on other things; namely watching tennis. I had a cold beer in me hand and a joint in me ashtray. Like I said, happy days.

Next thing I know there's a knock on the door. I couldn't be bothered to move, so Sirus says, You gonna get that? All sarky, like he does. He didn't look like he was movin, so I step around the boxes and piled up videotapes and open the door. There's a deliveryman standing there. Had the whole thing, the little grey jump suit, the peak hat, the clipboard and name badge, the lot. Delivery for Mr Dino, he says. Nah, mate, I tell him, I didn't order anything. He says, that's not what it tells me on this delivery form, and he shows me so I can see me name. There it is, bold as brass, Mr Terence Dino. Print and sign here, he says, pointing a skinny pen at the little black crosses. That's when I see the two other geezers standing behind him with a box taller than all of us. Am I supposed to be paying for that? I ask the deliveryman, who was actually more like a boy. Nope, it's all paid up, he tells me. Then I'll take it, I say, and sign.

They wheel this massive box in and I can see the sticky tape they've used has COMET all over. Who the hell bought me a fridge-freezer from Comet? I'm asking myself, cos it's the only thing that monster of a box could be. Sirus is sitting there trying to hide the joint, but it's no use cos the flat stinks of hash and the blokes wheeling the monster box in couldn't give a shit. They dump it in the kitchen, take a look at all the stuff I've crammed into the house and leave with a nod. I shut the door and crash onto me sofa.

That you an your fuckin itchy spider? Sirus says, sparking one up.

I s'ppose, I tell him. I'm still a bit shocked.

Thought I saw you scratching away, lucky git, he says, grinning now. Do you know what it is yet?

I think I've got an idea, Rolf, I reply. It's probably a fridge-freezer innit?

That's Sam then, don't you reckon? Daft cow's lost the plot and bought you a fridge-freezer.

Yeah, I say, the thought sinking in that he was probably right.

You're bound to get admirers in my line of work. Dealing with the public like we do, it's only natural. Me and Sirus have been selling antique goods on Portobello Market for fifteen years. Everyone knows us and everyone who don't wants to. It's a great gig, setting up bright and early every weekend, having a laugh and a cup ah tea with the other stall holders, nattering with the public and getting on with business. All the years we've been at it, running the stall never feels like real work, especially with me old pal Sirus by me side. We piss about for the most part, have a bit of a dance to the music coming from the CD stalls, chat up birds and make money. Happy days.

The only thing is, you can't get away. People know where to find you and often do, using you like some kind of agony aunt or shrink, telling you all their woes. The amount ah people that come to me in the early hours of the morning saying they got six months to live. Or they're having an affair with the wife's sister. Or they've tried to chuck the coke but can't do without it. Terrible it is, the things you hear, not that I'm complaining cos I believe I've seen the rich tapestry of human life in all its colours; but, Jesus, you see some things.

Samantha was one of those things. She come to the stall with her husband wanting to buy this huge statue of Ganesh I brought back from Thailand last year. Made from iron this thing was, fuckin heavy too, could sit on your mantelpiece if you had space for it. Anyway, hubby wasn't having any of it, he thought the thing was ugly and un-Christian but she wouldn't give in, so they spent half an hour going at it in front of everyone, arguing in that middle-class way, you know, whispering at each other with red-faces; *I'm* not *being unreasonable*, you *are* – stuff like that. Cos I've seen a lot of couples come and browse my stall, I can more or less tell whether a relationship's good or bad from how they shop. If they can discuss their differences and decide to buy or not through mutual agreement, they'll do well. If they can't, they won't. Young, budding relationships can be more giving. Older couples often find it difficult to communicate, as though the years have stretched their patience to breaking point. Gay couples of either gender are usually better than both, saying stuff like: *What do you think? No, what do* you *think? No,* you . . .

Sam and her husband fall into the second bracket. They've been married as long as I've been running the stall, have four kids and fell out of love ages ago. Sam's husband clearly wants to wear the pants and I think that grinds her down. They argued back and forth until he put his foot down and stormed off. Sam shrugged at me and Sirus then went away. Two customers later, we'd already forgot 'em.

Next day, I was standing on the stall scratching me palm when Sam comes back on her own. She marches right up to me, points at Ganesh and says, I'll take that please. She seemed so different I hardly recognised the woman; her shoulder-length blonde hair was loose around her shoulders, and I'm not the type of man that can usually tell, but I could've sworn she was wearing make up. It made her big blue eyes seem even bigger. Sirus was on lunch so I couldn't even ask whether I was right as soon as she scarpered; though I suppose that was for the best. I wrapped and bagged Ganesh and when she give me the money she kissed me on the cheek. Nothing major, just a quickie. We said our goodbyes and it was only when I was putting the money in me pouch I saw she'd slipped a piece of paper between the notes. *Call me* it said, next to her mobile number. Being a smart bloke, I followed orders – when a woman asks you don't think twice. The day after that, while hubby was at work, we did the wild thing all over my flat. Happy days.

All that happened a month ago. She'd been round mine once a week since then, and, much as I'd enjoyed myself, something didn't feel right. My spider hadn't itched until that afternoon watching Wimbledon. That kinda freaked me out. It made me think what I was doing might be wrong on some level. I'm not usually such a moral soul, but there you go.

You keepin it? Sirus asks, passing me the joint. On

the TV behind him, there's a grunt and the Umpire yells, *Duece*.

Let's take a look and I'll see, I reply.

So we get up and strip the box away to reveal a brand-new shark-grey Zanussi with an icemaker and a water dispenser and enough space to stick a side of beef inside if I ever wanted to. The thing was huge. I kinda resented the Comet men not installing the whole thing, but I like to DIY. We spent the next few hours removing my old fridge-freezer and replacing it with the new 'un, which we wheeled into the kitchen with a metal trolley I keep in me attic. We exchanged all me foodstuffs, connected her up, switched her on, then stood there with satisfied smiles when the Zanussi started to hum.

Very Notting Hill Gate, says Sirus. Pimm's ah clock, I think.

I agreed one hundred percent.

Sitting on the sofa with our glasses of Pimms and lemonade on the rocks, courtesy of my brand new icemaker, I realised we needed to get rid of me other fridge. It was an old model I'd found on the street and liberated for me own use; now it was time to set her free. I wanted to throw her back onto the pavement outside me house; give some other local the opportunity of experiencing her charms. Sirus was having none of it.

Take it to the dump, he tells me. You can get rid of the rest of this junk too.

I wasn't really happy with his use of the J-word but I had to admit he was right; my flat was more like our antique stall, mixed with a bit of car-boot sale, mixed with a bit of bric-a-brac. There were VHS videos, lamps, books, a chest of drawers and clothes, and a single-bed mattress leaned against the wall behind the sofa. Broken chandeliers and fake marble statues in a corner. Futon frames and miscellaneous boxes I hadn't peeked inside for months. Every nook and cranny of that room was inhabited by some item waiting to be sold, or chucked out; I liked it that way, no one else did. Even though I was enjoying the Pimms and the tennis on me telly, I knew a clear-out was well overdue. I drained me glass until ice was numbing me lips, slammed it on the coffee table.

Right then, I said.

That was how we found ourselves motoring towards Wandsworth and the biggest commercial, industrial and household tip in that part of London; the Western Riverside Waste Authority. When I got started in the game you'd often find big junkyard dealers wandering around the outskirts of the tip, looking for easy bargains. There were guys who spent years sifting through the rubbish and selling what they found to the people that sold to you. Many an antique or even some humble second-hand item has been liberated from that stinking mass of dirt and grime to find its way into the homes of Portobello Road or Camden Lock. These days, the council's cut that trade down to a minimum, but if you're a dealer with the time and van space, Western Riverside's the place for you. I hadn't been there for years, and I was feeling pretty excited. Even as a kid I'd loved to wander around the local tip, burrow into rubbish and find that special object some idiot had thrown away.

Sirus thought I should phone Sam and thank her, but I was having none of it. I appreciated the gesture, and I loved my new fridge-freezer, but I still thought she was going too far. Last thing I wanted was to get involved in breaking up her marriage. A feeling told me things were heading that way. I liked her a lot, the sex was great, but I didn't want to be with her. I wasn't sure exactly how she felt about the matter, although the appearance of me new fridge-freezer was a clear indication it might be time for us to talk.

We paid our toll and trundled through amongst the rubbish trucks and lorries. There was rubbish heaps twice the size of my van. It didn't really smell of anything other than old dustbins, but Sirus rolled up his window all the same. We drove around looking for the smaller heaps where people dumped household goods. The sound of hydraulics, air brakes and reverse-warning messages echoed.

Once we found the right place, getting rid of the stuff – including my old fridge – was easy. It didn't take longer than fifteen minutes. Sirus was looking at me with a gleam in his eye.

Wanna take a butcher's? He says.

That's what I like about old friends. They know what you're thinking before you do.

Sure. See you back 'ere in twenny?

Make it twenny-five, he says with a wink and walks off towards the big rubbish piles.

I picked around our heap for a bit, but there was nothing but broken TVs and metal chairs, clock radios and stained bed mattresses. I looked at my watch. Five minutes killed already. I took a wander around the back of our heap where the medium-sized piles were. I wasn't looking for anything in particular, of course; I was just enjoying the atmosphere and the feeling of space and the cloud-filled sky above. It's rare to see an uncluttered sky in London, unless you go to the park. There were small puddles of rain created by tyre-treads in the rust-coloured dirt that made up the path between the rubbish heaps. Swarms of buzzing insects floating above the water like miniature clouds. Barking dogs from somewhere far away and cats lazing on black plastic bags, or prowling the dump looking for mice. Although it wasn't hot, whenever a cloud moved I could feel warmth on my skin. It felt good to be out and about. Away from the Bella in relative quiet. It felt peaceful and reminded me of when I used to go rambling by myself in the little bit of woodland left in North Acton, the bit that was now a housing estate.

I saw something that made me smile at the bottom of one of the rubbish piles. A huge, industrial freezer like the ones in the Iceland frozen-foods store, about the size of my Zanussi, only horizontal. God, that brought back memories. Playing with me mates in the dump pretending to be vampires, using the freezers as coffins and weaving a game of tag around our imaginations. Lying inside and counting to a hundred, sitting up with our arms outstretched. *Comin to get you!* Daft, right? We'd seen the adverts about playing on dump sites, but we also saw the ads that said don't go on the train lines, or mess around with fireworks, or take drugs; never stopped us. I walked closer to the thing, ran my hands along the smooth surface. It must have been a recent dump; it looked almost brand new. The glass wasn't smashed and there was no rust. I moved the door back and forth, testing it out. It squeaked a little, was otherwise fine. I was grinning by then. I would've put it in the van but Sirus would've killed me. I had absolutely no need for another freezer, I just had the urge. The urge was why I'd stopped coming to the dump in the first place.

Before I could second guess meself, I was going around the other side of the freezer, climbing in. I'm not the tallest of blokes, so I could stretch my legs out pretty easily. There wasn't really the space to move my arms, and I soon discovered there wasn't much space at all, not like when I'd been a kid. There was that strong smell of plastic you get from the inside of fridges that I'd forgotten about, although it was soothing to look up and see the clouds roll past, a random bird swoop by, wings outstretched. I tried to take a deep breath, but the smell was stifling. I tried to turn so I could get out, an bumped the side of the fridge. The glass door trembled, fell closed.

Instant panic. That was the first thing that hit me as I pushed and struggled to get the door open. I had a flash of memory, when one of me mates had been stuck that way, in an ordinary household fridge-freezer. We'd left him for a bit, laughing and calling him names from outside, let him out when we thought he'd had enough. He was red-faced and gasping, tears staining his face. We'd been in hysterics, thought it was a great laugh, and were still curled up on the floor when he ran home. Poor sod never came out to play again. There'd been five of us that day. I only had Sirus, and he was probably miles away.

It was getting hot. The air was stifling. The glass began to grow cloudy. I tried to sip thin breaths between my lips but it was a difficult job. I banged on the glass, only to imagine me actually breaking it and huge shards piercing my belly, my groin. It made me thump lighter than I would've done, although the way my air situation was going I probably wouldn't care soon. Nothing made any difference; that bloody door stayed put.

I tried not to panic because that would just make things worse. To breathe slower and force my heart-rate down. It felt like ages before the thump in my chest decreased into something that didn't feel so terrible. My head began to swim. I assumed that was the lack of oxygen. I knew I had to stay awake, but there was a heavy feeling above my eyelids. They began to lower, much as I tried to force them upwards. The world outside me makeshift coffin went dark.

At first I didn't know where I was but then I recognised the Monet hanging directly opposite me. I was back in the flat, lying alone on me bed. It was strange, because apart from that print there was nothing else in the room I owned. Something was scratching me chest. I realised I was stark bollocking naked, apart from a coarse red and black blanket wrapped just beneath me nipples. I almost panicked again, but then I could hear movement from outside the room, smiled to meself. Soft music, jazz piano. My smile grew wider. I knew who that was. Sam innit?

I put me arms behind me head, content to wait. When I heard the footsteps I turned to see her; if there was one thing I loved about Sam, it was that body.

Sirus stood in the bedroom doorway, stark bollocking naked too, apart from the tiny black apron around his waist. He was holding a bottle of champagne on a tray and two glasses. Alarm sounded inside me but me arm still reached out, me fingers beckoning him closer. Sirus crossed the room. His skin was tanned, and his body was covered in dark black hair, much like mine. The lust was an entirely foreign emotion, but it belonged to me. It was good. He reached for me then, put down the tray, leant over, began to press his lips against me chest. I watched the faded blue waves of his Poseidon tattoo writhe as he moved along me body, and reached for the back of his head, stroked his hair.

He bit me. The pain was sharp and I felt the tug of me skin between his teeth. I gasped, mouth open wide. He was laughing. I opened my eyes, laughing with him. The smile was still there when I realised I was back in the dump, stuck in that fridge.

Sweat rolled behind my ears, from my armpits and down my back. My hands were prickly with heat. I was disoriented, and as soon as I realised I'd been dreaming I started to kick and yell as my lungs began to burn. I reached down with an unconscious hand, started to scratch. It took me a moment to notice.

Me head fall back, and I allowed meself a long wheeze, even though I knew I shouldn't. But I trusted it. The spider had never done me wrong. It was only another minute or so before a grey-haired bloke looked into the glass, shaking his head. Hands wrestled with the door clasp, and then it opened and sweet, fresh, cool air was flooding into me nose, me mouth and lungs. An arm thrust into the fridge. I ignored it, not out of malice, but because me limbs were weak beside me, paralysed by relief. For the next few seconds all I could do was scratch me palm and suck air like a baby taking its first taste of the outside world.

I thought I'd only been trapped in the fridge a matter of minutes or so, but when I went back to the van, Sirus was gone. I looked at me watch. Twenty-five minutes. Lucky wasn't the word. I should've been dead, though I tried not to dwell on that too much. The silence of the dump felt like a cemetery. There was goose bumps on me arms and me heart pumped like mad.

I thanked me saviour, an old bloke in a fluorescent jacket over orange overalls with the Western Riverside crest stitched into the breast pocket. He stared like I'd just escaped from St Mark's Psychiatric. I was a little embarrassed, though I didn't much blame him. He watched me all the way out the dump.

It was a long walk from there to the bus stop. I had change in me pocket for the fare, so that was all right. It was only when I felt in me jeans I realised I'd had me mobile on me the whole time. Scared meself for nothing. I ran hands through me sweaty hair, looked up and down the street as a dust black HGV rolled by. I stood with me phone in one hand, letting the thunder of the lorry wash over me.

Anatomy of Man

He'd long known that the upper end of Westbourne Park Road, council blocks on one side and million-pound flats on the other, was a pick-up point for prostitutes. What surprised him was the sight of Teri, stalactite high-heels, short dress and a tiny handbag dangling from her elbow like an afterthought. She was so intent on peering into car windows she didn't see Mike on the council-block side, speeding up his normally slow gait, willing her not to look. He stared until she was far behind, turned at the second corner and hurried into his flat. He was breathing as though he'd run all the way, and kept seeing Teri pacing the curb in his mind's eye.

The off-licence that used to be on the corner of his road had sold up a few years ago; where it once stood, there was an upmarket bathroom retailer. After sitting on his sofa for a good ten minutes, staring into space, still seeing Teri, Mike snatched his keys and slammed out of his flat, the building. He walked to the corner of Westbourne Park and All Saints, his nearest offie, bought four bottles of Budvar, one of E&J. When he tried to make conversation with the man behind the bulletproof plastic, the man looked at Mike as though he'd lost his mind. Mike took the plastic bag and walked home, head down so he wouldn't have to look up the block where Teri, for all intents and purposes, could still be.

TV couldn't distract him. *Eastenders*, *Pimp My Ride*, other cheaply made US programmes. He flicked the remote until he got the children's channels, popped his brew and called Cheryl. She took so long to pick up he began to think something might have happened. There was a click and silence.

'Hello,' he said, thinking 'wrong number'.

'*Ssssh* . . .' Cheryl had always been demanding, even when they were kids, even though she was younger by four years. 'Bethany's sleeping. I just put her down.'

'Very humane. I wondered when you'd release her from the misery.'

'Hardy, ha ha. You've inherited Mum's wit.'

'That and her perfect legs.'

'Do tell. Can't say I noticed.'

'That's probably a good thing, right?'

'Probably. What's up?'

'Oh nothing,' he said, and knew he wasn't fooling her. Cheryl was silent, breathing into his ear, and he could picture her, tucked inside the little nook beneath her stairs, brow lowered, lip jutting.

'I suppose I'm not feeling the best . . .'

'Go on . . .'

'It's just work. You know how it is . . .'

'It's the business, Mike. It's what you chose. You can't help the people; you just have to remember they're not your friends.'

'Then who is?' he said quickly, regretting it when he heard the silence. She was thinking. He could tell because he couldn't hear her breath.

'Why don't you take a break? Go home. Mum would be over the moon.'

'Yeah . . .' he thought about small brick houses, pubs that smelt of old beer, money ploughed into the city in the run-up to the Olympics. He thought of going out on a Saturday night in a shirt and no jacket, and shivered. 'Guess who I saw about half an hour ago?'

'Who?'

'Teri Judet.'

'Oh.' Mike waited to see if Cheryl was going to say something else. She didn't.

'Isn't that weird?'

'She is.' Long pause. 'Did you talk?'

'No, I wasn't even sure it was her. I was on the other side of the road.'

'Yeah, best to keep it that way, I reckon.' Cheryl tried for a laugh, kept her voice bright, but Mike heard the strong undercurrent. 'She was always trouble, right?'

'Certainly was,' he said. 'How's Bethany then, and Jack?'

They talked about the subjects most dear to his sister's heart: her four-year-old daughter and husband of six years. His sister had done well to marry a chartered surveyor and move to Cornwall almost ten years ago. Jack was a well-mannered guy, slim and tall like a scarecrow. He obviously doted on Cheryl. Whenever Mike came to stay, which had been regularly, he and Jack would sit up drinking JD and Coke, watching football with their feet up. Bethany was a self-proclaimed princess in the nicest possible way, a textbook child who was polite and clever, studious and athletic, and generally did no wrong. On his visits Mike would take her to the park, spend the day amongst climbing-frames and sandpits, friendly dogs and proud parents, meet Cheryl for a coffee later.

When Bethany was about eighteen months they'd gone for creamed teas at a café named The Full Frog. They sat on a marshmallow-soft couch by the front window surrounded by stuffed amphibians of all hues and sizes. Tomy Water Toy games where leaping frogs deposited coloured balls into numbered sections, pictures of the number-one frog of the walk, Kermit *the* Frog, everywhere. When Mike went to the toilet he was greeted by a porcelain toad (he noted it was too big to be an actual frog), which must have been fitted with a sensor, as it went *ribbit* when he passed. He tested it out, going back and forth in front of the toad until he got bored. There were little green seats and frog board games and by the time he came back to the soft couch Mike was thinking it was all a bit too much.

They ate scones the size of breakfast baps, thick with Cornish cream and homemade jam, and left just as the café was closing. Cheryl led them towards the pay-and-display car park, Mike pushing Bethany's Bugaboo and feeling right with the world. There was a taste of sea on his tongue, his belly full of scones and hot tea. The sun was weak though the sky was blue, and a Muslim family across the street piled into a car, waved hello. They were strolling along a road with no pavement when a silver Clio roared past, veered directly in front of them and slammed on the brakes. Cheryl clutched his arm. Her eyes were like sea-washed pebbles, her attention on the Clio. White reverse lights shone. For one horrible moment Mike actually thought the car was going to back into them, into the Bugaboo.

A man on a daffodil motor-cross bike came to a stop behind them. Mike craned his neck.

The biker wrenched off his helmet. 'What the fuck d'you think you're doing?' he yelled. A few of his teeth were missing, and his skin was like waxed cheese. When neither Mike nor Cheryl said anything, he pointed at the Clio. 'The man's trying to park!'

They turned to the car. A huge bald-headed man who looked twelve-months pregnant squeezed himself out of the driver's side and came towards Mike. His eyes were stone blue, his beard a meagre Gandalf imitation.

'What the fuck are you doing?' he said, standing over Mike. 'I'm trying to park.'

'Yeah? Well, I'm trying to walk.'

'You could've stopped and let us by. Then you could've parked,' Cheryl told him.

'Yeah, well you could've fuckin well gone round.'

Mike felt his breath catch, fingers tighten on the buggy handles. He wanted to look around to verify what he already knew, that there was no one else but them.

'I'm pushing this buggy, and you park right in front of me. Why should I go around? That's just plain ignorant – and rude.'

'You callin me rude?'

'Yes I am.'

'That's not rude, all right?'

There was less than a foot between them. Tension filled the empty space, bouncing like atoms.

'Well, I'm telling you it is. You're bang out of order . . .' Mike said, steering the buggy around the Clio, on towards the car park. Behind him he could hear the biker swearing, occasionally laughing in a self-conscious way that let Mike know he wanted to be heard. He couldn't tell what the bald-headed guy said in return, if anything. He became aware of Cheryl's fingers on his arm.

'What was that all about?' she whispered. He shot a glance at her, almost angry, caught himself. She thought she'd married out of the deal, had for the most part. Those rednecks yokels weren't to know Mike and Cheryl weren't a couple, couldn't see they were related, probably wouldn't care if they had.

'You know damn well what that was about,' Mike said.

They removed Bethany from the buggy and strapped her into the *Star Trek*-style car seat then didn't say anything until they arrived at the house. Jack stood by the front door, waving.

The phone slipped. He jerked into the moment, the darkness of his flat.

'What was that, Chez? I was practically nodding off.'

'I said, "You could always come down." If you want. You know you're always welcome.'

'Yeah . . . I will . . . Soon . . .'

'Don't stop living . . .' Cheryl said. 'Never let it stop you.'

'You're right,' Mike told her, feeling ashamed. 'An I will, I promise. I miss you all. Well, Jack and Bethany, I miss them.'

'Screw you, pal.'

'I'm not even going there, Sis.'

'All right, that's enough. Call me soon?'

'Will do. Love you.'

'Love you too.'

Mike rang off, looked around his living room. It had grown too dark to see. He liked it that way.

He played with his phone, sent a few texts, got some replies. Elected to go to meet Chris at the Market Bar, their favourite Portobello haunt. It was only when he'd made the ten-minute walk that he remembered it wasn't the Market Bar anymore, it was O'Leary's. The outside was painted green, Irish flags and Guinness banners strung. When he entered, everything was exactly the same. The flat-screen TV, the Thai-food menus, the weeping wax candles, staff, punters. It reminded Mike of himself, outer garments changed in pretence of being a Londoner, a Manchester boy on the inside.

Chris had found a table not far from the toilets and was sitting with two pints, wriggling foot perched on one knee as he read the *Metro*. Mike sat down.

'Awright, fella.'

'Nice one, geezer. Got you a Budvar.'

'Nice.' Mike nodded towards the flat-screen, the flailing figures. 'Who's winning?'

'The one with the most goals.'

'Like that is it?' Mike said, raising his glass.

'It is when you're broke and they get three grand a week. It is then.'

'Aye,' Mike said, and drank half his pint. 'Any news?'

Chris huffed, shaking the paper like a victim. 'People asking where they were when Michael Jackson died, how ridiculous is that? A year today they reckon. Like we should give a damn.'

Mike felt his face grow hot. 'Yeah, Elvis ODed on the pot weighing God knows how many pounds and no one commemorates him. Why should we remember Jacko?'

He downed the rest of his pint, slammed the glass on the table. Chris looked at the floor.

'Want another?'

'Yeah ta, same again.'

Chris went to the bar. Mike knew he didn't mean it, actually didn't resent his opinion. He was just tired. Tired of being on the defensive, of letting things go. Tired of compromising, of criticising everything he laid eyes on. Nothing seemed to fit; not this city, his job, or even the people he came into daily contact with. He felt pent up, clogged with frustration, unable to escape as there was no place where things were any different.

Chris came back with their pints. They saluted each other, drank.

'Did you call that number I gave you?'

'Yep.' Chris put down his glass, changed his mind, went back for more.

'What d'he say?'

'No new work; the jobs he has are already full.'

'Shit. What about that exhibition Dawn promised?'

'No dice. Slept with her cousin.'

'Chris mate . . .' Swapping grins. 'Isn't that meant to be a good thing?'

'Not if you don't call back, get caught snogging

some other bird in the Goldbourne.' Mike sagged, held his head. 'What can I say? I've low self-esteem – she raised it.'

'You need to raise your tax bracket.'

'So I can hold a light meter for some idiot with less talent than me and you combined, make teas and grin? Watch him flirt with clients an sniff coke in the toilets? Go to shit parties with shit people an shit attitudes?'

'See? Passion's all you need.'

'All I need is income support and a shag every once in a while . . .' Chris was looking around the bar, eyes narrowed. 'Less stress.'

'It's a thought,' Mike said, turning in his seat. A blonde and a black woman, Portobello Gold. Like the early days of prospecting when dreamers would arrive at streams and underground seams and the metal would lay there, glittering in thankless sun. 'Can I ask you something? Suppose you were walking along Westbourne Park Road and you saw an ex-girlfriend you hadn't met in years, maybe twenty or so? She's walking up and down, looking in car windows, clear heels, all that. Would you talk to her, ask what she's doing? Would you care?'

Chris thought about it, Mike gave him that, rolling the pint between his palms and staring at the table. Lager sploshed against glass. He sat back, looked at the ceiling. 'Fit?'

Mike slumped again. Should have known. 'She was. Back in the day. I didn't look close.'

'Yeah, well I'd ask for a discount,' Chris smiled, eyes over his shoulder. 'For old times sake.'

* * *

Nothing for a few days, then another job. A magazine shoot in the Great Eastern hotel, celebs everywhere, public relations officers eating dry sushi and spitting rice darts while they ordered techs around. Art Directors getting into a strop over every little detail; Mike's worst nightmare. He was in a darkened room that contained the biggest bed he had ever seen, pale blue wardrobes matching bedside lamps, and way too many people arranging, chatting idly, stealing bathroom toiletries when no one was looking. Mike tried to get on with the job. The room was filled with battered suitcases that looked like they'd been stolen from a props department (and probably were). Each case overflowed with wind-up toy puppies. Some of the cases had been left open so puppies spilt onto the floor. There were puppies on the bed, puppies on the bedside cabinet, puppies on the floor. Some female techs cooed and stroked the coarse fur, kissed the toys on the nose. Mike saw more than a few men put puppies in their pockets for their own girlfriends.

Their celeb, a C-list author whose publicist managed to squeeze him into the shoot at the last minute, entered and hadn't been impressed. The Art Director, Gary Janssen, an idiot savant Mike had worked with in the past, explained his idea. A travelling salesmen who can't sell his product ends up in a snazzy hotel room. He's miles from home, frustrated beyond repair, surrounded by the evidence of his ineptitude. The only flaw in Janssen's vision was the product placement, not suitcases or puppies, but the designer shirt and black-and-white chinchilla fur the author was asked to wear. He clearly didn't have time to explain how a poor salesperson could afford such things, as he had another shoot going on in another room, and yet another later that evening on the far side of the city. The author, who frowned through Janssen's speech, scratched his neck and looked at all the puppies, sucked in a breath and told the room that while he couldn't suspend that much disbelief, he'd be willing to give it a go.

The room breathed out. The author sat at the end of the bed, on the floor. Puppies were scattered on his lap, forced into his hands. The lights went on and Mike read the meter. He winked at the author when he got close, knew he shouldn't have but couldn't help feeling he should communicate his own thoughts, even if no one else would. The author gave a wan smile, rested the back of his head on the edge of the bed. He was sweating, mainly because he was wearing a fur coat in a closed room filled with a forest of two-hundred-watt lights. Mike told Janssen, who told one of the girls, who dabbed away the sweat with all the precision of a surgeon.

They got ready to shoot. Took a roll. One of the girls elbowed the Art Director, pointed discreetly. Mike got closer to his colleagues, heard whispers. The author had a hard on. The roll was useless.

'Uh, we're gonna have to scrap that roll,' Mike told the author. He was sitting with his legs crossed, seemingly guessing what happened. Sweat rolled down his temples and collected in his neck, dampened the designer shirt collar. None of the girls wanted to tell him, and as the only male bar the Art Director, who wasn't going to say anything deemed negative, it had been left up to him.

Mike dabbed sweat with rough fingers. The author flinched. If Mike saw anything twitch or grow he was likely to scream.

'Why, I thought it was good. What's the problem?' The author trilled. He had a nasal voice and earnest, squinting eyes that always looked serious.

'The light reading was wrong. We're really sorry.'

'Didn't you take that reading?'

'Yes.'

The author scowled him all the way back to Janssen. The Art Director put a hand on Mike's shoulder.

'Natives getting restless?' He felt his insides jump, but didn't want to look at Janssen, feared what he'd see. 'Never mind, thanks for taking one for the team Jim. Appreciate it.'

'I'm Mike,' he said, and walked to the other side of the room where there were piles of jackets, M&S sushi boxes and more suitcases. The assistant was cute, pale and sparrow-tiny, a thin white T-Shirt daubed with a teen vampire hanging from bony shoulders.

'I'll give him twenty more minutes, max,' she said, speaking low. He could smell her deodorant and a vague scent of perfume, Chanel No. 5. Teri used to wear that, didn't mind that her mother and grand-mother before her did too. He moved closer.

'I'd say ten,' Mike said, breathing her in. The assis-tant looked over her shoulder, gave him a smile as though she knew. She went and stood by the author and rearranged puppies.

Forty-five minutes passed. The room sweltered.

They tried take after take but it didn't look right. That lasted fifteen minutes. Then the electricity died and the room went dark as Mike's flat. Twenty minutes were eaten up waiting for the hotel electrician to replace a fuse, and the next ten trying to help the author find his 'motivation', which had seemingly escaped under the cover of darkness. He scowled his way through shot after shot until Janssen called Mike over and asked him to take a look. What he saw looked like a mug shot. Mike told Janssen, who cupped his hand over his mouth, swore into his palm.

'You're meant to look deflated, not murderous,' he called in no particular direction.

'I'll murder you, gimp bastard,' the author said, glaring at Janssen, who ducked his head, retreating into the bathroom.

'What now?' Mike said.

'Call the publicist,' Janssen said. 'See if she can housetrain him. I dunno . . . Give some chav a fur and they don't know how to wear it. Give him a drug dealer's jacket, some hoodie with the brand name stamped all over and he's happy as a pig in the parlour.'

Mike stood rigid for a moment, left. Came back with the publicist, another sweet, skinny, pale girl, this one strawberry blonde with freckles.

'What's the problem?' she asked.

'He's not co-oporating,' Janssen said. 'He's messing up this shoot, and another.'

'Have you tried *asking*?'

Janssen gave her a look. The publicist left. She was gone another twenty minutes. There was shouting and the laboured yap of a toy dog, which ended in a bang as something hit the bathroom door, then a whine and the crunch of metal. Everyone looked at each other, said nothing. Janssen did a line, offered no one. The publicist came back.

'He won't do it.'

'Why not? Janssen seethed. 'What did he say?'

'He says your concept is somewhat degrading, as it suggests some level of subservience and doesn't take into account his award-winning status, and the fact that he turned down an OBE. He said, "I didn't turn down an OBE for this shit." He says your concept alludes negatively to the fact that he's a working-class writer from the streets, being that the fictional character you've created is attempting unsuccessfully to *ply his trade* and that this comparison is insulting in the extreme.'

'What does that mean?!' Janssen screamed. The pale assistant was trying, unsuccessfully Mike thought, not to laugh.

'It means he won't be completing your photo shoot,' the publicist told him. 'He also told me to tell you he heard your comment about restless natives and bitterly resents being labelled as such. He says you're racist.'

'I am *not* racist,' Janssen yelled. 'My great-grandmother on her father's mother's side was half-Polynesian. I sit next to black people on the tube!'

'Be that as it may,' the publicist said.

'Bloody ignorant . . . Yo!' Janssen spat.

'You rest his case,' the publicist said.

'They say that in *The Wire*! And in Spike Lee's *Clockers*, they say Yo all the time!'

The publicist turned her back on Janssen, faced Mike.

'Talk to him! Change his mind!'

'I think he's already gone,' the publicist told Mike.

'I'll talk to him,' the assistant said, already moving.

'You stay put!' Janssen cried. 'Jim, you're from the street. You talk sense into him.'

'Sure,' Mike said, and went into the room. It was empty apart from open suitcases and toy dogs, blazing lights. He collected his jacket and rucksack, left trying not to trip on the broken pup, metal innards exposed like road kill. He might have been able to charm the publicist's number from her if he'd been feeling better, didn't have the energy to test his theory. At the lifts he thought Janssen might come after him, maybe even the assistant, but the hotel corridor looked like a modern remake of *The Shining*. A bell chimed, doors opened, Mike stepped inside. The author stood in a corner, sheepish, gave him a dour glare.

'You have to press the floor you want,' Mike told him, touching G.

'I know that.' Mike ignored him, looking at numbers. 'I do actually.'

The lift hummed.

'They didn't think you'd actually walk.'

'Yeah, well if they think I'm taking that crap they can think again.' The author was fight-faced, neck stiff, eyes darting. 'They don't know who they're dealing with. I won a Betty Trask!'

'It was a good book.'

That took a second to sink in.

'You read it?'

'Part of it. Then my cat peed on the rest and, you know, it was pretty tough to unstick the pages so I never found out what happened, but I liked what I'd read.'

The author gaped. The lift rocked and steadied.

'That was a joke.' Mike saw he wasn't buying it, tried again. '"Marvin ran into the night, away from his hopes and resolutions towards the darkness, which embraced him like family." *Night Dreamers*, right? Last line.'

'OK, OK. I believe you.' The author eyed him, hands in pockets.

'They're pretty much used to everyone doing what they're told,' Mike said. 'You know, chain of command and all that.'

'Do you know what they said when I walked into that room, before you got there?' The author waiting for Mike to shake his head. 'That Janssen, came right up to me, shook my hand like a sailor, said, "Jim, pleasure to be working with you again.' I said, "The name's Range actually," and without missing a beat he says, "Range, pleasure to meet you, amazing book! Meet Emma, she'll take care of you from here on in." Then off he goes, out comes the dolly assistant. I was dying to see who the other black guy was . . .'

They laughed until the lift doors opened and continued across the lobby. At the glass doors, they wiped their eyes.

'My name's not even Jim . . .' Mike said in a high voice.

That set them off again, loud enough for bellboys to stare, some with frowns, most smiling in a manner that suggested they weren't sure if they were allowed.

'What the hell is it then?' the author managed when he'd regained control.

'Mike Lynott,' he said, offering his hand.

'Range Cassidy,' Cassidy replied, turning his hand into a fist and bumping it with Mike's. There was a card between the author's thumb and first finger, which he waved at him. 'I'd better wait for Amy but you give me a call, let's go for coffee. Got to stick together, right?'

'Sure do,' Mike said, and put the card in his back pocket. He walked out of the hotel, stopped a few steps from the doors, looked at the sky. It was raining again, the wet pavement dark as the clouds.

Chris, when he was told, thought the whole thing was hilarious. He sat in Mike's living room and helped him finish off the bottle of E&J he'd bought a few nights back. Mike stood by the window, short glass in hand.

'So he really called Janssen a gimp?'

'Yep. Walked right after that, left the gimp pulling his hair out trying to explain why.'

Chris roared harder. Mike had a feeling he was still bitter, as he'd worked for Janssen years ago, back when he'd been a young photographer on the up, full of promise. They'd got into an argument over the layout of some model shoot. Chris had been drinking that day, so when Janssen refused to back down he gave him an open-palmed slap to the ear. It perforated the Art Director's eardrum and left him slightly deaf. Chris had been unemployed with a penchant for wine and drunken bar babes ever since.

'And Janssen didn't call for an explanation?'

'Yeah, a couple of times, but when I never answered

it was all the explanation he needed . . . I mean, what else could he think? He kept calling me Jim.'

Chris shook his head slowly, chuckled. 'You've done it this time. You're rank-and-file unemployed and unemployable, a branded troublemaker. Janssen'll tell the world and its orphans you sided with a no-hope has-been author who has the misfortune to be named after a road vehicle.'

'He is? How d'you know that?'

'You know me. *Trivial Pursuit* UK champion 1988–91. If it's an obscure fact no one gives a damn about, I'll find it.'

Mike turned Cassidy's business card between his fingers. It was brown, the author's name embossed in white. In smaller type below his name the card said: *Novelist, Poet, Playwright, Screenwriter, Literary Philanthropist.*

'What's a Literary Philanthropist actually do?' Mike asked.

'Dunno. Philanthrop Literaries?'

He gave a mock smile, turned to the window.

'So much for the champ.'

'What you gonna do with that anyway? Call him? Offer to chronicle his life from now until death through photographic imagery?'

'I was thinking maybe author photos . . .' Seeing his disbelief. 'Or something. I don't know. It's a long shot.'

'Yeah, well, I can't believe you actually remembered that last line. That was pretty quick thinking . . .'

Chris held up the yellowed, urine-stained novel. He tried to run his thumb along the closed pages but they hardly moved. The book looked like a paper brick.

'Good thing I managed to tear it out and have a look before I left the house, that's all. I swore he could tell I was lying.'

'A very good call,' Chris looked up. 'Hey, what happened to the cat?'

'Oh. Ran away. Came home one night and it was gone. Bastard didn't even eat the discount food I'd bought, three kilos of the stuff. It was on offer.'

Chris was grinning.

'That's why I like cats. Law of the jungle, no bullshit, if it don't work they're out of there. *Vamoosh*. Gone.'

'Like Teri,' Mike said, returning to his window vigil. He couldn't tell if she was there or not.

He woke in his bathtub the next morning, one leg hanging over the side, mouth feeling like moth wings and his head like he'd swallowed a police siren. There was an empty wine bottle in his lap. Mike recalled the vinegar taste of cheap stuff, opened months ago and left in his fridge until the night before. He tried to climb from the tub, remembered. It was his birthday. Might as well stay put.

When he closed his eyes he could see everything. First meeting in the student bar, drunk with friends, being introduced to Teri, seeing that crooked smile and thinking how odd it looked, how appealing. Finding themselves alone in the town centre long enough to flirt, swap numbers, walk her part-way home, a fleeting kiss, her running for the night bus, him watching her bum writhe. First date, a trip to Chinatown and the cinema to see *Batman and Robin*, missing the film because they were kissing furiously, hands foraging in each other's laps, Teri's skirt around her hips, her hand in his trousers up to the wrists, Mike thinking he'd struck gold. Teri calling the house, his sister answering, passing the receiver while glaring at him, coming into his room afterwards, telling him rumours he'd already heard. First argument, her flat, Teri throwing plates, lamps, anything that came to hand and when nothing was left launching herself at him, scratching his face with psychedelic nails, Mike prising her off, throwing her to the floor, Teri bouncing to her feet, leaping on his back. Having to slam her into the wall until she gasped and sagged, running for the door. Making up, arguing again. Making up, arguing again. Mike clubbing with mates, seeing Teri with one leg wrapped around a guy's waist, the guy holding a tanned thigh, staring into her face until Mike's fist crashed into his temple. His mates trying to hold him back, the guy trying to fight Mike and Teri off, confused, not quite sure what had happened. Teri and Mike thrown out by bouncers, laughing about it, going back to her flat where they tore the place apart with violent lovemaking. Mike moving in. Teri moving out. Mike going to the guy's place after a few weeks, hearing they'd fought, she'd left. Seeing her in the town centre with another guy, tattoos and muscles, giving up. Calling her mobile until she agreed to meet, telling her about his University place. Teri crying. Mike staunch. Going back to the flat to move his things to his mum's, Teri turning up. Violent lovemaking. Goodbyes. London.

Mike let his head fall against the bath, heard a satisfying thump. The years had passed and nothing changed and now there he was, thirty-seven that morning, looking out of the window at the same square of grey that was there the day he'd arrived. He thumped his head again. And again. Closed his eyes, remembered their lovemaking. Sometimes it had hurt just like that, pain all over but especially his head. Teri had done that. She'd done that and he'd escaped and yet there he was, three years shy of forty, sitting in his bathtub with the same old ache, the one he remembered, and he hadn't been near her in nearly twenty years.

He thumped his head one last time, climbed out of the tub. Pushed the plug in, turned the taps, got undressed.

He walked to the upper end of Westbourne Park Road that night. There were girls, none pretty, none Teri. He stood on the opposite side of the road and watched so long one of the girls stared back, disappeared and returned with a tall skinny guy in a fitted cap and leather aviator jacket. Mike pushed himself from the cold railings of the estate, walked to the off-licence on All Saints and bought a quarter bottle of E&J.

He went back every night for two weeks, didn't see her. His eyes grew tired and red. On the first night of the third week he was scratching dirt from beneath his nails when a Mercedes-Benz pulled up. Teri got out. The driver waved, drove away. Teri waited for the car to turn a corner and looked up, right at him. Mike had been so surprised at her sudden appearance he hadn't even bothered to hide. He watched her unseeing expression, the second glance, eyes widening, a slim hand cover her mouth, dropping as she mouthed his name. The other girls faded into the overhanging bushes of front gardens. Mike kicked off from the railings, crossed the road.

'Teri.' It was an immense pleasure saying her name, a release. Even better, she still had that lop-sided smile.

'*Mike Lynott* . . . Well . . . Long time.' They looked each other over, both grinning. 'So, this is where you moved to?'

'And you it seems . . .'

'Oh, this is temporary. Can't afford it. Might go to Brighton maybe.'

'Oh.' Rejoicing his good luck in finding her. 'You look good. Older, but good.'

'You look the same.'

'Do I?'

'Oh yes. You haven't aged a bit. Just hairier.' She giggled, reached to touch his beard, caught herself.

He looked at paving slabs. 'You aren't busy are you? Fancy a quick drink?'

'Well . . .' Wrist raised, looking at her slim watch.

'One or two. Go on. It's been nearly twenty years.'

A sigh, a full smile. 'Well . . . All right then. Just a couple, OK?'

'Sure. Any preferences?'

They walked to the Cow, a little farther up the road and packed as usual, though they squeezed through bodies and managed to find spare seats. It was half an hour until last orders so Mike bought four double brandies and Cokes, piled two in each hand and weaved his way back to Teri. Her hair was tied back. She looked elusive, more self-contained than he remembered, and he wondered if he'd made a mistake. The Teri Judet he'd dated and the one that sat before him seemed so dissimilar he almost believed he'd made her up.

'You drink brandy, right? Double no ice?'

'Wow. You remember. Thanks, Mike.'

'No problem. So, what are you doing with yourself in London?'

She peered at her drink. Mike saw embarrassment, shuddered. She was actually going to tell him.

'Don't laugh.'

Laugh? He could hardly breathe.

'Course I won't.'

'It might be a bit of a shock.'

'I can handle it.'

'I'm a poet.'

That seemed like a joke until she met his eye. There was fear reflected in them, the most he'd ever seen her own.

'Well, at least you know it.'

'Still a sarky bugger aren't you?'

'I am that,' he said. 'What made you go in that direction?'

'Mike. You make it sound like a road map.'

'Sorry. Didn't mean to.'

She was smiling over her brandy glass. Mike, too, couldn't help it.

'It's not even like I "went in that direction". It just happened. Kinda like puberty. I got older, looked around and realised that's what I'd become. All the scraps of paper I used to write on, all those books I read . . . '

'But you always said you'd never write back in college, you said all the writers you knew were broke.'

'Yeah, that was true,' she laughed, took a sip. 'More true than I knew.'

'You said I was the dreamer, not you.'

Teri faced him. Her eyes were light brown, her pupils tiny dots.

'I was wrong about a lot of things back then Mike. A hell of a lot.'

Teri lowered her eyes. He placed a hand on hers, surprised when she never moved it.

'Does your boyfriend mind you being out with other guys?'

'My *what*?'

Face pinched, half laughing.

'Boyfriend. The guy in the Benz, the one who dropped you off?'

Teri barked another chuckle, a sound more like a cough, squeezed his fingers.

'That was my agent, silly. We had dinner to discuss the book. I'm single, Mike, I think that's best for me, don't you?'

A bell rang behind the bar, an Eastern European girl calling time. The noise grew louder. Mike's hands felt damp.

'Wanna go someplace else?'

'Mike . . .' Now the hand was removed, the feel of the table beneath his palm cold in comparison. 'It's pretty late.'

'So. Neither of us have to get up for work do we?' He grinned, knowing she'd always liked his smile. 'Just one more place, for old times sake. I promise I won't bother you again after that. Unless you want me to.'

She was squirming. 'I don't get *up* for work, but I am working . . .'

'Go on. One more.'

Teri arched her chin towards the ceiling. Mike watched, strangely devoid of nerves. Her neck was slender, loose hair falling around her collar. He could have easily watched her all night.

'OK . . . OK . . .'

They downed their drinks and left, Mike leading the way. As they crossed blocks and cut through quiet back roads, Teri linked an arm through his and told him about her work. She was compiling a collection of poems themed around the oldest profession in the world, she said, what she saw just blocks away from where she was staying. She'd been working on the book for the last three months, was house sitting for a friend while they visited parents abroad, which gave her ample opportunity to see how things worked in London. So far she'd been observing the trade in Westbourne Park Road, Kings Cross, Streatham Common, Brixton, and of course, Soho. She'd talked to the girls and some of their pimps, had gained their trust and sometimes even been granted the opportunity to stand on the corner with the Westbourne Park girls, only because the friend who owned the flat was close with one of the pimps, Teri stressed, and even then she couldn't be out too often.

Mike nodded, grunted replies, kept his eyes on the road, believed none of it. He'd seen her looking in car windows, getting out of the Benz. She had to have known seeing him wasn't a coincidence; other girls, the pimp, had noticed him. He listened to Teri speak about poems she'd written, things she'd seen and felt amused by her attempt at subterfuge, to mask what he knew her to be. She had changed, grown up somewhat, but her ability to tell convincing lies was undiminished. Mike squared his shoulders. He'd grown up too, knew better than to believe her after all that had gone between them, all those years. He pretended to listen, steered her towards a block of shops.

They entered the after-hours bar, a former fifties blues spot where drink was sold and weed openly consumed, reggae blasting from wardrobe-sized speakers. Scattered men lounged on chairs around the small dance-floor while a gathering of Rastafarians, middle-class out-of-towners, old West Indians and young couples moved to the music. Mike was pretty broke, glad when Terri paid for sweating Red Stripes and brought them back, lop-sided grin almost falling from her face. It was like being propelled back in time; they were students again, locked inside the basement of some Caribbean restaurant in Moss Side, the perfume of Overproof Rum, Lambs Bread and Chanel No. 5 competing for his attentions. They popped ring pulls, moved from foot to foot, tentative. He was a terrible dancer, not like Teri, but she'd never seemed to care, passion had always driven their movements, she made him do things he wasn't even aware he could. She placed her arms around his neck. He could feel the cold perspiration of the Red Stripe cooling the heat from so many warm bodies together in so little a room. They slid against each other, backed away, came together and it was that same combination of soft and firm that beguiled him all those years ago, and he wanted to cry out in memory but he bit his lip, lowered his head to her neck, pressed his mouth against the beat of a pulse so quick it felt as though it would burst, and Teri sighed then, only he didn't hear it, just felt the rush of breath against his own neck, so he slipped his knee between hers and they moved against each other as though they wanted to grind themselves into dust, as though they wanted to absorb the essence of each other via osmosis until nobody would know whether Mike was Teri, or Teri was Mike.

They stayed that way for many hours, from song to song until they ran out of money. They held hands and climbed the stairs that led to the street, breathed thin clouds that emerged into the cold air like speech bubbles. Arm-in-arm, they walked towards Mike's flat, which was only a block away.

Inside, he found alcohol – an old bottle of Jack. He poured for them both, handed Teri the glass. She was standing by his window.

'You can see the corner from here,' she said, when he gave her the glass.

'Can you?'

Teri gave him a look. If she wore glasses, she would have been peering over the rims.

'What were you doing out there tonight?'

He frowned, emerged from his drunken fog. Got what she was saying.

'Coming home,' Mike said, looking right at her. 'Then I saw you.'

'Really?' she said, her tone light. Mike realised she

was more beautiful than ever. The white street lamp lit one side of her face, highlighting cheekbones, her lips. He didn't want to lose her, not again.

'Yeah . . . I mean . . . I'd met a friend for a drink in town . . . I walk home that way all the time . . .'

'Isn't there a bus stop on this block?'

'Yeah, but . . .' Floundering, thinking hard, knowing how it looked. 'I stopped to pick up a pizza from Domino's, but the queue was too long . . .'

Teri sat on his sofa.

'Really?'

'Why d'you keep saying that?'

She patted a sofa cushion. He crossed the room, lowered himself next to her. It was amazing how she made him feel like a guest in his own home.

'I'm not the person I was, Mike.'

'How d'you mean?' Trying to erase panic from his voice.

'When I was a kid, when we were together, I was pretty messed up. But I'm not that person anymore. I just want you to know that.'

'I do – I mean, I can see that, it's obvious,' he said in a rush, thinking he should have anticipated the curve ball, had time to think of something better to say, though she nodded and gave him her down-turned grin again.

'That's good,' she said. 'That's good.'

She put the glass on the coffee table, took his and placed it beside hers. She leaned forward and kissed him. It was the softest kiss he'd ever felt, a light pressing of lips against his, mouths closed, a few seconds and it was over. She leaned back.

'You've always been kind to me, Mike. I trust you,' she told him.

Mike ran a hand along her leg. Edged closer, bent towards her.

He dreamt them both on the corner, him wearing the fitted cap and aviator jacket, her in the striped chinchilla fur, black-and-white stilettos. He was leaning against a wall while Teri approached passing cars, bending to talk into the passenger window, exposing knickerless flesh. She was just about to jump in when the Benz pulled up. A huge man dressed in a salmon-silver suit leapt from the car and rushed Mike, bellowing for his money. Mike was running and didn't know why, trying to move faster and not knowing how, the Silver Pimp grunting and huffing like a bull, so close Mike could feel hot breath tickle his ear.

He woke with a start, not knowing where he was, one hand clasping his bed sheet to his chest, panting and covered in cold sweat. He sighed, fell back against his pillow, breathed out long and slow. The heat from his window was pleasant. The night before rushed back, memories overpowering the dream. He rolled over, reaching. She wasn't there. He threw the bed sheet from him like an enemy, got up, paced the flat. Teri was gone. He rubbed his head, thinking. Guessed she'd left a number, went back to the bedroom to find it.

The first place he looked was his bedside cabinet, the most obvious place, but there was nothing. He was so consumed by what he wanted to see he didn't notice what was there until they fluttered, fell to the floor. Not many, three as far as he could tell. Notes. When he bent to pick them up there was another on the floor beneath his bed and a sheet of torn paper. He scowled, turned the paper over.

Thanks for a great reunion. I needed that. T xx

He looked from the paper, to the cash. Four twenty-pound notes. Teri had left eighty pounds and he'd said he was broke the night before, but she'd never mentioned a loan.

Mike walked out of his bedroom to the living-room window. It was only there, looking out at the empty morning corner, that he realised, and he looked at the money in his hand, out at the corner and back to the dusty, second-hand interior of his flat and threw back his head and laughed. He laughed until his jaws ached, until his sides hurt, until he collapsed onto his knees pounding broken floorboards with a fist. He laughed to erase the hurt and almost succeeded.

The Chase

A thin wall of drinkers separate us, but I can't find the courage to approach. I crane my neck, try not to look obvious, peer at loosened ties below red, exposed throats, dark thunderclouds of hair and the rolled-up arms of shirts. Others in un-ironed khaki shorts, T-shirts emblazoned with logos. The women wear one-piece dresses I might have tried some way back and the music as always is too loud, too repetitive. A business trio camped behind my table lean over the scattered debris of pork scratchings, the spider-webbed crust that line pints. We smile, mime apologies. I sip my Mojito, watch people trip on the businesswoman's feet.

There are so many mirrors it's difficult to avoid my reflection. Difficult not to like what I see, despite it all. To see is to accept, or at least be confronted with the obvious, and it has been such a grand day, one of the few to be found in London when the sun has shone from the moment it cleared the litter of rooftops, and remained with us. You can see the change in temperament, the surprise on people's faces, unspoken thought; this might be it for the year. We guzzle sunlight as though last orders will be called any moment, and we might be thrown onto the streets, dazed and inebriated, feeling a slight chill as we're wearing summer clothes.

Still, no matter how much I attempt to deny it, here I am. All long, all thin, moonlight skin and shepherd's delight hair. A green sleeveless vest and jean shorts. Freckles like distant constellations. There are more details, more than what I see in a cloudy mirror, but this is enough for me, for now.

I am pleased and dismayed. It's a relief to verify my existence, a burden to acknowledge my change.

And what of you? Sometimes there are flashes of designer clothing, of laughter, urine-coloured liquid raised high, the off-beat composition of meeting pint glasses. Vibrant and young, you and your friends are all beautiful in dissimilar ways; there is something warm to be found in you all. Yet it's your face that awakens memories, your eyes I recall gazing into. You don't remember me, and why should you? It was so long ago, I hardly remember myself.

After the first Mojito I made a trip to the loo. There were only two men at my table, though I was grateful as I could ask them to watch my bag. The bar wasn't as packed, and walking as I tend to these days, head down, hair obscuring my face like a particularly shy breed of sheepdog, it was inevitable I bumped into something. That something was you. You were so busy watching football you hardly noticed; I leaned into you, you steadied me, half-looked into my face and said *sorry*, then it was back to the screen, back to your mates, back to yelling at the figures chasing the ball as if they owed you money. I kept walking, slower now, turning around to be certain, already sure.

In the ladies, jean shorts meeting chalky knees, I read bold inscriptions etched into cubicle walls, unable to forget the magic conjured by your features. A rustling of bed sheets, summer leaves at midnight. Mingled sweat, warm spring rain. I closed my eyes against lurid messages, sat with my head cupped in my hands. I flushed and didn't move.

The bar seems to have crammed in more people and my second Mojito is finished. When I turn towards the flat-screen, you're still there. I sigh and look at my sliver of a watch; this is stupid. I ask the business three-some to save my seat, go back to the bar and order another.

The barman, young, skinny. High on the confidence of resembling every other guy with his job. Bottle-green eyes, attractive smile. Stubble like a hairbrush. Don't appreciate the way he looks at me, as if the conclusion's foregone. I wait for him to throw ingredi-ents together, exchange conversation with the blonde barmaid, ignore her stunning figure, shake up the mixture, throw it over his shoulder, pour. I'm trying not to look in the mirror so I dip my head and read elongated wood grain, only look up when he gets to the pouring.

There you are. Beside me. A crisp, shrimp-flesh note between slim fingers, hips rocking to the thump of music. Skin like grain in the palm of my hand, grown and warmed by the sun, and my heart's going so hard I can't tell the difference between the beat from the speakers and the one inside me. I remember how it felt to be powerful, to recognise that yearning, and know I could answer the call if ever I wanted, to be in control. I'm wondering whether my own bottle-green matches those of the barman, who is handing over my cocktail and making them converse with mine, making them glint and throw back dim bar-lighting, and if it wasn't for you I might have agreed, just for old times sake.

I take the drink, lower my head and slip the straw between warm lips, gently inhale. Let sweet liquid saturate my tongue. When the barman leaves I slide my hip along the bar until it meets yours. Rest. You jerk a moment, most likely from shock, but then I feel the returning fuzz of heat, hesitation before you relax. We don't talk. Don't look at each other. That small protrusion of flesh, a mere two inches, says everything. It is our introduction, our shaking of hands, a warm greeting.

I wait for you to order, sip for courage and the pretence of something to do, head down. When the blonde with the stunning figure brings your drinks and makes her own eyes dance I almost panic, bail out. Your hip leans against mine with even more force. I close my eyes, dizzy. When I open them, she's gone. I stare straight ahead until I feel you look. There are drinks before you, four piss-coloured circles, and you haven't moved. I turn, try for a smile. See that moment of sheet-lightning disappointment, tell myself it's nothing, a window of regret smaller than the flesh that opened this dialogue, although it's difficult to erase once noted. I feel my own remorse for not making more of my time, not being secure with my body instead of wishing I could trade it for another; more curves, bigger boobs, cuter face, less freckles. Better dress sense, or at least a figure that could wear those clothes. Now, when I look at photos taken then, I can only think *you fool*. It's a mistake I knew I was making, impossible to act otherwise. We're so consumed by the present we leave it unopened, gaze at the wrapping for an age before we place it to one side in hope it will remain unchanged.

Something of the girl I was remains, because you look into my eyes and it's so familiar I find it difficult not to blurt out everything, to ask if you recall. That would be ridiculous, I already know you don't, something would have been said, so we keep smiling and sipping drinks, shake hands, exchange names, bad jokes, the usual. Although I am out of practice this works in my favour; I seem less the vamp, more the alluring older woman who would never pick up a young man in a bar, never force our bodies together like magnets of equal polarity, never keep pushing despite the invisible energies that force us apart. You are charming, this is true, and the fact you are attractive goes without saying. I watch the muscles in your forearm flex and un-flex as you drink until the glass is empty, you drink as if there is very little time, and when your friends come looking for their own pints you hand them over without apology, order a round for us.

I see their faces as they catch sight of me; incredulity, distaste; one takes in my breasts and legs with open lust, winks. I'm grateful to see you take no notice, credit you with the maturity they lack and retreat into my shell, a lumbering, scaled animal. The later it becomes, the more drink consumed, the more people crowd the bar, the longer the stares. Blonde barmaid gives me a probing eye when she thinks I don't notice; I see it all in the mirror. The barman with verbose eyes refuses to let them meet mine, his stiff-lipped silence says everything. As we bend our heads to catch each other's words I see frowns crash around me like thick, foaming surf. I hear the roar in my ears, feel hot. This Mojito, the one you have bought, tastes sweeter than the others, which I don't like as much. I say very little, listen to you talk of Howard Barker and Rupert Thompson, and other writers I've never heard of. This is something new, this artistic bent I've discovered, and I let your enthusiasm wash over me like low tide. I force myself to lie still, endure the cold, imagine what it might be like if the water was deeper. You say none of your friends are like you. They share your appreciation of such things, not your experience. You tell me how rare it is to talk with someone who understands. I wait for the words to escape, for the slow leak to reach its end, for you to look at me, smile, raise your glass and call a toast. I lean into your warmth and stare into the dark full stop of your pierced ear, ask if you will come home with me.

An old lover, way before you, told me the thing he liked most was my ability to describe emotion using the senses. It wasn't something I normally share, yet we discovered the oddest connection, one that seemed to transcend the time we'd spent; at that stage about two months, probably no more than once a week, always at night, always at my place. Though we termed it casual there had been nothing less so in my entire life. Magnets of differing polarities, we didn't so much meet as collide, and the connection was so intense we repeated it via physical contact, in debate, in the bedroom. The friction created by our violent exchange felt so good it took some time to realise it actually caused pain. With our energy expelled, separated on my bed, he would ask me to describe the rotting smell of anger, the sharp-edged texture of joy, or the smooth cylindrical hum of content.

I feel stars crackle and spit like eggs frying in darkness, squint them into focus until they become scattered dust motes. The music is distant, lost below the resigned sigh of the wind; every now and then a faint song emerges. The throaty voice of an organ, four repeated notes at most, an acoustic rendition of club music. I know there are people down there, can hear excitement in children's laughter, though for all intents I am alone. Flashes of supernova spark from some lonely point, so distant I'm tempted to pinch them between my fingers, experience spiked pain. My Ferris wheel has halted. The clouds are close as siblings. I sit at the highest point, look on the fairground beneath me with dispassion, a mite of fear. Gears yawn themselves out of sleep, lurch forwards. I am descending. I curl my toes, clutch the metal bar until my fingers seize.

You walk around my living room, half a pencil line almost crossing your mouth, not quite. I offer you a drink, strain to remember whether I have any brandy, go and take a look. I am trembling. Many full moons have passed since anyone visited my housing-association flat, let alone a man. I pour full measures for us both, bring the glasses into my living room where you stand back, a full pencil line now, turning left to right, nodding as if I make you proud. You say you didn't know I was an artist. I say, how would you? You nod, we laugh, I hand over the glass. Cheers.

My photographs come from all over the world. A packed, dusty coach, sweating heads in the central aisle, grime-faced workers travelling through Yucatan to Belize. Islamic schoolgirls, headscarves waving like cats' tails in the sea breeze of Lamu Island, Kenya. A small child, eyes wide, mouth open in delight as the colossal geyser of Stokkur, Iceland erupts, dwarves him. The tense faces of prostitutes looking straight into camera, the grandeur of the hotel lobby behind them a faded blur, Rostov-On-Don, Southern Russia.

For a long period of my life I was a nomad, hawking snapshots of experience from thin park railings on gloomy Sundays, funding further travel. I would come home and exhibit, take commissions and dine well. I would attend parties and take lovers and try not to think. So much time has passed I barely remember the majority of those photos. Hours have been spent staring at the images, a mug of tea beside me, waiting to see if anything comes back.

We sit at opposite ends of the room, give each other space. The brandy is sweet as my last Mojito, but this is better, there is a bite I relish, savour. You ask about my work and I feel something inside me protest; that's not what we're here for. I realise it is part of the game and hope you're not really interested, that would be disappointing. You seem well travelled. I attempt to steer conversation in that direction, while you insist on talking as though you'd like to manage me and my photos, you speak of exhibitions, competitions, newspapers and journals, book covers, record covers, the world in my hand. I don't have the heart to say I've already visited that continent, returned fully aware I'd never go back for good. There are day trips and weekend visits, I admit. Just last month I displayed a selection of Hackney photos in a small gallery not far from the main street. You seem frustrated by my lack of excitement, puzzled. Lucky for me, intrigued.

I take the measure of you as we talk about your exploits. Young warrior, a dragon slayer, out to rescue maidens and carve your name into the annals. Your mission to reshape the world through artistic terrorism makes me smile into my brandy; this I remember well. Your eyes are speaking, shouting actually. Your hands are like frenzied birds more scared of what's beyond the cage than what might happen if they remain behind bars, and although this is your chosen method of mooring yourself to sanity, the rope is already creaking, is strained. I lose the smile and listen harder. What you have seen and described is truly disturbing, this is no tabloid headline, no shocking sensationalism, it's real life occurring as we speak, the world beyond thin, glistening metal. You speak briefly your childhood and I flinch; am aware of the gaping void, the years. My fingers grow numb from the chilled glass. You sculpt wretched nightmares into beautiful ornaments.

I put down my glass. Stand. You've bowed your head and all I see is dark hair, the pale eggshell smoothness of your neck. I close space between us, take your hand. You are looking up, serious now, and it is difficult to look back, not be overrun by what I remember, what you do not. You stand. Let me lead you from the room, so young, so trusting. I take you into my bedroom, caress your fingers, let go. Sit on the bed, say nothing.

You're also silent. Spinning on one foot, turning slow as the earth. One wall, to another, to another, to the last. A small revolution, back. Here are the memories that never escape, though I almost wish they would. These are the portions of my life I relive daily, that have me clutching my pillow like a living body I hope to squeeze lifeless, unaware what I'm doing until the moment has passed. I watch you, feeling my own wince, bracing myself as you step closer, scan the photos on my walls, pick a framed shot of us together and hold it closer. Your back is turned and those long seconds when I can't see your face are the worst pain, the worst that has happened. I almost wish it would end right there. I hardly breathe in all that time, hardly make a sound. The soft thud of a rocking bed against my adjoining wall, that ridiculous gentle bass, can be heard above the silence. I listen, count lover's time, wait.

He was peach melba to your grain, at least that's what I remember. Never told him in case I sounded stupid; another regret. It would have been nice to know whether he agreed. We promised ourselves bright moments, as there were others who wrestled for our time and we didn't care about them, or our studies, only us, only that feeling. I loved to watch him walk the corridors between lectures, create fierce discussion in the lunchroom, sit with a hand on his ridged forehead in class, biting his lip, pen scribbling. Saw the world in his movements, felt that deep hum. Once he came to college with you in tow and even that didn't make me feel bad about him – or me, or anything – it just reinforced what a good man he was. That was the power your father had, to make people believe he was always right. His viewpoint erased any guilt I might have felt about you, or even your unseen mother, somewhere far in Never-Never Land.

I expect to see shock, maybe even your friends' disdain, but this barren silence throws me. You sit in the chair as if you have staked some claim, and even when I stroke the back of your hand, you don't look. I refill your glass, take the seat that is mine by default. The two-tier whistles of young men are like birdsong outside my window. Darkness seeps into the room. You sit with brandy between your fingers, head bowed, still. You down it in one, so I give you more.

To fill the silence I explain how we met, what we meant to each other, how many years it's been. Your head is low; I can see the inert whirlpool of your crown, even so, I can tell you're listening. I talk of the times our paths crossed and you look up, eyes painted in rogue mascara. You're searching your memory for some trace of what I'm saying, some recollection of me. I already know it's useless. You were a small child, your father protected you from his misdeeds, refused to even smoke or swear around you. I was filled with a weighty sense of his nobility, so much so that keeping myself in the shadows seemed right. Hadn't counted on losing that surety as the years passed and the distance grew, of becoming another woman.

I recount the time he brought you to class, the joke our lecturer asked you to tell. We were discussing the ability of the smallest child to tell stories, the lecturer saying a joke is the shortest short story in words. You sung a naughty rhyme about Kermit the Frog and Miss Piggy that made the class roar. I came up afterwards to congratulate your father for producing such an intelligent son.

You stare. It actually begins to frighten me. Your mouth is a full dark line, thick and straight. You say you do remember and describe what I wore right down to the navy blue plimsolls. I'm stunned. You say you always remembered because I'd looked like I wanted to cry, even though I kept my smile busy. You say I don't look like I did, that your father is dead.

You're waiting for my reaction so I nod, study bubbles in my glass. I'm prepared for this eventuality, but no amount of reasoning can remove what I see in my head. Bubbles launch themselves from dimpled walls and hurtle to the surface, explode. The glass falls, my feet are wet, I hear nothing above the distant call that shakes my ribcage and causes my arms to flail. I can feel you trying to push it all back, can feel you trying to contain this ghost I've trapped inside me, and though I fight and resist and panic, I know it needs to escape and go back, escape and go back, just like the air in my lungs.

Pagan idols line my bathroom shelf. Squat, mean, faces blank with indifference. Round shoulders and Mediterranean skin, plump with possibility. I see my future inside their opaque bodies, am never blessed with the same vision twice. I worship three times daily, meditate for at least an hour afterwards. Sometimes more. Most days I don't feel better but the medicine man tells me this is normal, and so I continue to pray.

I know you've seen my shrine. You asked to use my toilet and when you came back you wore an expression I've seen before. Either you don't believe in the power of my idols or you're dismayed that I use them in order to survive. When you return the thin line of your mouth is gone and your eyes have become soft as broken eggs. I see your father's face in yours, and my past life is so familiar I almost break once more. If you can deal with it, with me, then I must.

My mattress is hard, although when I push against it there's some yield. I test my theory, smile. It is as it was. I curl into a porcupine ball, shudder tense convulsions, stretch, relax. Beside me, on your back, you cast a military gaze at the ceiling. Long seconds pass between each blink. I stroke your arm until your head turns. You'd forgotten I was there, busy reshuffling what you thought you knew, replacing ideals with what you've discovered. Your stomach makes a long growl. You ignore it. I think about food, going to the kitchen. My limbs grow heavy. I'm just about to force myself up when your arms wrap around mine and I fall back, give in.

When I told you I was ill, you asked how I felt about dying. I made a flippant comment, something about people running from the thought even while others are forced to admit its imminence. Your father, me; the troubled, the war-torn and the afraid. I said that the proximity forces us to take courage, face truth in the eye. And you looked at me, that bold glint of youth infuriatingly close, asked whether our truth was no more than the absence of hope. I thought about the eight year old singing a lewd nursery rhyme before a classroom of adults, of me congratulating your father with that lucent sheen in my eyes, and couldn't say anything. You apologised and I accepted, but there was no need.

We lie on the bed, hold hands. Dawn is an arm's length from us, just beyond my window.

Gone-Away Boy

Stella got the giggles twenty minutes after, lying on the sofa pounding cushions and holding her belly. Davis watched. He was laughing too, less so, as he was struck by her expression. She hadn't looked that way since they were teenagers.

He crawled on the sofa next to her, snaking his legs between hers, back turned, facing the television. It was on and loud, though neither was watching. The room was dark, apart from intermittent flashes. Stella put her arms around his waist. He could feel her warm breath on the knob of his spine, which perfectly matched the warmth at the centre of his forehead. He let his thoughts drift, eyes open, dappled light playing on his cheeks. He heard a deep hum from his wife.

'*Mmmm,*' she said. 'That's good.'

'It is.'

'We need music.'

'We do.'

'Want to get some from Barry's room?'

'Does that mean you want me to get it?'

'No. Yes. Yes and no. Oh, I don't know.'

She giggled again. The room was moving slowly to the left, like a child's carousel.

'Are you even sure you want to hear Barry's music?'

'What?'

'I said, "Are you even sure you want to hear Barry's music?" Cloth ears.'

'You're slurring, that's why. And yes I do. Maybe it'll sound better.'

They wallowed in the drift. Car engines rose and fell. Apart from that and the whistle of their breath, there was silence.

'I'll go,' he said, struggling to his feet.

The world around him spun, but he had that under control. He hauled his own bodyweight upstairs, feeling his heart pound at the top, put his hand out for the light and then Barry's door. Going in, he was amazed at how tidy the room was, yet again. That wasn't inherited from him, or his mother. Surfaces were free of dust, books alphabetically shelved; the computer desk was empty apart from a notepad and pen. Davis had an insane urge to open the drawers and throw clothes around, pull down the books, grab all his CDs and spread them across the floor. It looked like a room kept just so because someone had died, not because they had gone away. It made him scared. He told himself it was paranoia, just like he did in uni, but the feeling wouldn't leave him alone.

He ended up taking a handful of CDs without even looking at the contents and brought them downstairs to Stella, unable to stem a hunter/gatherer's pride. He put the first into the deck and pressed play. Who knew what kind of music it was. Dirt, grime, footstep? It was the kind of music they were used to hearing from behind their son's closed door, or on the cable shows he sometimes watched, or in the car, a full-to-capacity beat and bass that made them feel tired and old. But tonight they listened. Tonight they were re-living their youth, what they had felt and thought when they first met and were open to each other because they were open to the world. They nodded their heads and shuffled their bums on the sofa, and when Stella got to her feet with her hands outstretched he rose to meet her, and they danced together, fingers entwined, palms joined, throwing all of their energy into matching the beat, Stella laughing with her head thrown back, laughing harder then she had in months, and he felt a twinge of worry again, was this too far? He was like this most of the time, searching beyond a smile, beyond the crinkle of her eyes as if he could see past skin and bone to read the flashes of electricity that sparked thoughts, searching for a place beyond the immediate, a desperate farmer scanning clear skies for rain. Sometimes she would laugh so hard and later go to bed early, leave him facing the TV. If he went upstairs he could stand by the door and hear her cry in the darkness. He would turn away, go back down, face the TV and not watch. He would wait a few hours before he went upstairs and slipped beneath the sheets.

Tonight they were time travelling, so he forced his mind from worry. He swung her arms and laughed with Stella, and when the song came to a close they fell against each other, panting and chuckling like years before. Their bodies came together and their sweat combined and their hair rested against skin.

'Is there any more?' she said.

He sat back down, fingered the thin plastic bag.

'I think there might be one.'

'Let's smoke it.'

She sat next to him, all big, earnest eyes.

'He'll be cross.'

'We'll buy more.'

'From *where*?'

'OK, we'll give him the money.'

'Oh, so now our son's a drug dealer?'

'It's only this *once*,' she said, eyes bright, skirt high on her thighs, and then he couldn't help it. They leaned forward of one accord, pressing against each other, removing clothes, writhing on the sofa. Afterwards she said nothing, just lay with her toes brushing polished floorboards, staring at the ceiling. He wanted to ask if she was all right, was tired of being repetitive. He felt he might be crushing her, so he eased away, picked up the thin plastic bag. He rolled like an expert, as though it hadn't been decades.

Once he was done, Stella put on her clothes. She rested her head on his shoulder.

'Let's go to the caravan.'

He had the joint in his mouth, lighter in hand.

'Tonight?'

'*Please*. Let's get out of the city. Just for the weekend. Just *go*.'

Davis had no arguments, bar the time of night. He took the joint from his mouth and slipped it into his pocket.

The roads were empty, their journey much reduced. They drove with Miles Davis – his father's favourite musician – hypnotised by the glowing lights and signs of the motorway. The cat eyes were like bread-crumbs leading the way. Service stations beckoned, were ignored. He relaxed on the headrest, let his body fall into the seat, Stella's hand on his thigh for most of the drive, talking little. She drank water from her thermos, looked out of the window. If she caught his eye in the rear-view she would smile at Davis, a steady, knowing grin. When the CD stopped, she played it again.

They'd listened to Miles four times over when they pulled into the caravan park, with its bumpy, unlit roads. Davis steered from memories of long weekends in the early days when Stella's parents would babysit; summers spent later, when Barry was a toddler; of outings with close friends while their son was away on school journeys, stolen slivers of time. They pulled up outside their caravan and took in the silence.

Stella inhaled a few puffs of the joint, passed it to Davis. An owl hooted. That made them laugh. They unlocked the van and took a good look, unsurprised that nothing had changed. Davis made the bed. Stella made tea. As he fluffed up sheets, Davis thought he heard her walk onto the steps and stopped what he was doing to listen. Quiet. A bad sign. He shouldn't have left her alone with so little to do. He should have made the tea. He'd thought he was being helpful when he was just negligent. Stella wasn't good on her own.

She'd been on her own when the pain came, that was the trouble. Six months after Barry left for Bristol a small bump rose under her dress like baking bread. She'd held his hand, moved it. *To replace our gone-away boy*, she'd said. She'd been joking, but Davis could see truth in her eyes. They decided not to tell

Barry in case he was diverted from his studies. He'd be worried for his mother, at her age. He might even want to come back.

A month after, she'd been running a tap in the kitchen when she felt cramps. Fell to the floor, dialled the ambulance on her mobile. He'd been at work, his phone switched off, couldn't help it, those was the rules. Tending other people's children.

Davis smoothed a hand over the duvet, plumped up pillows. He sat on the bed and let the drift carry him, body limp, gliding with the current, thinking of everything and nothing at all, sightless eyes on walls the colour of dried tangerine. When the owl hooted again, a soft cry in keeping with the run of his thoughts, he realised how long he'd been there. He heard the mournful sound of another animal, a cat or maybe a fox that reminded him of a child startled awake somewhere distant, maybe in a caravan across the park. He imagined opening his eyes to endless darkness, not knowing why. He let his head drop, stomach churning. He squeezed his eyes shut and whispered her name so low even he hardly heard it. Nina. He gasped and clutched his belly and tried to chase the last sight of her from his memory, but it stayed.

Outside, the night was silent, the darkness like a walled maze. He could smell damp leaves and mud, a faint pong of cows. Davis walked down the tiny steps, hoping to see her resting against the caravan, but she wasn't there. He tried not to panic, kept going. Sometimes he stumbled in the mud and even thought he should go back for his walking shoes, but he didn't want her alone a moment longer. Once he was away from the lights of his caravan and the spots of his next-door neighbours, the night came down like a fallen brick, and having his eyes open was no different to having them closed. He moved like a toddler, unsure, legs wide apart, arms in front of him, trying to use his feet as feelers, dragging them through the unseen tall grass.

He waited for his eyes to adjust, although nothing happened for a long time, and the dark seemed to spring back when he touched it until he felt as though he'd been consumed by it all; his daughter's death, his wife's grief, his guilt. He was tempted to just give up, to sit on the cold damp of the mud beneath him and wait for whatever judgment he was due. He even stopped and looked around, knowing there was nothing to see, caught a glitter of silver he almost took as an illusion. When it happened again, Davis saw he was squinting at the reflection of moonbeams. Of course. The lake. He pretended he hadn't been scared, hadn't forgotten, smiled to himself.

She was at the water's edge, a photonegative silhouette, as if she'd been cut out of his vision, balled up, thrown away. She was smoking a cigarette with her back to him, the mug of tea between her feet. She was shaking, and at first he hoped it was because she didn't have on a jacket. Davis heard her sniff, stopped a few feet away. Waited. She didn't seem to have heard him, even though she wasn't crying loudly. He looked at her feet and saw a droplet splash into the mug. Raised his chin to the sky. No rain.

He moved towards Stella and put his arms around her. They circled her waist easily, that hadn't changed.

She gave a masculine grumble, like she had on the sofa. Davis squeezed tight, turned her.

'Look at me, Stella,' he said. 'Please?'

A cloud passed above the lake. It grew difficult to see her. There was no light, no sound, just them.

Passive Smoke

He needed to quit the cigarettes. It was beginning to get to her, especially since she'd begun to exhale smoke. The first time Evie had been getting out of bed when she felt a tight pain in her chest and the urge to cough, followed by two dry bursts. The tiny puffs that escaped her mouth and the ashen taste on her tongue stopped her dead, one foot caught in the duvet, the other on the carpet, stunned. She remained there, a hand to her burning throat for the next five minutes, unable to believe what had happened. She instantly knew Max was to blame.

The simplest thing would have been to tell him, but the notion was ridiculous, she already knew that. She threw herself into her dressing gown and marched downstairs, through the living room and into the back garden. Sure enough, there he was: leaning against the garden fence enjoying his first of the day, having a laugh with the neighbour. She stood by the open back door, dressing gown clutched in a tight fist, hissing like a snake.

'What d'you think you're you doing?'

Max jumped out of his skin. He shot a look at Clyde on the other side of the fence; he was already smiling.

'What?'

'You're not trying very hard are you?'

'I am. I'm cutting down.'

'In what way?'

'I didn't have one last night.'

That was true. She was too upset to credit him for honesty.

'I want you to put that out, right now.'

'Get stuffed,' he muttered into his neat-trimmed beard.

'I beg your pardon?'

She was almost shrieking by then, stood on bare tiptoes, leaning as far into the garden as she dared. Clyde was red with suppressed laughter. Heat rose on her face.

'Yes, dear, whatever you say, dear . . .' He took three big drags, admired the dwindling butt, took one more, pursed his lips and blew. This time there was no doubt; the hit struck Evie deep. She turned her head, coughing into the clean living-room air, expelling a brackish grey cloud that swirled above her head. Evie could literally feel Max stare in her direction with that look in his eyes, the one she hated, narrow eyes and set jaw, a wolfish sneer. He didn't even seem to notice the strange absence of any smoke around him.

'It's not that bad. Why do you always have to exaggerate?'

She thrust her head out of the back door again, lunging, spitting venom.

'And why d'you have to be such a pig?'

'Oink, Oink,' he said, dropping the butt and crushing it flat beneath his heel.

'You better put that in the bin!' Evie screeched. She turned and stomped upstairs to the bathroom.

* * *

Sitting in front of her desk, Evie tried to concentrate on what she was doing, but could only focus on Max. Their relationship seemed like an exercise in incompatibility. He smoked, she didn't. She worked, he didn't. She liked theatre, film and books, he didn't. Evie answered the phone and directed calls to relevant members of staff, speaking in a dull monotone. Yes, it had been fun back when they had first started dating, but if she was truthful she'd known he was boring even then – good looking, perfectly groomed, but still boring. Of course, in those early days he'd been polite too, nothing like the obnoxious swine he had become. After a run of violent boyfriends, Max had seemed the safer option. Evie hadn't imagined she could bruise without fists.

She began to feel pangs of hunger close to her eleven-fifteen break. When she looked at her watch Evie saw she had ten minutes left. There was a somewhat familiar tickle and she felt that lurch in her chest, then there was the hit, and she couldn't control her own body. She started to heave dry coughs. The year-ten head, Edward Draper, was stood at the Headmaster's pigeonhole at the time, a handful of files and letters in hand. He dropped them at once and ran to her side as she coughed and retched and wiped stinging tears. He even thumped her back, which was thoroughly irritating, until he smelt the smoke. Draper backed away. He was sniffing the air, eyeing Evie with contempt.

'I know you're fully aware of the ban; I think you

should wait until your break to smoke, especially around the older students,' he told her, thick eyebrows clashing. Evie suddenly understood why she'd overheard the kids call him 'Crouching Caterpillar'.

'I . . . don't . . .' she wheezed, just as she blew out a huge plume of smoke. She looked up at him, eyes bright, in desperation. 'I don't smoke . . .'

Draper didn't believe her, even though he'd never seen Evie with a cigarette. He peered at her fingers and even into the bin under her desk for evidence. Finding none, he looked around the small room as though he wanted to call for help, but it was empty.

'I think you'd better get some fresh air and a glass of water, don't you?' he said, an unconscious hand to his throat.

Evie jumped to her feet and pushed past Draper. She ran along the corridor, down the stairs three at a time as the pips went for morning break, her mouth covered with one hand. In the playground she leant over, hands on her knees, coughing so long and loud she attracted a group of sympathetic kids. They rubbed her back and offered cans of soda, which she took, but nothing made any difference. When the kids saw cigarette smoke belch from her open mouth, they backed away as though she had fangs for teeth. By the time morning break was over, both her coughing fit and the crowd of students were gone.

He had to be told. She couldn't risk losing the best job she'd ever had, or becoming a freak to anyone that might potentially witness her puffing like a cartoon dragon. It was demeaning, a smear on her character, especially as a non-smoker. All afternoon, even during her hour lunch break, Evie sat at her desk typing with tentative fingers, the office window pushed wide open in case she felt that uncontrollable twinge, oblivious to the head's complaints about the draft. Whenever she began to feel that foreign tickle, she jumped out of her seat and hung her head outside, mindful of passing staff members, blowing rolling plumes into the air. He'd been lying. Max wasn't trying to give up, no way. Every cigarette he smoked was expelled from her virgin lungs in violent bursts. Evie imagined that the Marlboro Lights, his brand of choice, tasted like mountain air on his tongue.

She fumed over his deceit all the way home, felt even worse when she stormed into the living room. Max had his feet up, wireless gamepad in hand, face contorted as he wrestled with that stupid football game on his Xbox. She had to stand at the door for at least five minutes before he even noticed she was there. He gave a mute wave and a grunt before he returned to the TV.

She decided to bide her time, going upstairs to change out of her work clothes and get a quick shower, brush her teeth. Hungry, she threw together dinner and ate alone at the kitchen table until he wandered in, drawn by the smell. They sat across the table in silence, Evie watching him eat, Max wolfing it all down as though it was his first meal of the day. Looking at the empty sink, she guessed it was. One of the things she'd loved most back in their early dating days was his appreciation of her cooking. Now it was just another irritation in her chest, something else that made her want to retch.

Plate clear, Max leant back, eyes at half-mast, hand resting on a bloated belly. She narrowed her eyes over the remains of her own half-eaten dinner.

'Do you want to tell me anything about the smoking?'

He stared back, uncaring, picking at food between his teeth with the outer tine of his fork; more bad habits, the offences stacked like dirty wares. Shook his head.

'So you've nothing to say?'

'Nope.'

'Even about this?'

A pack of twenty, the white packet bright between her fingers. The box was open, half the cigarettes missing.

'Sneaking about in my drawers are we? Nice to know I'm trusted . . .'

'Well, how can I if you're taking me for granted? Lying to me? How can I believe you then?'

'It's none of your business! I'm a grown man, what I do is my concern . . .'

A shift in the air; raised tensions creating heat between one body and the next; clenched fists, protruding tendons, red faces.

'None of my . . . This is *my* flat! *I* pay rent while you sit on your arse all day, doing nothing . . . *I* have to breathe in your smoke . . .'

'Well leave then! Or I will! Either way, I'm not listening to this crap . . .'

And that was the end, Max slamming his offending fork onto the plate, causing a painful clatter in her ears. He stormed out the front door leaving Evie with a half pack of twenty and anger for company.

That Saturday evening Evie dressed in front of the mirror. She'd chosen her tightest purple dress with the shortest hemline. Damn Max if he didn't know what he was missing, she'd show him anyway. The frosty atmosphere had lasted ever since their argument. They were both so busy maintaining hostilities they'd forgotten the invitation extended over a fortnight ago, when they'd asked their next-door neighbours Clyde and Sonia over for dinner.

Evie applied a little make-up and went downstairs to find Max scrolling through his iPod with a lazy thumb. He wore jeans and an old T-shirt that continually escaped the wash and didn't react when he saw her sheer purple dress. Yet another dirty plate.

She retreated to the kitchen, pretending to watch the butternut soup until their guests arrived bearing bottles of sparkling wine. Clyde was a six-foot oaf in Max's vein, albeit without the looks. No wonder they got on. He kissed her on the cheek and leered at her cleavage even when Sonia noticed. His partner was a miniscule sweetheart, polite, humble and funny, painfully beautiful. She snatched the bottle from Clyde's grasp, ordered him into the living room with his playmate, popped the cork and poured for herself and Evie. They sat at the kitchen table, fully prepared for a good old gossip.

'How's things?'

Evie stirred the soup, lifted the lid on the saucepan

of stewed fish curry. She was struck by the insane urge to cry.

'Oh, the usual,' she told her, back turned, spoon lifted to taste. 'I shout, he ignores me. I'm surprised you haven't heard.'

'Well . . .' her neighbour gazed at her glass.

'So you already know. That's about the size of it.'

'Men aren't generally easy to live with,' Sonia conceded, forming her words slow. 'Look at Clyde. I used to wonder why he wasn't sensitive and considerate, then I realised guys like that already have boyfriends.'

'Yeah . . .' She was supposed to laugh, she knew that. Sonia was smiling, encouraging, but she was so tired she couldn't muster strength. 'It's just that most of the time I don't know why I bother. Surely that's not good?'

'Yeah, but still . . .'

The men strolled in, just in time for dinner, as was usually the way. Evie spooned food and sat submerged in conversation, feeling as though she'd been ducked beneath shallow water. Everything seemed muffled, far away. Max was shoveling mouthfuls and cracking the same old jokes, talking about the same old topics. Clyde complimented her cooking and felt Sonia up under the table, making her jump and slap him every few minutes or so, even while he made eyes at Evie like a dog mesmerised by an out-of-reach bone. Sonia attempted to angle the conversation Evie's way but it was a losing battle she'd lost the heart to win. She sat there, dazed, wondering what had made her want to invite her neighbours over when she despised Clyde so much. Then she remembered. She hadn't. It was Max.

She'd bought dessert from the local supermarket, a small strawberry cheesecake Max usually loved, but the men were up and out before she could even get to the fridge, heading for the back garden. Even though she knew why they were going, knew she should find some excuse to leave the kitchen, Evie stayed.

'You know, you don't have to do this to yourself,' Sonia whispered, half an eye on the kitchen door.

'I know.'

'It might seem as though things aren't the best between me and Clyde . . . He's a pig, we both know that, and my family is always going on about how much better I could do . . . The thing is . . . I feel stupid saying this . . .' Sonia shifted in her seat, allowed a small wince of embarrassment. 'I love him. Bottom line, I truly do. Warts and all. So you have to ask yourself the question, is he worth it? And if not . . .'

'. . . I know what to do . . .' Evie said.

'Exactly.'

She felt a sudden pang for the creamy taste of cheesecake and got to her feet, turning towards the fridge.

'You're right. I know you are. I just feel it's like the song says, you know . . . "I'm not in love. . ."'

'". . . But you're open to persuasion?"' They laughed, perhaps more heartily than the words allowed. 'That's cool. That's normal. But is he doing a good job? Persuading?'

She found the cake and searched for a knife, some plates. Peered out at the garden door. Max's laughter drifted into the house.

'*Noooo* . . .'

'Well . . .' Sonia lifted her slim shoulders and let them fall, sipped more wine.

Evie was smiling, thinking how cute that miniscule gesture looked on Sonia when it happened. The hit. This time it was so deep in her chest she almost gasped, her shocked reaction making her bend over, suck in air, almost drop the packaged cheesecake to the floor. Sonia half rose to her feet, unsure what had happened, and then Evie rose again, eyes wide, grasping her throat with one hand, and bellowed a thick blast of grey smoke across the table right into Sonia's stunned face. Directly after that came the coughing, so fitful and loud she was forced to put down the dessert, sit at the table. Sonia came to her side, rubbing her back while she belched more smoke into the kitchen, again and again. It went on until the coughs began to subside in force, died into nothing. Sonia ran cold tap water into a glass and handed it to Evie. She gulped it down, breathing weakly, a hand still rested on her throat, almost face down on the table.

'Oh my *God* . . .'

Sonia was peering. Evie avoided her stare, ashamed.

'Sorry about that . . .'

'Sod that, babe . . . Was that *him*? Max, I mean.'

Her throat was burning, so she nodded.

'Have you told him?'

She shook her head, twice.

'Oh, Evie, you have to. That's really bad.'

Evie sat up, feeling shaky. It was a struggle, but she was so surprised she forced herself.

'You saw it? I mean saw the whole thing, not just the smoke.'

Sonia's expression morphed from concern into annoyance. She made to speak, thought about it, started again. 'I believe what my eyes tell me, babe. You don't have to worry about that. And you know it's true. Do something.'

'I will,' she croaked. They held hands.

The men came back, laughing overbearingly loudly, smelling like bonfire. Clyde looked at the women and sniffed the air, gave Sonia a questioning look. Max, oblivious as usual, flopped into the seat he'd vacated, spotting the boxed dessert. 'Ah, yeah, strawberry cheesecake. My favourite! You dishing it out or staring at it?'

Another roar from both men, Sonia shooting daggers at Evie. Max and Clyde clutched each other and laughed.

She lay in bed the following morning with her boyfriend snoring beside her, staring at the ceiling. The sun was rising. The birds were chirping into life, though Evie hardly heard them. Every so often Max would grunt and throw an arm across her body, which she would immediately remove. Despite her anger, she was happy. Someone had seen. And she'd had an idea.

After some time she decided he could stay in bed, leaving him to sleep while she showered and dressed. The local supermarket opened late on Sundays, so she was there when they raised the shutters, looking amused at her impatience. There were half-sized trolleys not far from the entrance. She took one, rolling up and down the aisles, filling hers with as much food as she could find, everything from cakes to sausages and Gammon steaks, to ready meals and pies, nothing remotely healthy. She scanned packaging for E numbers and additives, the more the better. When she'd piled the trolley high, Evie paid with Max's credit card. She took her massive haul home.

He came downstairs to the smell of a full English breakfast. Fried eggs, sausage, bacon, mushroom, beans, black pudding and toast. He was rubbing his hands together in glee as he entered the kitchen, just in time to see Evie clearing her plate.

'Wow, smells lovely!' Max wore a wide grin. 'Where's mine, in the oven?'

'Yours? Oh sorry, love, I thought you'd still be full after last night, so I made breakfast for myself. Is that alright?'

'Well . . .' Max looked around the room, confused. '. . . I thought . . .'

'You sure you're not full?' Evie said, staring at him, eyes gleaming. 'I could've sworn you would be.'

'Well . . .' Max flopped to the kitchen table. He lay back in his seat, hands resting on his stomach. His eyes looked vague, distant. He seemed sleepy. 'Come to think of it, I do feel a little bloated. Dunno why.'

'Thought you might.' She smiled for the first time in months. 'Would you like a cup of tea?'

'No thanks, I couldn't stomach anything.' He looked at her, suspicious. 'What you grinning at?'

'Oh nothing. Just feel good today. You don't look so well, actually. Maybe you should go back to bed.'

'Yeah . . .' Max said. He was beginning to pale. 'I don't really feel the best.'

'You do seem a bit peeky.'

'Yeah.'

He got up, stumbling out of the kitchen. Evie's smile grew. When she was sure he wasn't coming back she opened her laptop and located the Ocado website. She ordered more food and put it on Max's card.

Evie did the same thing every day for the next three months. She ate a massive breakfast, lunch and dinner, making sure she snacked in between each meal. Full English breakfast, bacon double-cheeseburger and chips with a side order of onion rings for lunch, Sunday roast for dinner most days. King-sized chocolate bars, family-sized packs of sweets, grab-bags of crisps, as long as the latter were full of MSG, none of that organic stuff. She bought ready-meals and ate them at work, or when Max was out of the house. Every now and then she would feel the hit. She'd run to the bathroom, lock herself in and wait for the spasms to pass.

Somewhere along the line Max seemed to notice that although he hardly ate, he was putting on an extraordinary amount of weight. His cheeks and throat swelled as though he had mumps, and his stomach began to push against his jeans in protest. By the second month he began to find nothing fit him like it had. When he went clothes shopping he was dismayed to discover he'd gone up a size. Max had always been quite fanatical about the fact that he could eat whatever he liked and not gain pounds as long as he exercised. Now Evie could feel the difference when he climbed on top at night, saw how hard he laboured once he was there. It pleased her to know she could affect him too. It was all she could do to keep the secret.

Still, it didn't take long for him to realise he had
hardly eaten a thing for over three months, while Evie,
normally a miniscule eater, was putting away huge
plates of food three times a day and not gaining a
stone. She was having her now-usual full English in
the kitchen one morning when he came down and
slid into the chair opposite her. The skin on his face
was sallow, puffy. His normally bright brown eyes
had become submerged in flesh. His arms and shoulders had gained in width and the T-shirt he wore was
baggy enough to hide the growing ball of his previously non-existent stomach. Evie fought down a smile,
concentrated on pork sausages.

'Good morning.'

He leveled his face with hers. Leaned across the
table. 'What's going on, Evie?'

She was chewing, voice muffled by her full mouth.
'With what?'

'You know what, Evie.'

She sat back, swallowed. Almost closed her eyes, it
tasted so good.

'Max, I'm really sorry. You're right; I never should
have done it. I'll make some brekkie for you too, all
right?'

He slammed his hands on the table, palms down,
making her jump.

'I don't want breakfast, Evie. I don't want it because
I'm not hungry. I haven't been hungry for the last three
months. Doesn't that make you concerned?'

Shrugging, maintaining a casual expression. 'No. I
just thought you weren't fussed.' Evie gave him a quick
flick up and down with her eyes, waited a beat. 'You

certainly don't *look* as though you're starved . . .'

It was all she could do not to laugh at the look of indignation that crumpled his face into a petulant frown of uncertainty, a schoolboy's sulk. Max unconsciously put a hand across his stomach, saw she was watching, took the hand away. She lowered her head towards the plate and cut a piece of bacon into a manageable portion. Added beans. Lifted the fork to her mouth. Opened and swallowed.

'Have you put Obeah on me?'

This time she did laugh. 'I thought you called it superstitious nonsense. Group hallucinations of the highest order, didn't you say?'

'I did. But my grandmother believed. I'm prepared to admit I could be wrong.'

She dangled a piece of sausage in front of him like bait, but he couldn't even look, his face turning green at the sight of the meat.

'Really? What a shame your admittance couldn't be stretched further than duppy power . . .'

'*What?*'

'Could be the first step on your journey, you know.'

'Evie. You're not making any sense.'

She pursed her lips, feeling powerful.

'I didn't use Obeah on you, Max. I wouldn't fool with that stuff, even if I knew how.'

Max slumped against his chair. She found it strange that he believed her totally, didn't think for a minute she might lie. It struck her then how much Max trusted her not to harm him, all the while throwing mental barbs for most of their relationship.

'So what's happening to me?' he said. The fear on

his face was genuine. He looked as though he might cry. 'I see myself in the mirror and don't recognise who I am, and when I try to eat, I can't. I've put on three stones in the last few weeks; I've never put on that much in my entire *life*. There's more food in the house than we've ever had, and when I come into the kitchen you – skinny you – are eating like a monster. You've got me searching the house for a bowl of sweat rice hidden in a cupboard . . . This is weird stuff, Evie, it's making me scared.'

She was finished, the plate before her clean, and yet she felt light as air, content but hardly stretched. Max, on the other hand, had that sleepy-eyed look of a man who had downed more than he could handle. He leaned back, burped long and loud, covered his mouth with a hand and looked very uncomfortable. Evie wiped her mouth with a tissue. She was stern, deadly serious.

'Light a cigarette.'

His eyes widened, though he tried not to.

'I don't have any.'

She sighed. 'Come on, Max, don't treat me like a fool. I know you're still smoking.'

They stared at each other until he puffed a huge breath, reached into his pocket and pulled out the pack. Another search for his lighter, then he was leaning on his elbows with both items in one hand.

'Sure about this?'

'Go on. I wanna show you something.'

She wasn't sure if it was for her benefit, but he took it slow, placing the cigarette in his mouth and letting it hang limp, spinning the cheap lighter wheel as softly as he could, letting the flame burn a few seconds before he bent it towards the tip, the glow and crackle as it caught, the race of red light. The hit was less of a blast and more of a tickle; she could feel it, but her lungs did not have the urgent need to expel the foreign object like they once had. Max took the smoke down, held it. Thus, so did Evie. It had happened. She'd got used to it.

When he exhaled, of course, nothing came out. She could feel his warm breath caress her skin like it did in the old days, when they had made love, him looking down on her with clear intent. Evie let the memory play for quite some time. It was good. She opened her mouth and let out the smoke. Max immediately reared back as though he'd been slapped, eyes closed. She blew it all from her, everything he had given until there was nothing left. Then she sat there and said nothing, point made. It didn't surprise her to see tears roll down his cheeks, even though his eyes remained shut. At this stage in their relationship she guessed, after everything that had happened, nothing would.

'How long?' he said, eyes squeezed tight.

'Four, five months. I can't actually remember.'

'And you didn't say anything.'

'I was hoping you'd notice.'

He had the good grace not to reply, just nod his head and weep.

'We can't keep doing this. To each other, I mean. You know that, don't you?'

'Yes.'

Evie stood and put her plate, knife and fork into the

dishwasher. Went back to the table and laid a hand on his shoulder.

'I'm leaving, Max. I think it's for the best. So do you, really.'

She let him grasp her hand a moment longer and when she could take no more, carefully removed it. She went upstairs to pack.

The Bright Side of the Moon

Maybe her initial misgivings had been correct, she was thinking as she went for breakfast, although that didn't necessarily make him a bad person. She'd just been lucky on this particular trip, that was all. As soon as she'd checked into her Nairobi hotel she met a couple she'd suspected were having an affair, but were welcoming towards her. On the bus to Mombassa she'd spoken with an old woman who said she liked her smile and told her all about her former life in London, before she got tired of the cold. And then there was Shella. Palermo. She couldn't help smiling about the night they'd spent in her dark, humid room, the smooth contours of his skin, the way his hair scratched against her shoulder, a welcome pain. Palermo was the real reason she felt strange about Robert. Whenever her memories conjured his image, all thoughts of the American faded, good looks drowned by her feelings for a man she hardly knew.

Or maybe it was just Malindi. The tall, colonial houses, lobster-coloured tourists in shorts and trainers, the way the African men stared. Tired of having to cover up in Shella to appease Islamic tradition, Shalini hit the streets in her own tight shorts and a miniature T-shirt that barely covered her belly. She regretted it as soon as she saw the looks from passing men; hers was the only foreign brown skin for miles. Feeling their hunger, wanting to escape the eyes, she ducked into an Internet café to find the power down. That settled it. She walked a further four hundred yards, where she found a restaurant with open white shutters and, inside, slow-turning fans. She read the menu and liked what she saw, mostly pasta dishes, which made sense in that part of town and so she entered. Obviously she should have known better. Half an hour later, while dining on spaghetti, a man sat at a white concert piano and began to play. As if from nowhere, lobster-coloured tourists appeared from doors she hadn't noticed until the restaurant, which she realised doubled as a hotel, was full of Italian voices and laughter. Shalini ate with her head down, marooned in a European sea. The only people of colour were the waiters, dressed in white shirts and black trousers, looking at her curiously when she asked for the bill. She left with her head straight, damning herself for the tiny shorts, muttering inward promises to keep them for the beach next time.

It was more than likely just the way he smiled, she concluded, crossing the empty tables to greet him. He was young and blond, the surfer type she'd loved as a teenager; his hair was shaved, stubble carefully groomed. His eyes were a still blue that reminded her of calm seas; she felt at peace looking into them, she could admit that. Shalini sat next to him, enquiring how he'd spent his night, lying about hers (saying she'd lazed in bed with a good book), talking a little about travelling, the usual stuff. Breakfast was good in the African Pearl, a hotel she'd chosen on a whim and the only one owned by Kenyans. They ate fresh fruits and hard-boiled eggs with bread rescued from a trail of ants, leant back in their seats and drank tea.

He was leaving the next morning. Although he didn't ask to stay in contact, she was sure he wanted to. Shalini told him about Khalid and the family, the problems with the farm and its surrounding land, inviting him to come and see both. She wasn't even sure whether her objective was a change of subject, or if she said it because she felt sorry for him. Before she could decide, Robert accepted. They agreed to meet for lunch in town that afternoon, followed by the trip to see her cousin.

That night, sitting on her terrace reading the novel Robert had given her, Shalini caught herself glancing at her phone. It was early days, and he was still in Shella, but she was wondering why Palermo hadn't called. Maybe he'd taken their liaison as a one-night stand. Maybe he'd met some local girl and forgotten her. She shook her head at her own morbid imagination; he was probably just trying to give her space. Her smile returned, remembering a joke he'd made. She forced Palermo from her mind.

Malindi, she'd found, was a segregated town in a divided country. Tribe, race and gender all mattered, despite, or maybe due to, a long-standing history of hospitality. The inland side of town was where you found hotels and places of business catering to tourists or ex-pats. The seaward end was filled with crumbling old buildings, dark skins and hijabs, cheap eateries full of locals consuming spicy curried chicken and roti. Walking that way after her meal at the Italian hotel the previous night, Shalini stumbled into a world very much apart from the place she'd left. She'd wanted to go inside for a cool drink, but the eateries were full of dark-eyed men who'd already noticed her. Very much aware that she was a woman travelling alone, Shalini returned to the African Pearl.

Her ten days in Shella reminded Shalini of a T-shirt she'd bought from a Bangkok market years ago – 'Same Same, but Different'. The locals distanced themselves from their brothers and sisters on Lamu, a mere half-hour boat ride away. There were Miami-style mansions people claimed were built by Mafia dons while young *dhow* captains slept in their vessels at night. Still, the beauty of that limitless powder-white beach had kept her enthralled, as did the smiles of beach boys and the ornate Islamic buildings. She'd even found beauty in the hesitant call to prayer that woke her every morning, sounding like none she'd heard anywhere in the world.

Robert had been sitting by the poolside bar when she'd first met him, reading Ngugi Wa Thiong'o. The bar also doubled as the breakfast area, though she hadn't noticed him before. There were only two other guests, a middle-aged Australian couple engaged in conversation with the Kenyan bar staff, two good-looking, agile young men. Shalini ordered a cold coke and sat on an empty sofa, eavesdropping. The woman was flirting with the Kenyans, though her husband seemed not to mind. She tried not to notice Robert, curiosity raised by the fact he was reading *A Grain of Wheat*. Shalini was impressed, despite herself. The young man, noticing Shalini, smiled when she caught his eye and eventually came over.

He was an NGO on leave working in Mombassa with one of the local tribes, teaching English and computer skills. He came from Rockville USA and had been journeying through Africa for eighteen months. Shalini thought he was shy until they got talking about African novelists, his passion ignited by Wa Thiong'o. Shalini had only read *The Wizard and the Crow*. He insisted she take his novel, claiming to have devoured it three times already. Shalini liked his easy generosity, even though it was only a book. She liked his jokes too, which were funny when they weren't forced and flowed even better once he'd downed some Tuskers. They talked until three, longer than she'd intended, enough to give him the idea that she might like his company more than she actually did.

The next day she avoided him without admitting it, spending the afternoon on Watamu beach, the evening in an after-hours bar Khalid knew, frequented by local prostitutes. By the time she got to the African Pearl it was past four. The lights in the bar were out. She'd felt guilty about being mean when he seemed like such a nice guy, and resolved to be kinder the following day.

Lunch was in one of the eateries, served by a Gujerati Muslim who constantly called her *beta*, Shalini relishing the roti with stewed meat and rice, glad she hadn't missed out. By the time they stalked shoestores like big-game hunters looking for a pair of sandals to match Shalini's tastes, Khalid was already calling. They agreed to meet in a café next door to the after-hours bar. She told Robert about it on the way, snapping shots of the sea road with her Canon. He was grave when she described the music and prostitutes smoking cigarettes with the air of movie stars, nodding with a noncommittal air, saying it sounded like fun. Shalini stifled her guilt.

Khalid was late, but that was to be expected. As he swivelled past tables, smiling at friends, Robert shrank in his seat like a puppy backing away from a stranger's hand. She waved at Khalid to reassure the American, feeling faint emotion, the urge to protect her cousin stronger than the night before. Then, sitting amongst weeping beer bottles and slow-drifting smoke, she'd tried not to look shocked at the glaze in his eyes, how skinny he'd grown. She relaxed as they spoke about family and Kenyan life, Shalini realising he was still the same Khalid who'd taught her to ride a bike outside her grandfather's house, shouting encouragement until she turned to see him standing fifty yards behind her. She'd immediately wobbled and fallen.

Khalid's smile looked painful, thin skin wrinkling as it stretched over his skull-like face. His eyes were bright, as though he'd slept well. Someone at a table behind them shouted his name and within five minutes there was a Tusker on their table. Robert shook her cousin's hand with a firm grip, impressed. Khalid raised the other hand in silent thanks, capped his beer and raised that too. He poured his drink onto the concrete beneath their feet before his first sip and talked exclusively with Robert, asking where he was from, how long he was staying in Africa. As they began to discuss

NGO work, local Malindi politics and Kenyan politics in general, she left them to it, ordering more beers. The pale brown sea crashed against the shoreline opposite the restaurant, vomiting Tusker bottles and driftwood onto a forlorn, empty beach.

Khalid asked if Robert would like to see the farm. She was grateful he didn't hesitate after everything she'd said. They downed their drinks and settled up while Khalid made a call. After half an hour, while Shalini was purchasing the perfect pair of hand-made leather sandals, Muli's *tuk-tuk* pulled up. They squeezed into the backseat while Khalid slapped palms with Muli, a tall, thin guy who looked Indian too, or at least mixed-race like her cousin. She was slightly uncomfortable to be in such close proximity with Robert, his bare thigh resting against her linen trousers. Robert didn't seem to notice, watching everything, saying nothing. Khalid saved the day, much as he had done when they were kids, climbing into the tuk-tuk between them, smiling his painful smile.

An expansive, lurching U-turn, then they made their noisy way along the sea road and out of town. Along a dirt road that took them into the bush. She didn't recognise the route but wiped that from her mind; after all, she hadn't been to the farm for years. Muli goaded the *tuk-tuk* through thick bushes that looked and smelt familiar, until they stopped before a small house, more like a hut. He climbed from the *tuk-tuk*, spoke in Swahili, disappeared.

Robert was smiling, eyes closed, inhaling. They talked marijuana strains until Muli returned with a bundle about the size of a small envelope wrapped in newspaper. He turned the bike around, re-started the engine.

They roared along the Mombassa road, overtaking beeping Matatu's and rickety old trucks, turning onto another dirt road. This time the going was tougher; the bike lurched this way and that, and they were forced to hold onto the metal bars above their heads, or else they would have been thrown. Shalini's bones rattled. She looked ahead, seeing dips in the road that looked deep enough to swallow the *tuk-tuk*. A few kids, some of whom seemed to know Khalid, ran by their side, laughing. The bike lurched forwards, almost pitching them into Muli's back. The kids roared. Tyres spun and dirt flew. The kids stopped laughing, running to a safe distance. They got out, standing to one side as Muli turned the bike around, back the way he had come. Collecting dirty notes that resembled strips of old leather, they paid.

Khalid suggested a walk to the farm; it was all his land from there on. She looked at Robert to see what he was thinking, but there was no chance of that. He was probably more used to that type of thing than her, she thought. Khalid was striding into the bush, thrusting stray plants from his path while Robert followed, the trusting puppy now. She tried to keep up and maintain a similar air, but the linen trousers that seemed so practical in Malindi became her flaw. Creepers hooked into the pockets. Her sandals struggled to find purchase on dry, crumbling earth. She found herself wishing for the shorts and trainers she'd been so set against two days before.

A sweet smell of bud. Robert stopped and passed

the joint while Khalid kept going, way ahead. She was slightly annoyed; how were they meant to find him? She inhaled smoke and displeasure, feeling a burn in her chest. Birds sang and the hum of the crickets was a continuous buzz that almost seemed unreal. She could hear crashes and footsteps from somewhere unseen, felt bad for being angry when Khalid obviously wasn't that far away. Her linen trousers got tangled. Sweat ran down her temples, between her breasts. She tugged uselessly until Robert came back, freeing her trousers, leading her by the hand. His palms were softer than she would have imagined, less sweaty. They held hands the rest of the way.

The first clearing was filled with knee-high plants. She wasn't sure what they were until she squatted and saw tiny red chillies. Khalid explained how a local company had given him the seed; Shalini was proud until she bent closer. Many of the chillies were withered. Some were overripe, presumably because they hadn't been picked. She looked at Robert to see whether he'd noticed. He was standing with his hands on his hips, a little way from them. Shalini pointed out that some of the plants were dying and her cousin smiled, saying yes, he wasn't quite sure whether chillies were the right crop for him. He puffed on bud and walked into the bush.

At the next clearing they emerged into the shadow of a baobab tree, hulking like an ancient God. This one stood alone, surrounded by miles of bush, hidden from the eyes of all but the intrepid. They gasped, placed their hands against bark while Khalid looked pleased. The trunk was five times the width of any oak, big enough for her to climb inside had there been the means. She pried her Canon from its case, began taking shots. The sun was falling, spreading shadows, causing the clearing to shift and grow less inviting.

Shalini strained her ears; the birds seemed to have flown, even the hum of insects had ceased. The air was cool. Khalid, being his usual generous self, offered to take a photo of Shalini and Robert together. She almost shot him a bad look, caught herself, gave her sweetest smile and posed beside the American.

They were obviously uncomfortable, made worse by Khalid's urges for them to stand closer, put their arms around each other. She settled for leaning on his shoulder. At the last minute he turned, looked into her eyes, causing Shalini to feel a light flutter of nerves. For a moment there was nothing but him and something undeniable, some moment of communication. Of what, she wasn't sure, or maybe didn't want to admit, but it happened, and for a minute she was unable to hear Khalid say what a great picture it was, even though she looked at the view screen and nodded her agreement, telling them she would email it to him.

She hung the camera around her neck like a medal she'd won for valour. They walked close for the few hundred yards it took to reach the farm. A grass path brought them to the cow enclosure; before she knew it she was stopping, crooning, stroking soft heads, marvelling at maple-brown eyes. Khalid kept walking, greeted by dogs and farmhands, several young Kenyan boys nodding shy hellos. Unlike the cows at home, Khalid's seemed tense at the sight of humans and eventually turned their backs. Shalini felt slighted for no good reason, even more so when Robert laughed. She followed the path into the farm, nose pointed high. Robert stayed with the dogs.

Her cousin shouted orders at the young men, who gazed as though she was some princess from a mythical realm, causing her to wrap her thin shawl across her open blouse. One was taking a shower in a stone cubical just past the cow enclosure. She averted her eyes from his nakedness, too late; curiosity made her peek at the glistening, dark body, and she felt another shiver run through her like the water that turned dry earth to mud beneath her feet. She gazed at the farm. It was difficult to hide what she felt. Mud was everywhere. On the floors, the bare concrete walls of the farmhouse, the iron fencing of the enclosure. On the farmhands, the dogs and the goats. The farmhouse looked as though it was about to fall in on itself like the crumbling buildings of Malindi's Islamic section. Dogs ran everywhere, puppies, Mongrels, lumbering Alsatians, sometimes darting through her legs, almost tripping her. She stepped carefully to where Khalid was sat on a small concrete bench, also mud-ridden. He was tipping a steel jug of jaundiced milk into what looked like a baby bottle. Apparently, if the young cow drank directly from the mother, there would be no milk to sell. Shalini nodded as though she understood.

There was an open doorway before her but no door. When she looked inside she saw nothing but darkness, the solid edge of large objects. She wanted to venture further, couldn't bring herself to. She sat and watched Khalid approach a tethered beige calf with the baby bottle; it was possibly the cutest animal she'd ever seen.

Shalini had heard all the stories and refused to believe. How it was rumoured that Khalid had gone mad. That the family wanted the farm back, even though it had been left to him in their grandfather's will. That her uncle, Khalid's father, had slapped his drunken son, and Khalid had punched him back. All she could remember was the cousin who'd been so happy to see her whenever she'd visited. He was seven years older, and she'd always looked up to him. She didn't want to think about her father telling her mother he was glad he hadn't stayed and married a native, like his brother. That he'd chosen to practise medicine in the West, rather than Africa where they had no respect for science, just superstition. She'd always disagreed on the basis that her father was wrong, and yet here she was. Linen trousers dragged through the mud, concrete against her behind.

Robert came to find her, yapping dogs in tow, a black moon puppy cradled in his arms. The dog looked half-asleep, content. If the American was fazed by their surroundings, she couldn't tell. Once again, she told herself that he'd probably seen the equivalent, or worse. Together they went to check out the beige cow, stroking the nubs where his horns would grow, taking turns to feed him from the baby bottle. The calf seemed to like her, bleating in languid fits whenever she stopped rubbing its flanks. If she walked away he tried to follow until the rope tugged him by the neck. She took more pictures as the sun set, half worried about how they would get back. Khalid and Robert said they'd be fine. The farmhands watched, amused.

They smoked a few joints before Khalid said they'd

better leave. There was a path that cut through the trees, leading to the main road. Night had fallen like a blanket thrown over the bush and Robert dropped back with a farmhand who joined them, leaving Shalini stepping ahead with her cousin. Khalid was full of good cheer, talking of plans for expansion, the difficulties selling milk in an already cornered market, the fight he would have retaining the farm from the clutches of the family. Through it all he seemed lucid, passionate, and most of all sober. The full moon hung above them. Shalini would never have believed how illuminating that reflected light could be, or how far away it seemed back home. She reached for Khalid's arm, leant her head against his shoulder and let her cousin guide her steps, happy to hear him breathe.

Discography

While this list is not exhaustive, I'd like to acknowledge all the musicians who've helped inspire this collection. All of these artists were on my rotating playlist while I wrote, and probably many more. So creative good wishes goes out to:

Abram Wilson, Afronaught, Ahmad Jamal Trio, Al Green, Alice Coltrane, Aloe Blacc, Amel Larrieux, Ananda Shankar, Angie Stone, Animal Collective, Anita Baker, Antonio Jobim, Arthur Verocai, Autechre, B.B. King, Ba Cissoko, Barrington Levy, Bob Marley, Basement Jaxx, Skream & Benga, Bert Jansch, Bernard Purdie, Big Daddy Kane, Big Youth, Bilal, Billie Holiday, Björk, Black Sheep, Black Star, Bobby Byrd, Bonobo, Branford Marsalis, Brother Jack McDuff, Bud Powell, Burial, Cameo, Cannibal Ox, Cassandra Wilson, Charles Mingus, Charlie Parker, Cheikh Lo, Chick Corea, Chico Buarque, Chris Clark, Common, Curtis Mayfield, D'Angelo, Dabrye, Demon Boyz, Devin the Dude, Devendra Banhart, DFRNT, Doug Carn, Domu, Donald Byrd, Donny Hathaway, Dr Who Dat, Drake, Dubbledge, Duke Ellington, Erykah Badu, Eska, Fela Kuti, Flying Lotus, Frank Walton, Fred Wesley, Fugees, Gene Chandler, Georgia Anne Muldrow, Ghostface Killah, Gil Scott-Heron, Gotan Project, Herbert, Herbie Hancock, Horace Silver, Howlin Wolf, Hypnotic Brass Ensemble, J Dilla, J-Rell, Jaguar Wright, Janelle Monáe, Jay Electronica, Jay-Z, Jean Carne, Jean Grae, Jean-Michel Bernard, Jehst, Joe Harriott, John Coltrane,

José James, Kaidi Tatham, Kanye West, Karen O, Kate Daisy Grant, Kelis, King Britt, KMD, Konono N°1, Little Brother, Lil Wayne, Lonnie Liston Smith, Madlib, Mandrill, Maxwell, Mazzy Star, MF DOOM, Michael Jackson, Miles Davis, Morgan Heritage, Mos Def, Mpho Skeef, Nicolette, N.E.R.D., Oh No, Ohio Players, Omar, Ornette Coleman, Osunlade, Peter Tosh, Peven Everett, Pharoahe Monch, Philip Glass, Prince, Radiohead, Raphael Saadiq, Rashaan Patterson, Ravi Shankar, Rick James, Rodney P, Róisín Murphy, Roots Manuva, Roy Ayers, Self Scientific, Shackleton, Shuggie Otis, Silhouette Brown, Sizzla, Slum Village, Soweto Kinch, Talib Kweli, Teena Marie, Terri Walker, Thelonious Monk, Weldon Irvine, Wiley, Wu-Tang Clan, Wynton Marsalis, The Zombies, 9th Wonder, 4hero.

Many apologies if you have been unintentionally omitted. I'm truly indebted to everyone I've listened to and without your work mine would not be possible. Thank you.

Acknowledgements

Certain stories in this collection were previously published as follows: 'Spider Man' in *African Writing Online*; 'All Woman' in the print edition of *580 Split*; 'White Goods' in the online edition of *580 Split*; 'Re-Entry' in *Antiques Children*; 'Passive Smoke' in *The Writer's Hub*.

Love and thanks to Sharmila and Senenti for providing me with even more purpose.

To Marlene Denny for your strength and guidance, even from afar.

To Will Mackie and everyone at Flambard for your easygoing manner and the Arts Council of England for generous financial support.

To Sherin for all the Skype chats and stories thrashed over; most of all for a great cover.

To Miriam Nelken, many thanks for commissioning me to write 'All Woman', 'White Goods' and 'Underground', stories that made me aware I had a growing collection.

To Glenn Benson and the Friends of Kensal Green Cemetery for all your help with my story and providing such a brilliant, spooky venue for the reading! And Terry Dino for allowing me to take artistic liberties with your livelihood and name.

To Jake Polley, Rupert Thompson, Sarah Hall and Lemn Sissay – thanks for the peer-to-peer support.

And to my lovely cat, Tashi – though you were my inspiration, you're nothing like the cats in these stories. Promise.

Also by Courttia Newland

The Scholar
Society Within
Snakeskin
The Dying Wish
Music for the Off-Key